Clan Rebel

Highland Heroes Series: Book 3

Theo Mann

The Invisible Publishing Company

Highland Heroes Series

Contents

Chapter 1

Echo Boxwood squinted up at the White House perched on top of Capitol Hill. "Are we really going in there to meet the President of the United States?"

"We better be," Dead Betty replied. "He did call us here to meet him today."

"We better NOT be, you mean," Echo countered. "If he's calling us to meet him, then Liam Barnett is right. The President is ordering us back into military service. We could be going into another war zone."

"You realize how unheard of it is for a unit as small as ours to visit the President, right?" Zero added. "How does he even know we exist?"

"The President was the one who ordered Liam to take the Last Division back in time to Scotland," Betty replied. "Lady Rhona Armstrong is his own relative and we're supposed to save her."

"Not exactly," Echo countered. "Liam only took Lily Dindle back in time. He was never supposed to take the whole Division."

"So why did he take Snowflake, too?" Betty asked. "We're down two members, not just one."

"He took Snowflake to find Lily and bring her back," Zero pointed out. "They're on a rescue mission."

"I'm not so sure." Echo eyed the White House one more time. "Something about this doesn't add up."

"What are you saying, Echo?" Zero asked. "We all heard what Liam said."

"That's what *he* said. What if it wasn't just a rescue mission? What if his plan was to take us all back in time? What if he lied to get Lily and Snowflake there together?"

"You're talking about his sister," Zero argued. "Why would Liam take Lily to Scotland to put her in danger and then do the same thing to Snowflake?"

Betty lowered her voice to a tense murmur. "Don't look now, but he's coming up the street."

Echo spun around and her scalp prickled when Liam Barnett strode toward the three women. He wore casual khaki pants and a nice white button-down shirt. He looked much nicer and better groomed now than he did when he first broke into Ironforge to spring this mission on the Last Division.

Something about his eyes and face made him look older and more weathered. He looked like he hadn't slept in a while and.... were those bruises on his neck and the sides of his head? He looked like he'd been in a fight, but that might have been a few days ago.

He pulled up in front of the three women and beamed at them like he was their best friend. That smile gave Echo the creeps.

"What are you doing here, Liam?" Betty demanded. "You're supposed to be three hundred years in the past with Lily and Snowflake."

"I was, but I came back here to get you three."

"What for?" Echo asked. "If you couldn't save Lady Rhona with Lily and Snowflake, what makes you think you can do it with us?"

"And don't tell us you need us to rescue Lily and Snowflake," Betty added. "You took Snowflake to rescue Lily. If you tell us Snowflake needs rescuing now, too, that makes you the worst mission commander in history."

He laughed. That sound set Echo's nerves even more on edge and she wasn't the only one. "What the hell is so damn funny?" Zero snarled. "Do you think it's a joke that you took two of our teammates back in time and lost them?"

"Lily and Snowflake aren't lost," he replied. "They're in Scotland carrying out the mission, but we need you three to come, too."

"How do you figure?" Betty asked. "Did you find Lady Rhona Armstrong?"

"Not yet. We're still trying to find her, but we did find a few other crucial pieces of the puzzle. Lily and Snowflake are working on them now. We need you three to come through the portal so we can finish this once and for all."

"Forget it," Echo snapped. "None of us is going anywhere with you. How do we know Lily and Snowflake aren't dead back there and you want to lead us into danger, too?"

He didn't act at all offended by her accusation. "It will be dangerous. It *is* dangerous. I wouldn't lie to you about that. Lily and Snowflake have already been dealing with dangers and so have I. It isn't the safest environment if you know what I mean."

"Why should we trust you, then?" Echo asked. "Why should we agree to go anywhere with you?"

"Because you've been ordered by Felix Margoles to go with me. I can prove it. If it makes you feel any better, I'm going to take you somewhere to prove that everything I'm telling you is true."

The three women exchanged glances. "I don't like this," Echo murmured. "This is not the way to conduct a mission."

"Just come with me and I'll explain everything," Liam added and he motioned behind him.

"Wait a minute," Betty countered. "We're supposed to meet the President."

"Not anymore. You were only ordered here to meet me."

"I don't believe you," Echo told him. "You took Lily without telling her or any of us about dragons or wizards or anything like that. How do we know you aren't lying about other stuff?"

He waved toward the White House. "Okay. Go ahead. Go to your meeting with the President. I won't try to stop you."

Echo and her companions looked at each other again. She saw her own thoughts written on their faces. Why was Liam being so agreeable all of a sudden? She had a bad feeling about this.

She, Betty, and Zero turned back to the White House, but all three of them kept casting backward glances at Liam as they walked away. He only smiled and trailed them at a safe distance.

"Let's ditch him," Betty muttered. "He's a creep."

"Let's see the President first," Echo replied. "The order to find and save Lady Rhona came from him. He must want to see us about something related to this mission."

They agreed and approached the front gate of the White House where several armed Marines stood guard. Betty gave the three women's names and appointment times to the sergeant on duty.

He checked the computer in his security office and came back holding a white envelope with the White House seal on it. "The President left this for you."

"Don't we have clearance to go in?" Echo asked. "We have an appointment."

The sergeant pointed at the envelope. "My orders are to give you this. It should explain everything."

Betty scowled at him while Echo got busy ripping open the envelope. She unfolded a single piece of paper that did NOT have the White House seal on it.

Last Division ordered to attend Liam Barnett on rescue mission according to previous orders by authority of Felix Margoles.

Liam materialized out of nowhere. "Now do you believe me?"

Echo rounded on him. "How do we know this is legitimate? You could have planted this yourself?"

He motioned toward the sergeant. "Ask him if I planted it."

Echo glanced over her shoulder. The sergeant and the other Marines stood around listening to their conversation and she knew in an instant that the note was legitimate.

No one in their right mind would plant something saying that the Last Division was under orders from Felix Margoles.

These Marines probably didn't even know what Felix Margoles was. Heck, not even the Last Division knew who or what Felix Margoles was. No one knew if it was a person or just a shadow department of the government that answered to no one else.

"You guys better come with me," Liam added. "I can explain everything, but I can't do it here. Come on."

He turned away and now Betty, Echo, and Zero had no choice but to follow him. They wouldn't get their questions answered at the White House.

Of course they wouldn't. The President of the United States wouldn't be able to admit in a public setting like this that he sent people back in time to fight wizards and dragons to save one of his ancestors. No one would believe that. Echo wasn't prepared to believe it herself.

Liam continued back down the street in the direction from which the three women had come. He returned to Pennsylvania Avenue and turned off into a nondescript building. He guided the three women into a large room. It was totally empty.

"Well?" Betty blurted out. "You said you'd tell us everything. We're listening."

He took out the small copper box that he used to open the time portals. Echo recoiled from it. "No way! You aren't taking any of us anywhere! You already made two of our comrades disappear with that thing. You aren't activating that until you give us some answers."

"Don't worry. I wasn't going to activate it." He put it on the floor and pressed some of the strange symbols on its sides. The box snapped and started to glow. "This will explain everything."

He took a step away and light started pouring out of the box. What looked like colored laser beams pivoted around the room in strange patterns. After a few minutes, they formed a map showing a giant city with a river running next to it.

"Here's the situation back in Scotland," Liam began. "Two Clans are at war against each other—the Creightons and the Buchanans. This is the city of Kald and this estuary is called the Boundless. It separates Kald, which is Creighton territory, from Buchanan country.... which is over here. The Royal House of Creighton are dragon shifters. They can change into dragons whenever they want to, but only the Royal Family can do it."

"You're making that up!" Zero countered. "That isn't possible."

"Magic and time travel shouldn't be possible, either, but they are. The Buchanans are shifters, too. They can change into Highland tigers. They're large cats about the size of a dog and they can all do it—all of them."

Zero's hand flew to her head. "This is nuts!"

"The two Clans have been at war for eons, and about twenty years ago—twenty years ago in the other time period, I mean—Laird Balfour Creighton kidnapped Lady Ilisa Buchanan. She was the wife of Neill Buchanan, the Chief of Clan Buchanan."

"Why did he kidnap her—to stick it to his enemies?" Echo asked.

"As it turned out, she was his daughter. She was already married to Camdyn Carmichael in Tyrekirk, which is their big castle in the city of Kald. She had two sons with her husband—Grant and Elliot. The Laird thought the boys were a threat to him. He thought they would become too powerful and depose him, so he decided to kill them both when they were babies."

"Wow!" Betty breathed. "This Laird sounds like a raving asshole."

"He is. He's a tyrant. Anyway, Lady, Ilisa hid the boys from him. She got a wizard to mask their identities and then she gave the boys to a castle maid to raise as her own. They grew up in Tyrekirk never knowing who they really were....and they go by the last name of Ritchie."

"So how did Lady Ilisa wind up with the Buchanans?" Echo asked. "How could she marry Neill when she was already married?"

"When she wouldn't tell the Laird where the boys were, he threatened to kill her, too. She ran away to the Buchanans in their mountain fortress of Icemeet. Neill already had three children and Ilisa had another son with Neill—Duncan Buchanan."

"Hold up a sec," Zero interjected. "If his father is a Highland tiger and his mother is a dragon shifter, wouldn't that make him....?"

Liam nodded. "Duncan is a hybrid. He can shift into a dragon and he can also shift into a Highland tiger. He's the only person who can unite the Clans and end the war, but that means he has to depose the Laird. As you can understand, the Laird has been trying to find Duncan and get rid of him to stop that from happening."

"How does this help us?" Echo asked. "What are we supposed to do about it?"

"You three are coming back in time with me. Your orders from Felix Margoles are to support Duncan Buchanan to take the Seat of Armstrong and bring peace to the land."

As if in answer to his words, the lights flickering from the box coalesced into a different pattern. They projected on the blank wall and showed a family tree with Clan Creighton on one side and Clan Buchanan on the other.

Echo's eye traced all the names Liam just mentioned. The tree showed Laird Balfour Creighton and his daughters, Ilisa and Saundra, on one side with Grant Ritchie, Elliot Ritchie, and Ness Creighton beneath Ilisa and Camdyn Carmichael.

The other side showed Neill Buchanan connected to Caitrin Buchanan. A branching line descended from them to Colton, Reid, and Edeena Buchanan. A long line connected Ilisa Creighton to Duncan Buchanan through his father, Neill. It was all there laid out in flashing light.

Her eye skipped back to the map. She thought she knew enough about the layout of Scotland and this definitely wasn't it. She didn't recognize the mountain, town, and river names. This map represented a different Scotland—or maybe Liam lied about this country being Scotland at all. How could Echo be certain?

She didn't like to question Liam in front of the others. He must know something she didn't. Maybe she'd just forgotten this part of Scotland....but she doubted that.

Either way, Lily and Snowflake were there. The rest of the Last Division would have to go there whether it was real Scotland or something else entirely.

"We know that Duncan Buchanan ascends the throne and marries Lady Rhona Armstrong," Liam explained. "Our orders are to make sure this happens, but right now, we don't even know where Lady Rhona is. As far as we know, the dark wizard is still back in Scotland trying to kill her."

"Do you know who the dark wizard is?" Zero asked.

Liam shook his head. "Lily and I thought the Laird might be the dark wizard, but since we don't even know who Lady Rhona is or *where* she is, it's kind of hard to see how the Laird would be able to threaten her. As far as we know, Lady Rhona isn't even in Scotland."

"How are we supposed to find her, then?" Echo asked.

"I'm not sure. I only know I'm under orders to take you three back in time. Once you're all there, we can work on how to complete this mission and end the war with Duncan on the throne."

Echo glanced over at her two companions—the only friends she had left.

"So which one of you wants to go first?" he asked. "Only two of us can go through at a time, so I'll have to take you one at a time."

"Not so fast," Echo countered. "I don't trust you as far as I can throw you, pal. You've already lost two of our people with that thing."

"What more do you need to know? You're assigned to me by Felix Margoles. If that isn't enough for you, maybe you aren't cut out for this mission after all."

"None of us is going anywhere with you, Mister," Betty added. "We can still carry out our orders without you."

"How do you think you're going to do that?" Liam asked. "I'm the only one who knows how to work the portal."

"Then you can send me and Echo through first," Betty replied. "You and Zero can follow after, but we're going through alone first. None of us is going anywhere with you alone."

"Zero will be going through with me," Liam pointed out, but Betty didn't listen.

She pointed to the box. "I'm sure you can program that thing to send us through and then return here....so do it."

He smacked his lips and bent over to pick up the box. "This is stupid."

"What's stupid is that you're still in the US Military service after the crap you pulled on our team," Echo snarled. "If you were in the Army, you would have been court-martialed and imprisoned."

He ignored her comments and went to work on the box. He pressed a few more symbols on its sides. "I'm programming this to take you as close as possible to Duncan's location. He was at Icemeet when I left Scotland. Snowflake is there and she's married to the Buchanans' new Clan Chief—Neill's son Colton. She'll be able to help you make contact with Duncan if he isn't there, too."

Betty gasped. "She's.... married?"

"Lily is married, too. She's married to Grant Ritchie. They're in Tyrekirk and Grant is Laird Balfour's heir."

Echo and her friends looked at each other again. Sinking dread seized Echo's heart. What could possibly have gone wrong in Scotland to cause two of the Last Division's sturdiest members to turn their backs on their oath of isolation and retirement? Did Echo really want to go back there if the same thing might happen to her, too?

Liam put the box on the floor and it started to vibrate. Echo grabbed Betty's hand. Whatever was waiting there for them on the other side of that portal, at least Echo and Betty would be facing it together. They wouldn't be alone.

Betty crushed Echo's hand in a death grip and Echo clutched Betty's just as tightly. Echo didn't want to get separated from Betty in this madness.

Echo glanced over at Zero. Echo opened her mouth to say something. She wanted to reassure Zero that they'd be together on the other end, but Echo couldn't get her voice to work.

The box spun faster and faster sucking the whole room into its vortex. It seemed to pull all the air from Echo's lungs and then an explosion collapsed the room around her ears. The world slammed down on her and everything went black.

Chapter 2

E lliot Ritchie crouched behind a rock and peeked out at a herd of stags grazing in the forest. He gripped his bow tighter and started to rise on his knees to shoot at them.

His friend Evan grabbed his arm and pulled Elliot down. "Hold hard, laddie. Dinnae take the shot just yet."

"We winnae get a better shot than this. They dinnae ken we're even here." Elliot nocked his arrow and wedged his knees under him to get up again.

"Wait for Barclay to catch up," Evan argued. "He'll be surly if ye frighten the deer off before he gets his chance."

"He winnae be surly when he's eating the meat I've shot." Elliot shook off his friend's hand and straightened up a second time.

He planted his knees in the soft soil and drew the bow back to his ear. He sighted down the arrow shaft at a big stag right in front of him. The creature raised its head and pivoted its antlers in all directions to listen, but the stag still didn't see or hear Elliot. It was a perfect shot. Elliot couldn't miss.

He steadied the string by pressing his wrist against his jaw. He commanded himself to shoot when, without warning, a swirling whirlpool opened in the air itself. It rotated in a tempest wind and two figures stepped out of it.

The vortex startled the deer and they bolted into the dense forest, but Elliot barely saw them. Elliot's spine tingled as two women emerged from the portal.

He would recognize that spiraling tornado anywhere. He'd only seen it once, but that was enough. As soon as the two women came through, he recognized them, too. He didn't *exactly* recognize them because he'd never seen them before in his life, but he recognized everything else about them.

They dressed and acted exactly like Lily, the woman he'd met in Kald who got so friendly with his brother Grant. Elliot tried for the thousandth time to push all thought of Grant out of his mind, but these women wouldn't let him.

Their sharp, alert eyes flicked around the forest with the same flinty readiness Elliot had only ever seen in Lily. He'd never met any other woman who acted like that. Now he was seeing two more of them.

They both wore trousers. The taller one wore her curly blonde hair gathered in a messy plait down her back. She wore a tight-fitting jacket over a buttoned white shirt and boots up to her knees.

The shorter one was wider in the hips and bigger in the chest. Her small, peaked face turned toward him and her pearly skin glowed in the dim forest light.

Her long, straight dark brown hair hung loose and spilled over her shoulders. She also wore trousers with small black shoes on her feet. Her short jacket had a hood behind her neck.

He lowered his bow, got to his feet, and strode down the slope toward them. He walked right up to them and measured them down to the inch. The more he saw, the more certain he became that they were who he suspected they were.

They both stiffened and faced him as he got nearer. That proved it beyond all doubt. These women knew how to fight as well as Lily did.

He nodded to them both. "Ye're Lily's friends, I suppose. Have ye come here to find her, then?"

"You know Lily?" the dark-haired one exclaimed. "Where is she? Is she here?"

"Here? Och, no! She's back in Kald. I havenae seen her since I left the city. What brings ye here? Ye've come back in time the same as her, is that it?"

The blonde one gasped. "You know about that?"

"Aye. I was all mixed up in that business with Lily." He held out his hand to the dark-haired one. She was captivatingly beautiful in a small, pixie sort of way. "I'm Elliot Ritchie."

"Elliot Ritchie!" she blurted out. "You're...you're Grant's brother! You're...." She glanced over at her friend and clamped her mouth shut like she shouldn't have said that much.

Elliot compressed his lips. "Aye. I'm Grant's brother, but he isnae here, either. Ye lassies had best get yerselves under cover. It isnae safe out here for any strangers wandering about."

"*You're* out here wandering about," the blonde one countered. "Why is it safe for you and not for us?"

He laughed. He hadn't laughed in so long that he almost didn't remember how. His whole life had fallen apart when he parted ways with Grant. Elliot was the one who walked away, but he still blamed Grant for the breach.

He stuffed those thoughts down in the locked box where he kept all his thoughts and feelings about Grant. Elliot didn't allow himself to think about Grant if he could possibly avoid it, but he still found himself brooding about his brother in spite of himself.

Elliot jerked his thumb over his shoulder. "Ye lassies had best come with us. Are ye here searching for Lady Rhona Armstrong the same as Lily? We can sort out how to proceed once ye...."

Evan interrupted by storming out of the rocks. He barged up to Elliot and the two women. "What the devil are they doing here? Ye frightened off the deer, ye trollops! Now we havenae ought to eat tonight and Barclay will be on the rampage. Ye'll catch it when he comes in."

"Dinnae ye talk to them like that," Elliot snapped. "Mind yer manners and speak in a civil tone."

Evan rounded on him. "Do ye fancy a thrashing, lad?"

"From ye? I'd love to see ye try."

"From Barclay, ye mapit!" Evan bellowed. "Ye had a clear shot at those stags and then these two jezebels...."

"I swear to Christ if ye dinnae watch yer mouth, ye'll be cleaning up yer brains off those rocks over there," Elliot snarled. "Do ye think for a moment that they meant to frighten the deer?"

"What deer?" the dark-haired one asked.

Elliot and Evan both ignored her. "We've enough trouble keeping ourselves alive without a couple of...." Evan checked himself when Elliot glared at him in murderous fury. "I'm only saying Barclay winnae like it at all."

"I'll be the one to handle Barclay," Elliot countered. "Ye can run along home to yer mother's teat if ye cannae be a man and stand on yer own feet."

Evan glared back at him, but Elliot didn't care. He turned back to the dark-haired woman. "Ye didnae tell me yer name, lassie. Ye ken mine and this is Evan. Dinnae mind him at all."

"That's right nice," Evan huffed. "I'm only yer best mate."

"Not for long the way ye're going." Elliot turned to the dark-haired woman for the second time. "Ye'll have to excuse him. He doesnae ken how to behave around a lady. He hasnae barely seen one before."

Both women laughed and the dark-haired one's deep brown eyes twinkled. She flushed and her cheeks dimpled when she smiled. She really was one of the most beautiful women that Elliot had ever seen and her spirit shone from inside her just like Lily's did.

"I'm Echo Boxwood." She held out her hand to him. "This is my friend Dead Betty."

Evan snorted. "Ye're a liar as well as a hussy. Tell the truth and ye may yet...."

Elliot hauled off and punched him square in the nose. He flattened Evan with one punch and Evan collapsed bellowing on the ground. "Ye filthy, rotten bastard! I'll cut yer gizzard out for that!"

"That's yer last warning, laddie. Now shove along with ye and dinnae ye show yer face to these lassies again." Elliot pulled back his leg and kicked Evan hard in the rump.

Evan roared again and scrambled to stand up. He pressed his hand to his nose trying to stem the flow of blood. "Ye'll pay for this! When Barclay finds out...."

"When I find out about what?" a deep voice boomed out of the trees.

Everyone spun around to see two more men advancing through the forest. One of them stood at least eight inches taller than Elliot and the man was as big as a house. His hulking shoulders and tree-trunk legs dwarfed everyone.

The other man was a cringing scarecrow who hovered close to Barclay's elbow. The little man's eyes darted here and there and they popped nearly out of his head when he saw Evan with a bloody nose.

Elliot narrowed his eyes at the two of them. Barclay was a dangerous brute, but his partner Graeme was no slouch, either. He preferred cunning and subterfuge to brute force, but he could still do as much damage as Barclay.

Barclay pulled up next to Elliot and leered at the two women. "What have we here, then?"

Echo glanced over at Elliot at the same moment he glanced at her. Barclay was the last person alive that Elliot wanted to tell the truth about how Echo and Betty got into this forest. Elliot read the same misgiving written on both women's faces.

"We're just visiting," Echo began. "We were trying to find someone we know."

"Ye cannae go back to Kald," Elliot told her. "It isnae safe for ye there."

"No one goes back to Kald," Barclay boomed. "Anyone who leaves for the forest stays gone if ye dinnae fancy the Laird taking yer head off."

"Seriously?" She scanned each man one after another. "Is that why you're here—to get away from the Laird?"

Elliot jerked his thumb at the other three. "These three are fugitives from his service. They've fled Kald..."

"We didnae flee ought, laddie!" Barclay thundered. "We're revolutionaries."

Elliot rolled his eyes and the slightest smirk twitched at the corners of Echo's mouth. Her dimples appeared again. "They're renegades from the Laird's service. They're deserters from the war against the Buchanans...."

"We didnae desert," Evan interjected. "We're mounting our own campaign to wipe the Highland tigers off the face of the Earth."

"And a fine job ye're doing of it, too," Elliot sneered. "Ye cannae even shoot a deer for yer supper."

"He had a perfect shot, Barclay," Evan babbled. "He had a grand stag in his sights and then these two...."

He cut himself when he caught Elliot skewering him with another ferocious glare, but Barclay didn't notice. "How do we ken these two lassies arenae Buchanan spies infiltrating our territory?"

"Ye can see yerself that they arenae Buchanans," Elliot countered. "The Buchanans have a certain pattern to their eyes. These lassies arenae even native to this country."

"Maybe you can help us," Betty added. "Elliot was just telling us...."

"Elliot doesnae tell anyone ought," Barclay rumbled. "I'll be the one to decide what to do with ye."

"*You* won't decide what to do with us or anyone else," Betty growled. "You might be in charge of these men, but you don't decide anything about us. We have our own business to attend to."

"Ye're our prisoners." Barclay took one threatening step nearer to them. "Ye'll come back to our cave and we'll take ye in as our captives."

"I wouldnae do that if I was in yer place," Elliot warned. "Ye're making a mistake."

Barclay ignored him. He towered over to the two women and glared down at one and then the other. "Ye're both tasty treats, I'll wager. Me men'll appreciate ye when I've finished with ye."

"Back off, asshole," Betty snapped. "If you lay a finger on either of us...."

Her words set Barclay off. He raised one massive hand and clamped it on Betty's shoulder.

She reacted in a split second, seized his wrist, and twisted it backward with brutal force. He roared in pain and Echo lashed out.

She dropped into a crouch, swept her leg across Barclay's ankles, and toppled him flat on his face. Betty still held him by the wrist and wrenched his arm behind his back. She planted her foot on his shoulder and gave his arm a cruel yank.

She and Echo rounded on the other three men and Elliot recognized the tense flexion in Echo's knees. She braced herself to attack anyone who came near her.

A second later, she pounced on Barclay, drew his saber and dirk from his belt, and aimed both weapons at Elliot, Evan, and Graeme.

Barclay bellowed again, but Betty only gave him one more vicious jerk. "Take one step nearer and you'll get more of this."

Graeme cringed away from the two women. Evan stood rooted to the spot gaping at Echo and Betty like they were monsters.

"Ye foul witch!" Barclay roared. "I'll slit yer throat for this! Let me go! Elliot—do something!"

"I warned ye not to," Elliot returned. "Ye didnae listen."

"You traitor! You bastard! When I get my hands on ye...."

"When ye get yer hands on me, I'll thrash ye the same as I did last week." Elliot nodded to Betty. "Ye can let him go now, lassie. No one will bother ye anymore. I give ye me word on that."

She shot him a menacing glance, gave Barclay's arm a sadistic twist, and stepped away from him. Echo backed off still threatening everyone with Barclay's weapons.

Echo's eyes narrowed to slits as they darted from one man to the next. Her dark hair fell over her face and transformed her into a compact ball of fighting power. Elliot didn't envy Barclay at all. These women were nothing to trifle with. He learned that well enough with Lily.

Barclay struggled to his feet. He snarled at the two women and Elliot braced himself for Barclay to attack them in return.

The instant Barclay got his feet under him, Betty took a step toward him and kicked him hard right in the sternum. Barclay staggered back three steps trying to catch his balance, tripped over Graeme, and toppled flat on his back. He roared again as he and Graeme tried to untangle themselves from each other.

Elliot raised his eyebrows. These women were turning out to be something much more formidable than even he expected.

Barclay lunged to his feet, but Echo sprang forward in a heartbeat. She planted herself in front of Betty and brandished both her blades at all four men. Her wild, furious eyes locked on Elliot for a second. He hadn't moved since the confrontation started.

She immediately pivoted to cover Barclay, Graeme, and Evan, but Graeme and Evan were in no mood to stand up to anyone. Graeme retreated behind Barclay's bulk. Evan remained frozen in place, unable even to blink at the two women.

Echo kept jerking back and forth to make sure she kept all three men in sight at all times. Barclay snarled at the two women, but he wasn't stupid enough to go near them again.

Elliot approached Betty and Echo from the sides. "That's all right, lassies. No one will bother ye again...."

Echo whipped around and pointed her blades straight at his chest. Her countenance smoldered with deadly fury. He didn't doubt for a second that she would run him through if he threatened her.

He raised both hands where she could see them. "Stand down, lass. I mean ye no harm. Put aside yer blades and I'll take ye somewhere ye can spend the night. We've a cave near here with supplies...."

"Dinnae tell them that!" Evan blurted out. "They might be spies. They might be out for the Laird to track us down."

Elliot snorted. "No one from the Laird cares for a lot of slum rats like ye lads." He turned back to Echo. "Ye're all right, lassie. I mean ye no harm. Lay aside yer blades and talk to me. I may be able to help ye on yer mission."

She glared at him and then shot a sidelong glance at Betty. Betty nodded. Only then did Echo straighten up and lower her weapons, but she didn't relax completely. She kept eyeing the other three men.

"As I say, lassies, we've a cave near here with food and supplies. Ye can come there and we'll...."

"Ye winnae share our goods with the likes of them," Barclay growled. "They may not be Buchanans, but they're strangers nonetheless. Those goods are for our men and no one else."

Elliot turned around with exaggerated slowness. "Then we'll take them to the Serpent Cave. Will that satisfy ye?"

"What's the Serpent Cave?" Echo asked.

"It's a cave that doesnae belong to any group," Elliot waved at the other men. "We belong to a group of rebels out to unseat the Laird, but the Serpent Cave is for all to use."

"But you're obviously against the Buchanans, too," Betty remarked. "How can you be against the Buchanans *and* the Laird?"

"They're against everyone," Elliot replied. "They're against the Buchanans, the Creightons—ye bring it and they're against it."

"Are you one of them?" Echo asked.

Her dark eyes bored into his being and he squirmed under her scrutiny. "I am at the moment."

"You said your brother is in Kald. Why are you out here by yourself.... with *them*?" She nodded toward the other three.

Elliot looked away. "It's a long story. Come along, lassies."

"Hold it. We have to find someone...." Echo glanced past him at the other three, came to some decision, and blurted out the rest in a rush. "We heard that Duncan Buchanan is in these woods. We're trying to find him."

"Buchanan!" Barclay thundered. "If any Buchanan is in these woods, we'll hack him to pieces."

"We heard that he's a hybrid between a Creighton and a Buchanan," Echo told him. "He's half and half, which means he can unite the Clans and unseat the Laird. That should make him your perfect leader."

Barclay grumbled to himself, but he stopped short of actually voicing what he was thinking.

"If ye're right, it would solve a heap of problems," Elliot replied. "It would end the war."

"Exactly." Echo brightened up and beamed at him. Was she blushing? His heart flipped when she looked at him like that.

"Our source says your brother is a Creighton prince," Betty added. "We heard he's living in Tyrekirk as Laird Balfour's chosen heir. Is that true?"

Elliot snorted and turned away to hide his discomfort. "I dinnae ken where Grant is nor do I care. He's a lizard."

"That's a pretty insulting thing to say about your own brother," Betty countered. "If he's the Laird's grandson, don't you think you might be a dragon shifter like he is?"

He refused to look at her or Echo. Grant was the last thing in the world he wanted to talk about. "I wouldnae be at all surprised if he was living in the lap of luxury as the Laird's pet dog. It doesnae concern me what he does."

"We also heard he's married to Lily," Echo went on.

"I'm sure he is."

"Then they were...." Echo stumbled over the words. "Were they close when you saw them together?"

"Aye. That's one way of putting it."

Echo and Betty exchanged glances again and Echo cleared her throat. "Listen. Our mission is to find Duncan and help him overthrow the Laird and ascend the throne. Maybe you could help us since...." She glanced over at Barclay. "Since that's your aim as well."

"I dinnae ken ought about any Buchanan on this side of the Boundless," Elliot replied. "If he was here, his life would be forfeit as Barclay says. Every hand would be against him. He wouldnae stand a chance."

"Even if he was both a dragon shifter and a Highland tiger shifter?" Betty countered. "That might give him an advantage over anyone who might be trying to kill him."

"We were told we would come through the portal as close as possible to his location." Echo scanned the woods. "That would suggest that he's here."

"Unless he isn't," Betty pointed out. "Maybe the box malfunctioned. Liam said he would send us to Icemeet."

"Liam!" Elliot blurted out. "Is he involved in this somehow?"

"You know Liam?" Betty asked.

"He was with us in Kald —with me and Grant and Lily."

"Ye dinnae mean to take them to the Serpent Cave!" Evan interrupted. "This is all nonsense, Elliot."

"Ye dinnae have to come." Elliot waved to the two women. "Come along. It's getting dark. Ye must find a place to get under cover for the night. I'll show ye the way."

Chapter 3

Echo's spirits lifted when Elliot turned away to lead her and Betty to this cave he mentioned. She couldn't believe their luck that they happened upon Elliot Ritchie so quickly. What were the odds?

The three of them took a few steps when the wimpy guy started whispering in Barclay's ear. Elliot ignored them, but a second later, Barclay spun around to frown at his little friend. "Where?"

The smaller man pointed into the forest. "They're here!" Barclay spoke much more quietly than he had since he first showed up.

"Who's here?" Betty asked, but Elliot only shrugged.

Barclay and the other two hurried away. Elliot, Echo, and Betty didn't go after them. "Och, good riddance to them, anyway." Elliot smiled down at Echo and she got another heart palpitation at the suggestive glint in his eye. Was he thinking the same thing she was?

He set off in a different direction and Echo felt the same wave of relief. She wasn't sorry to see the other three go, but she hadn't gone more than a couple of yards when a commotion broke out in the trees.

All three of them looked over and Betty gasped. "Oh, my God! Are those......?"

Echo, Elliot, and Betty stared in astonishment as two large cats dashed across Echo's line of sight. They were much larger than normal house cats—about as big as large dogs just like Liam said. They were Highland tigers.

They sprang easily on furry paws and their long, striped tails stretched out behind them. They covered the distance with incredible speed.

Barclay and his two dopes chased the cats with drawn weapons—or at least the other two did. Barclay was unarmed, but he had picked up a big stick to use as a club.

The cats would have outstripped the men easily, but it wasn't to be. The cats got twenty yards ahead and the smaller one sprang off the ground with impossible speed and agility.

The cat collided with a nearby tree, bounced off hardly touching the bark, and soared straight into Barclay's face.

The cat landed on the big man's head, sank its claws into Barclay's bald scalp, and hung on while it kicked and shredded him with its claws.

Echo's jaw dropped watching the carnage. The cat yowled in spine-chilling rage and sank its fangs into Barclay's head. He flung up his hands to defend himself, but his club got in the way.

He grabbed the cat and tried to rip it off, but he only succeeded in bringing it within range of his eyes. The cat lashed out one more time and sliced its hind feet down Barclay's face. It caught his eyes in eight parallel gashes that ripped his eyes to shreds.

He screamed and let go of the cat to clutch at his eyes, but he only succeeded in dropping the cat where it could attack him again. The cat hit the ground, levitated against gravity, and struck him full force in the chest.

He tumbled backward with the cat latched onto his clothes. He hit the ground and the cat dove for his throat. In half a second, the cat's razor teeth slashed his jugular and whipped around searching for its next victim.

The larger cat raced past the tree its companion had used as a launch point. The second cat zoomed around the trunk in a tight curve, pelted back at the pursuing men, and charged the skinny guy's legs.

The cat coiled into a ball, rolled along the ground, crashed into the guy's ankles, and downed him in a second. The cat whipped around and tackled the guy onto his face.

Echo couldn't move watching the cat clamp its jaws on the guy's neck from behind. The sickening crunch of bone drifted through the forest and seemed to resound louder than it should have in the deadly silence.

Both cats stepped off their victims and turned to the last man standing—Evan. He stood frozen in place still holding his saber in front of him. He seemed to have completely forgotten it was there.

The two cats stalked ever nearer. Evan's eyes skipped back and forth trying to watch them both at the same time, but anyone could see he didn't stand a chance against both of them working together.

These cats made Echo shiver, but seeing the petrified shock in Evan's eyes snapped her out of her trance. She charged and skidded in front of the cats to block them from reaching him.

She dropped her weapons on the ground and held up both empty hands for the cats to see. "Wait! Please.... listen to me. We're searching for Duncan Buchanan. We want to help him. We heard he was in these woods. We want to support him and help him fulfill his destiny. You're his relatives, aren't you? Can you help us?" She thought fast. "We're friends of Snowflake's...from the future. We thought we were going to Icemeet to see her. Do you know Snowflake? She's married to your Clan Chief, isn't she? If you take us to her, she can tell you who we are. She'll tell you we only want to help Duncan."

The words tumbled out of her in a rush. She became aware of Betty at her side. Elliot stood off to one side staring at her like she had gone completely out of her mind....and maybe she had.

The two cats glared at her and she realized she may have just made her last mistake. She was totally unarmed facing two of the most effective killing machines she had ever seen.

The cats didn't move for a second. Echo's hands felt painfully empty without some weapon to defend herself. If they attacked, she would just have to fight them with her bare hands and hope for the best.

Without warning, the smaller cat transformed before her eyes. He straightened up, his fur vanished, and his tail pulled back inside his body.

He changed back into a man with light, sandy hair down past his shoulders and piercing brown eyes. He wore a black kilt cinched with a rough leather belt around his muscular waist. A swath of tartan covered his bare chest and he wore no other clothes or shoes. He was also unarmed.

He narrowed his eyes at Echo and her stomach clenched. Some kind of hidden ferocity smoldered just beneath his skin. It threatened to explode at any second....and then she remembered. He was the same tiger that just killed Barclay. He wasn't a man. He was some kind of feral creature from another time—another reality.

"Ye ken Snowflake?" he asked. "Did she send ye here to help us find Duncan?"

"Not exactly," Betty interjected. "Our people in the future told us he was destined to unseat Laird Balfour Creighton and ascend the Seat of Armstrong. We're here to help him take the throne."

The man snorted and looked back and forth between Echo and Betty. "Ye're a wee bit too late for that, lassie. We dinnae ken where Duncan is. We're here trying to find him ourselves."

"You are?" Echo asked. "Where is he.... I mean......?"

"He ran away from our Clan. He couldnae stand to live at Icemeet with the threat against his life....and I cannae say I blame him. Colton and I stood by him and gave him our protection, but he couldnae belong to any Clan that considered him a Creighton....as he is one. He doesnae ken where he belongs as he doesnae belong anywhere any longer." He turned to the other cat. "It's all right, laddie. They're friends of Snowflake's."

The other cat shifted in front of Echo's eyes. She shuddered when he changed into a much bigger man with huge, chiseled shoulders even bigger than his companion's.

He had sandy, reddish-blonde hair, too, and three days' growth of beard. Horrible burns covered half his face, ran down his neck, and across his burly chest.

The first man extended his hand to Betty and then to Echo. "I'm Reid Buchanan. Me brother Colton is Clan Chief in Icemeet. He's Snowflake's husband. This is me cousin Alastair."

"Aye," Alastair added. "Snowflake is our commander. We wouldnae do without her."

Echo softened to these men. She couldn't help but chuckle. "She never could walk into a room without taking over."

Alastair laughed outright. "That's her all over."

"Have ye seen Duncan in these woods?" Reid asked. "We tracked him here, but he keeps evading us."

"We just got here a few minutes ago. We were talking to...." Betty's gaze drifted back to Elliot, who hadn't moved or spoken through the whole encounter.

"This is Elliot Ritchie," Echo told Reid. "He's Grant Ritchie's brother."

Reid's expression hardened and he snarled through gritted teeth. "Is that so? We've had dealings with yer brother, laddie."

"Never mind about that," Echo exclaimed. "We can go with you. We can help you find Duncan. These rebels threatened him, too, so he won't be safe in these woods. We should find him and take him home where he'll be safe."

"I dinnae ken that he'll be any safer at Icemeet, but we can try," Reid remarked. "We were on our way to check a waterhole down the hill there...."

"Hold yer horses a moment, lassies." Elliot strode over to them and held out his hand first to the two women and then to the two Buchanans. "I dinnae say ought against yer Clan, lad, but ye lassies cannae go off with them."

"Why not?" Echo asked.

"I cannae wait to hear this," Reid growled.

"Ye cannae go with them because ye cannae travel the same as them. They're tigers and ye're human. Ye cannae keep up with them and it will be night soon." Elliot waved to the two women. "Come with me to the Serpent Cave and ye can get something to eat and some sleep while ye decide what to do."

"We ken what to do," Alastair countered. "We're off to find Duncan, and if ye belong to these rebels, ye're as big a threat to him as any Creighton. Ye can count yer blessings we dinnae end ye here and now to stop ye from going after him."

"I wasnae going after him or ye as ye've just now seen," Elliot replied. "I was simply trying to help these lassies as they're friends of a friend of mine as well as yers."

Reid raised his eyebrows. "Ye dinnae say so."

"He's talking about our friend Lily," Echo explained. "She's still in Kald."

"She's married to the Creighton prince," Reid fired back. "She's our sworn enemy. Ye cannae go there. Ye come with us to Icemeet. Snowflake will sort ye out right enough."

"But not tonight," Elliot argued. "These lassies dinnae run like ye nor live on the land like ye. Ye lads can come to the Serpent Cave, too, if it means that much to ye."

Reid scowled at him and then studied the two women. His intense gaze made Echo uncomfortable, but she noticed Betty smiling at him.

"All right," Betty decided. "We'll stay in this cave tonight and then we'll see about finding Duncan. If you can track him by scent, you'll have a much better chance of finding him than we will."

Elliot perked up and he gave Echo another one of his meaningful smiles. He wiped it instantly when Reid glared at him again, but at least the Buchanans weren't in any danger of killing anybody anymore.

The party started to turn away when Elliot noticed Evan standing there with his mouth open. He still hadn't put his saber down.

Elliot walked over to him. "I'll take that, laddie." He took the saber out of Evan's hand and then drew the dirk from Evan's belt. "Ye winnae be needing them."

Elliot and Reid exchanged a glance and then Elliot took Evan's elbow. "Come along, laddie. There's no sense hanging about."

He tugged Evan into a stumbling walk, but Evan kept gaping at the two Buchanans like they might tear him apart at any second.

Reid and Alastair gave Echo that impression, too, but then she saw Reid and Betty smiling at each other again. Echo deliberately turned away and pretended not to see.

This crazy country had some strange effect on the Last Division. Their oath to give up love, family, and society evaporated here. Lily and Snowflake had already found love and gotten married. Would Betty be next?

Echo's gaze flicked over to Elliot. He guided Evan in front of her and Elliot didn't turn around. He didn't cut as imposing a figure as Reid and Alastair with their bare chests and legs. They showed no sign of being aware of the elements and they walked easily on the rough forest floor. Their toes gripped the earth with practiced ease.

Elliot wasn't as tall as Reid or as bulky as Alastair, but she recognized the triangle of muscle rising from his shoulders to the back of his neck. His shirt did nothing to hide how muscular he was.

He didn't radiate the same animal ferocity that infused everything the Buchanans did. He seemed softer somehow but no less rugged and capable.

He cast one glance behind him to make sure the others were still with him. His eyes locked on her and they flashed with that suggestive glint before he turned away.

She felt herself becoming attracted to him. She shouldn't with the Last Division's oath hanging over her head, but if the others were all doing it, why shouldn't she?

Her mind teemed with questions about what he was doing here. Why had he left his brother in Kald? What did he remember about his life before he fled to the forest?

Liam's story about Grant and Elliot growing up as the sons of a castle maid piqued her curiosity. Elliot called his brother a lizard and Elliot seemed overly reluctant to consider that he might be one, too. Why resist it if it meant he could be royalty like his brother was?

Then she remembered the other missing detail. The Laird tried to kill these two when they were babies. Grant was living in Tyrekirk as the Laird's heir, but that didn't mean Grant wasn't still a threat to the Laird's rule.

The Laird would probably turn against Grant if it served his purpose, which meant that the Laird must be threatening Elliot, too. Was that why he fled from Kald?

Lily was living under the Laird's rule, too. She must be doing it to help Grant. That had to be hard on both of them.

Echo looked behind her at Reid and Alastair Buchanan. Finding them so quickly was another stroke of luck, but her elation vanished when she saw both men glaring at the back of Elliot's head. They hated him. He was a rebel, the group who had sworn to kill any Buchanan who set foot in these woods.

She didn't have to think too hard to figure out why they were going along with this. They wanted to stay near Echo and Betty. They didn't want to get separated from two of Snowflake's friends, but there was more to it than that.

They wanted to be on hand if and when the party found Duncan. Reid and Alastair wanted to keep an eye on Elliot to make sure he didn't do anything to harm Duncan.

Chapter 4

Elliot ducked under the overhang, entered the shadowy cave, and parked Evan on the floor. "Come along inside, ye lot," Elliot called to the rest of their party. "There's food and wood in here. We can make a fire and spend the night here."

Echo crouched down and peered inside. "It's pretty dark in there. How can you see anything?"

"Yer eyes get used to the dark after a while. Dinnae hang about, ye lads."

He did his best to keep his tone cheery, but he couldn't help seeing the two Buchanans glaring at him behind his back. They didn't try to hide it—not that he blamed them.

He didn't want to have anything to do with them, either, but if it meant keeping Echo and Betty with him, he could put up with the Buchanans, too.

Echo got too excited about finding them and going after Duncan. He didn't want to let them take her away.

He had to admit to himself that he cared a lot more about her than her friend, but they were a unit. He couldn't expect them to split up.

She stooped into the cave and squinted into the dark. "I'm over here, lassie."

Her expression cleared. His heart flipped when she smiled at the sound of his voice. Did she feel the same way about him? Did she feel this quivering excitement at meeting him?

She knelt down next to him and peered out through the cave opening. Betty, Reid, and Alastair stood outside talking. Elliot didn't want to think about what they were talking about.

"You're right!" Echo exclaimed. "I can see now."

"Good lass. Perhaps ye'd like to help me with this lot, then." He nodded down at a bunch of bundles and crates stashed at the back of the cave.

He opened one of them and took out a haunch of cured meat, a loaf of bread, and a round of cheese. "Where did this come from?" she asked.

"We supply all our caves so we have some place to stay when we go out hunting." He threw a tarpaulin off a pile of firewood. "Would ye prefer to cook or start the fire?"

"I'll start the fire. Thanks for asking." She shot him a knowing smirk and his stomach burned. She was flirting with him! He'd bet anything on that.

"I suppose that leaves me to do the cooking like the old fishwife that I am."

She burst out laughing, but a booming voice cut her off. "We'll take naught from the rebels," Alastair barked. "We'll sleep on the ground and hunt our own food before we touch a speck of their goods."

"I dinnae care if ye starve." Elliot jutted his chin toward the forest. "Go on with ye if ye fancy yer luck."

"No, no." Echo jumped up, grabbed Alastair's hand, and pulled him into the cave. "Don't leave, Alastair. You don't have to eat the rebels' food, but at least spend the night with us. We want to talk to you, and if we're all going to leave together in the morning, we wouldn't be able to find you."

He suffered her to tow him inside. She had to let go of his hand to build the fire. He scowled down at her and then at Elliot, but Alastair didn't leave.

Reid and Betty took longer to come inside. Whatever they were talking about out there certainly engrossed them. They engrossed each other. They didn't even hear what Alastair said.

Echo worked over the fire and finally lit the tinder with the flint from the rebels' stores. The flames licked up and she tried to pull Alastair down. "Take a seat, Alastair. You don't have to stand all night."

He didn't. He glared at everyone. He really looked hideous with half his head and chest burned like that, but he acted nice enough as long as Elliot wasn't around.

Elliot brought the food over to the fire along with a cutting board and a knife. He started by cutting off a section of bread, wrapped it around slices of meat and cheese, and held it over to Evan. "Here ye go, laddie. Build yerself up."

Evan didn't see the food. He stared into the flames consuming the wood. He finally shook his head and looked around with wild terror. He took one look at Alastair's burned face and then Evan spotted Reid and Betty coming inside.

Evan blurted out, "I cannae....," launched to his feet, charged out of the cave, and bolted into the woods.

"What's wrong with him?" Echo asked.

"Och, it's just as well, I suppose." Elliot held out the food to Alastair. "Take it, lad. It isnae poisoned."

Alastair scowled at him and then snatched the food from Elliot's hand. Alastair tore off a hunk with ferocious brutality and started chewing like he wanted to punish Elliot by eating it. Elliot chuckled and went back to cutting up food for the other three.

"What do you mean—it's just as well Evan ran away?" Echo asked. "Isn't he your friend?"

Elliot shrugged. "He's as good a friend as a man can have out here.... which isnae saying ought, I can tell ye. He's better than Barclay and Graeme, but then again, anyone would be."

"I've been thinking," she replied. "Maybe you could take us to Kald. If we can't find Duncan, we should go find Lily and follow up on Lady Rhona Armstrong. You could introduce us to your brother and...."

"Och, no!" he interrupted. "I winnae do that."

"Why not?"

"It's out of the question. That's why." He got to his feet and held out a sandwich of bread, meat, and cheese to Reid. "Take it, lad. Ye cannae hunt always."

Reid eyed him suspiciously, but in the end, he took it, too. Betty smiled at Elliot when he gave her one, too. "Thank you, Elliot. Thank you for bringing us here. We really appreciate it."

He smiled back at her. He was starting to like her, but she didn't have the same effect on him that Echo did.

He squatted down and started cutting up some food for himself.

"What happened between you and Grant?" Echo asked again. "He's the Laird's heir. You could be living at the castle with him instead of slumming it out here."

He didn't look up. He couldn't meet her gaze. "Och, aye, I'm sure I could. It's a hard life out here. Dinnae ask me what I'm doing out here for I dinnae ken meself."

"Ye lassies would much better come to Icemeet with us," Reid cut in. "Jaimee will be right pleased when she kens ye're in the country."

"Who's Jaimee?" Betty asked.

"Snowflake," Reid explained. "She goes by her own name now."

"Wow," Betty breathed. "She must have really changed since she got here. Now she's married and everything."

"She called herself Snowflake when she first arrived," Alastair replied. "Then, when she mated with Colton and joined our Clan, she said she wanted the rest of us to ken her as well. She doesnae keep any secrets from us any longer."

"Aye," Reid murmured. "She's one of us now."

Echo stared into the flames deep in thought. Elliot couldn't read her expression. The fire crackled and she added more wood to it.

"We'll leave for the Boundless tomorrow," Reid decided. "We dinnae ken where Duncan is at any rate. We'll take ye home to Jaimee and then come back out."

"Thank you." Betty beamed at him. "We'd still like to help search for him if we can, but we understand if you can do that better without us."

"You don't know where Duncan is?" Echo asked. "Can't you track him by scent?"

"Aye, but he has a strange way of eluding us. I dinnae understand it at all. We should have found him by now."

"I cannae understand why he crossed the Boundless at all," Alastair added. "He's more in danger here than anywhere else with the Creightons hunting him."

"He *is* a Creighton," Echo pointed out. "Maybe he wanted to try to get back to his mother's people."

"That makes no sense at all, lass. The Laird wants to kill him and the rest of the Creightons hate him for being a Buchanan." Reid waved at Elliot. "Can ye imagine a Buchanan descended from the Clan Chief walking into Tyrekirk and telling the Laird, 'I'm yer long-lost grandson'? It's preposterous!"

Elliot looked away. He didn't want to think about himself or anyone else walking into Tyrekirk. If he ever saw Grant again, Grant would probably try to kill him for pushing him away.

Then again, Elliot would want to kill Grant just as badly. Grant was a Creighton and Elliot hated all Creightons. He'd grown up hating them even when he worked as a soldier in the Laird's army.

Chapter 5

Elliot reentered the cave carrying a bundle of firewood. The party had already gone through the stores stashed here. Elliot would have to come back and replenish them once he dealt with these people. That was the rule. Anyone who used the supplies had to replace them.

His adrenaline started pumping again when he saw Reid, Betty, and Alastair sitting off to one side talking again. Echo sat alone by the fire and she smiled up at him when he squatted down next to her. "They're plotting me demise, lassie," he teased. "I'll be dead by morning."

Her eyebrows knit together in the middle frowning at him. "Is it as bad as that? Do you really think they'd kill you?"

"Perhaps. There's no love lost between the rebels and the Buchanans."

"Why? You're all against the Laird. Why don't you join forces against your common enemy?"

"Most of the rebels grew up in the Kald slums and fled the Laird's service to go their own way. They've all grown up hating the Buchanans. They dinnae change their stripes when they come out here."

She studied him more closely as though trying to decide something. "What about you?"

"What about me? Ye ken all there is to ken about me."

"I don't know anything about you except your name. How did you grow up? I heard you and Grant were raised by a castle maid at Tyrekirk."

"Aye."

"So? Why did you turn against the Laird? Don't tell me it was because you want to depose him."

"I never turned against the Laird. He turned against me....and Grant. We were doing our duty fighting Buchanans when he sent his wizards out to attack us. If he hadnae, I'd still be...." He trailed off. The memory was still too fresh and painful.

"You mean you'd still be with Grant?"

He tried to distract himself from her question started by breaking up the sticks he'd brought. "Anyway, we might have gone our separate ways anyhow what with him getting drawn in by Lily and all."

She gasped. "Do you mean she came between you? I find that hard to believe."

"Och, no! I'm saying naught against Lily. She's a fine lass. I cannae fault her at all and I dinnae blame Grant for falling for her. I might have done the same under different circumstances.... or someone like her. She's staunch through and through and never let us down once. It was just.... Well, one of us was bound to find a woman one day and then.... I suppose we'd have parted after all. It's the way of the world."

She kept studying him with that intense, unwavering stare of hers. She looked like such a pixie, but her eyes left nowhere for him to hide. She saw everything about him that he'd rather conceal and she heard everything he didn't say.

He didn't say that parting ways from Grant was the most excruciatingly painful thing he'd ever done in his life. He didn't say that he would never have parted from Grant under any circumstance—certainly not for a woman.

He also didn't say that he parted from Grant as much out of fear of Grant's dragon nature as from disgust at finding out that Grant was a Creighton and the Laird's own grandson.

Echo finally turned back to stare into the flames. The crackle of popping wood and the whispers coming from the Buchanans made the only noise in the silence.

"And ye?" Elliot ventured. "Tell me all about ye."

"What would you like to know? How much did Lily tell you about our life back home?"

"I ken ye belonged to some Division with ye and Betty and Lily and this Snowflake woman. I ken ye went into battle in the Army and suffered losses and I ken ye swore off love and society and all to help the poor. That's all I ken."

"If you know all that, you know just about all there is to know about me. There isn't a lot to tell, although it looks like the Last Division is finished. Two of our members are married and up to their eyeballs in a war between two Scottish Clans. I don't see Snowflake coming back to the States, now that she's fully a member of Clan Buchanan."

Echo glanced over at the Buchanans. "It doesn't look to me like too many people quit that Clan and run off to the forest to get away from them."

"Aye," he murmured. "They're a staunch Clan right enough."

They both fell silent. Elliot could think of a lot of things he'd like to ask her about her life and her past and the Last Division, but he kept quiet. If anything developed between them, he'd have plenty of time to ask later.

He thought for a long time about how to restart the conversation in a more casual vein and finally asked, "Do I get to ken ye're real name? Ye ken mine."

He expected her to throw up her defenses, but she only grinned at him. "Do you want to know a secret no one outside the Last Division knows?"

His eyes popped. "Ye'd go as far as that? I'm honored, lassie."

She only laughed. "My real name is Echo Boxwood. It's so unusual that most people don't believe that it's my real name. That's why I started using it as my codename in the Army."

He nodded down at the fire. "It's a lovely name. Echo." He listened to the sound almost as though it was making an echo in the cave.

She laughed at him. "Don't start saying it over and over. It's just a name."

"It's more than that." He beamed at her. "I'm honored ye told me. It's me privilege."

"Hardly. I'm not royalty like you are."

He looked away again. "I'm anything but that." She didn't press the point, so he changed the subject. "It appears yer friend Betty is forming an attachment for one Reid Buchanan."

"I noticed. I can't say I blame her. He's stunning."

Elliot gasped in mock horror. "Lassie! How could ye be so cruel? I'm sitting right here."

She laughed again and her cheeks flushed. "Shut up! You're just as good looking as he is."

"Och, no! Grant was always the better-looking one. The lassies couldnae get enough of him."

"I bet you had your share of them, too," she teased.

Now it was his turn to blush and he lowered his eyes to the flames. "I cannae say I didnae."

"I knew it! You look like a devil."

"Now ye're trying to hurt me. I cannae have fallen so far since I came to live in this forest. If I cannae call meself a ladies' man any longer, it's time I packed up and went back to Kald. At least I ken the lassies there. They'll have me even if ye break me heart."

They both laughed and then she got more serious. "I didn't mean it in that way. I meant you look like the kind of devil that charms women and breaks *their* hearts. You look to me like you could get any woman you wanted whenever you wanted."

He eyed her, but he couldn't joke about this anymore, not with her looking at him like that. "Perhaps not *any* woman I wanted."

She read exactly what he meant and looked away, but at least he said it. He would gladly give up every other woman in the world if he could get Echo, but that would probably never happen.

She was so much like Lily—not in her looks or her voice or her manner. In that way, the two women couldn't be more different. Lily never flirted with Grant like this. Lily didn't laugh and joke around. She was all business, but the circumstances never called for anything else.

Echo was just as tough and alert and capable. That was her charm. She could be all that and laugh and joke at the same time. She fascinated him beyond any woman he'd ever met, but why should she go for a rebel and an outlaw like him?

He was no royalty. Even if, by some fluke of nature, he turned out to be a freak dragon shifter like Grant, Elliot would never go back to Kald. He would never simper for the Laird—not for all the gold in the world.

Echo wouldn't want to live as a rebel in the forest. Why should she when she could have any man she wanted? She only had to look at him with those deep, soft eyes and he would melt for her. Any man would go to the ends of the earth for a woman like her.

Chapter 6

Echo woke up in the middle of the night and blinked into the dying embers of the fire before she remembered where she was.

The stone floor underneath her made her bones ache. She had been getting soft at Ironforge after spending years sleeping in a regular bed. Maybe the whole Last Division had been getting soft. They'd been living behind walls for too long. No wonder the whole thing was starting to fall apart if it hadn't already fallen apart already.

The way Reid and Alastair talked about Snowflake unsettled Echo more than anything else that had happened so far. They used her real name and talked about her becoming a full member of Clan Buchanan. That didn't sound like the Snowflake that Echo remembered.

It made sense, though. That must be why Snowflake started using her real name in the first place. She wasn't the same person she had been in the Army. She wasn't in hiding anymore. She wanted to be known for who she really was. The Buchanans must have affected her more than any of the Last Division could have anticipated.

Echo had no idea who the real Jaimee was and Echo wasn't sure she wanted to know. She had depended on Snowflake for years to lead the Last Division.

Was that the only reason Echo wanted Snowflake—so she could have a leader to make the hard decisions and take the responsibility off of Echo's shoulders? Echo didn't like to think of herself that way.

Turning her back on Jaimee now that she was no longer Snowflake would be a low blow. It would be cowardly. It would prove that Echo never really cared about Jaimee at all.

Echo sat up to add more wood to the fire and straightened the blankets that Elliot had given her. She smiled to herself when she remembered their conversation earlier. She enjoyed flirting with him and his suggestions excited her. She didn't know what she was missing at Ironforge. She had forgotten how much she enjoyed a man's attention.

She glanced over at his blankets still smiling at the thought of watching him sleep, but he wasn't there. She frowned. His blankets lay in a heap by the fire where he'd fallen asleep, but he definitely wasn't here anymore.

She looked across the cave to where Betty, Reid, and Alastair had bedded down and Echo stiffened. They weren't there, either. Betty was gone. Echo was totally alone in the cave.

Echo scrambled to her feet fighting down panic. What happened to everyone? Where was Betty?

Echo couldn't imagine the Buchanans doing anything to Betty. Reid had been just as taken with Betty as Elliot had been with Echo. After the comments Alastair made about Snowflake, Echo couldn't see Alastair doing anything to Betty, either....so where were they?

Echo peered outside into the pitch dark. Only a faint glimmer of starlight made it through the dense forest canopy. Wherever the others had gone, they had left the cave in the middle of the night.

She heard noises in the distance and her heart started hammering. Something was going on over there. The other four must be out there somewhere. She had to find them.

She went back into the cave and got the weapons she had taken from Barclay. She would need them if anything dangerous came along to threaten her in the dark.

She hesitated on the threshold while her eyes got used to the darkness. She scanned her vision back and forth across the ground. She might not have the Highland tigers' noses, but she could track well enough.

She found four sets of human footprints, but they all went off in different directions—or, to be more accurate, two went in one direction while the other two split off. The two that went together must be Reid and Alastair.

That left Elliot and Betty. Echo couldn't see which was which in the dark, so she tracked to the left for a while. She slowed when a fifth set of tracks joined up with this one. Who was out here in the middle of the night coming up on one of their party?

She paused to decide what to do when she heard it again—a faint mewing noise in the distance. She swiveled that way and picked up speed closing on the noise.

She climbed a small hill and froze when she looked down the other side. She dropped flat on her stomach and crept to the edge to watch.

Three Highland tigers pranced together in the starlight where the hill joined a grassy stream bank. The cats swirled around each other swishing their tails and touching noses.

They made soft chirping sounds, fluffed up their fur, and pounced playfully on top of each other.

Echo could see from here that one of the cats had most of the fur on his head and back burned off. Raw, scarred skin covered one shoulder and ran down one leg. It was Alastair.

Echo couldn't tell which of the other two cats was Reid. They looked similar and Echo's pulse raced even faster. Did Reid and Alastair find Duncan after all?

A flash of movement caught her eye and she narrowed her eyes at two men below her. They lay on their stomachs, too, and watched the cats from a hollow farther down the hill.

In front of Echo's shocked eyes, Elliot rose on his knees, brought a flintlock rifle to his shoulder, and took aim at the cats. Echo didn't recognize the second man, but she heard his voice whispering in the dark. "Shoot, laddie! Take them out now and prove yerself."

Echo gaped at them in horror. Elliot was about to shoot Duncan! What the hell was wrong with him?

She couldn't let this happen. She rose to her feet and took a firm grip on her weapons. She sidestepped along the hilltop until she positioned herself directly on top of Elliot.

She took a deep breath, raised her weapons, and launched herself off the hilltop to land right on top of him. Elliot and his friend kept all their attention on the cats. They never saw her coming

Echo launched herself into open space and left all her happy feelings about Elliot lying on that hilltop. He wasn't the man Echo thought he was if he could do something like this. He would threaten the one man who could bring peace and stability to this country.

She arched back to drive her blade into him from behind when a flying blur of movement rocketed out of the shadows. Echo was already sailing through the air and couldn't stop herself in time.

She caught one fleeting glimpse of Betty whistling out of nowhere before Betty collided with Elliot from the side. His gun exploded as he fell over and fire spat from the barrel.

Betty and Elliot bowled sideways and Echo heard Elliot yelling, "What the devil are ye....? Get off me, lassie!"

Echo couldn't check her flight now. The second man reared up to see what was going on and Echo landed right on top of him. She didn't know who he was and she didn't care. He was the one encouraging Elliot to attack Duncan. This man was Echo's enemy just as much as Elliot.

She slammed down on top of him, pinned him, and punched him three times. He collapsed back on the ground and his eyes fluttered closed.

She held her dirk to his throat while she looked around for Betty and Elliot. They were still scuffling several yards away, but Betty had already gained the upper hand. She pounded him a few times and he didn't fight back.

He held his arms in front of his face and yelled up at her, "Be done with ye, lassie! Be done!"

Echo glanced down the hill toward where the cats had been....and her heart sank. Alastair lay flat on his back with a bloody hole where his eye socket should have been. Reid knelt next to him holding Alastair's hand, but Echo could already see that Alastair was gone.

She let go of the stranger, hiked down the hill to Reid's side, and squeezed his shoulder. "I'm sorry. I tried to stop it...."

He shot to his feet and glared up the hill. "Where is the bastard?"

He didn't wait for an answer. He stormed up the hill clenching his fists in rage. Echo hurried after him, but she didn't much care to save Elliot from Reid's vengeance.

How could Elliot do something so stupid? He deserved the worst that Reid could dish out. If Duncan really had the power to save this country, then Elliot deserved a lot worse for trying to kill him.

Reid marched up the hill and found Betty still standing over Elliot. She held a fistful of Elliot's shirt in one hand, but she wasn't beating him anymore. Both of them had started to relax, but Echo didn't see the other guy anymore. He must have slipped away while Betty's back was turned and the gun was also gone.

Reid stalked up to Elliot and smashed his fist into Elliot's face with all his might. Elliot keeled over backward and Reid attacked him with frightening speed. He shouldered Betty aside, knelt down straddling Elliot's chest, and started pounding.

Elliot collapsed under repeated blows. His arms went slack and his body flopped every time Reid picked him up to punch Elliot again. Reid must have knocked Elliot out with that first punch, but Reid didn't seem to notice.

He snarled through gritted teeth slamming his fist into Elliot's face again and again. Echo reached Reid first, and a second later, Betty joined her.

They grabbed Reid's arms and struggled to haul him off. Even then, it took their combined strength to overcome Reid's fury.

"No, Reid!" Betty yelled. "Don't kill him yet! We need to question him first."

Reid fought them off. He threw elbows and toppled Echo before he lunged for Elliot again.

Betty darted in front of him. "Don't, Reid! You've done enough!"

He checked himself when he saw her face, but his rage didn't slacken at all. He glared at her with smoke billowing out of his ears.

She dared to take a step toward him and laid her hand on his chest. "He killed Alastair, but we need to find out why. He might be connected to our enemies somehow."

He still didn't relax. He shoved against her hand like he might push her out of the way and go after Elliot again.

Betty shot Echo a pointed look and took hold of Reid's arm. "Come on. I'll help you take care of Alastair's body."

He switched his menacing glare down to Elliot lying unconscious on the ground, but in the end, Reid let Betty draw him away. They headed down the hill to where Alastair still lay with the blood running out of his skull.

Echo let out a shuddering sigh. At least Elliot didn't hit Duncan—not that this situation wasn't an equally serious disaster.

She waited just long enough for Reid and Betty to reach Alastair's body. Then Echo turned her attention to Elliot. He was out cold with his face smashed in. Blood covered his features from his eyebrows all the way down to his chin.

This wasn't what she had in mind when she thought about watching him sleep. What in God's name could make him do something so stupid? She must have seriously misjudged him.

She couldn't leave him lying out here, though. She grabbed his arm, heaved him into a sitting position, and then hoisted him onto her shoulder in a fireman's carry. She lugged his bulky body back to the cave and lowered him onto his blankets.

She thought the matter over while she built up the fire and rummaged in the food supplies. She didn't expect anyone to be hungry after what just happened, but she had to do something to occupy herself.

She didn't look forward to the moment when Reid and Betty came back—if Reid came back at all.

Chapter 7

Elliot regained consciousness before Reid and Betty returned. He groaned, rolled over, and finally forced himself to sit up. He stared into the fire for a few minutes before he looked up and frowned at Echo.

She couldn't even feel happy about sitting next to him by the fire. Whatever she might have thought or felt about him before only proved how grossly ill-suited she was to going out into the world. She'd been living in a prison of her own making. Now she couldn't even judge a person's character on their first meeting.

His shoulders hunched and he buried his bruised face in his hands. "Och, lassie!"

She didn't say anything. There didn't seem to be anything to say compared to the colossal mistake he just made. Did he even realize it was a mistake? Did he even begin to fathom how close he came to destroying his whole country?

Footsteps distracted both of them when Reid and Betty entered the cave. They halted there glaring down at Elliot. No one spoke for a minute.

Elliot lowered his eyes before Reid's fury. Elliot refused even to look at Reid and Echo didn't blame him. Reid smoldered in volcanic rage. He clenched his fists, compressed his lips, and trembled all over while he fought to control himself.

Betty glared at Elliot, too, and when she finally broke the silence, she snarled low through gritted teeth. "Do you mind telling us what in the holy hell you were thinking? You killed Alastair and you almost killed Duncan. What in the world is wrong with you, Elliot?"

"Who was that guy with you?" Echo added. "Why was he telling you to shoot at the Buchanans?"

"It's Torran MacAllister," Elliot muttered without looking up. "He leads the rebels in this part of the forest."

"What the hell difference does it make who he is?" Betty snapped. "He didn't shoot at Duncan and hit Alastair instead."

"I ken, lassie," Elliot murmured. "I'm sorry...."

"Dinnae ye dare to sit there all sad and broken and say ye're sorry!" Reid hissed. "I swear to Christ I'll tear yer stinkin' muckle head off!"

Elliot pursed his lips and kept his eyes down.

"You still haven't told us why you did it, Elliot," Betty demanded. "Why would you want to kill Duncan? Do you have any idea what he could mean to this country if he unseated the Laird and took the Seat of Armstrong for himself?"

"Aye," Elliot murmured under his breath.

"Then what made you shoot at him?" Betty snapped. "Look at us and answer like a man, for God's sake! You're really starting to piss me off, Elliot, and if you don't sack it up and face us, I'll tell Reid to do what he wants with you."

Elliot's head shot up and he met her gaze. "I cannae tell ye why I did it...."

"Bullshit!" Betty roared. "You tell us right now or you won't live to see morning!"

He glanced down at the fire and then forced himself to look back up. "Torran.... Ye'll say I made it up to save me own life. I'm not a coward, but a man's got to live somewhere."

"What are you talking about?" Echo chimed in. "What could possibly justify you shooting at the one man who stands to accomplish everything the rebels want to achieve?"

"Torran didnae ken ought about Duncan," Elliot countered. "He didnae ken ought about ought, lassie. Dinnae ye see?"

"No, I don't see because you haven't explained it to us."

"Evan went back to the fort....the rebel fort where Torran rules. Evan told Torran all that went on when those two attacked Graeme and Barclay." He waved toward Reid. "Torran came out and found me. Dinnae ask me how."

"What does this have to do with you shooting at Duncan?" Betty asked. "Why would you shoot at him and try to kill him if Torran didn't know anything about Duncan?"

"He only kenned there were tigers in the area. Evan told him. I woke up in the night and found those two gone. I followed them outside and Torran came up on me in the dark. He demanded I shoot the Buchanans or he'd.... He said I couldnae ever go back to the fort meself without losing me own life and he'd see the Laird learned where I was. I havenae anywhere left to go in the world, ye see. The fort's all I've got."

"You sad sack of shit!" Betty snarled. "You could have killed Torran. You were out alone with him in the middle of the night."

"Ye dinnae ken ought, lass." Elliot went back to staring into the flames. "If I'd killed him, I'd have the whole rebel pack on me tail. They'd hunt me to the ends of the earth.

It's enough I'm already hunted by the Laird and cannae go back to Kald without getting me neck cut."

"You are a coward, Elliot," Betty returned. "You had the chance to do the right thing and you...."

"He could have had a hundred men in those woods! Ye dinnae ken ought about him. He put me up to the test. He would have killed me if I didnae pass it."

"Well, you didn't pass it," Echo added. "You didn't kill Duncan."

He hung his head. "I killed a Buchanan. He doesnae care about ought else."

Echo glanced up at Reid. He hadn't moved. He glared at Elliot like Reid didn't hear a word Elliot said.

Echo turned back to Betty to talk about how they were going to find Duncan when, without warning, Reid shot out his arm and pointed at Elliot. "I warn ye, lad, I'm leaving ye with yer head on for I dinnae fancy ripping ye apart in front of these lassies. If I ever lay eyes on ye again, yer life is worth naught to me. Do ye get me meaning clear enough? We arenae quits on this and ye can lay odds that every Buchanan on that mountain will ken yer name before the end of tomorrow." He shot Betty a furious glare and barked out the side of his mouth. "I'm off to find me brother."

"I'll come with you." Betty grimaced in Elliot's direction and followed Reid to the cave mouth.

Echo got to her feet to go with them. Her mission lay wherever Duncan was. Reid stood a much better chance of finding Duncan than the two women did alone.

She made it two steps before Elliot shot off the ground and grabbed her arm. "Dinnae walk away like that, Echo. I ken I mucked up, but ye dinnae ken what it's like living out here."

"I can imagine well enough. You came out here because your brother turned out to be a lizard. So what? Is this really what you want your life to be, Elliot—living in caves and hanging out with people who would rather kill you than stop the war? Don't you have any backbone at all? Isn't there anything in the world you care about more than saving your own sad, sorry life?"

He stared at her in shock for a minute. She didn't think before the words spilled out, but once she said them, she knew they were true.

If this was his life, she didn't want any part of it. If he could really raise a weapon against Duncan, then Elliot was the last person in the world she wanted to be anywhere near.

Echo turned back to Reid and Betty. "The question is how we're going to find Duncan again. Is there any sign of where he went?"

"He's long gone," Reid growled. "There arenae even any tracks for us to follow."

"What about the scent trail?" Echo asked. "He couldn't just vanish."

"He did vanish," Reid snapped. "I've been telling ye from the beginning. He can erase his scent trail somehow."

"That shouldn't be possible," Betty replied.

"Dinnae tell me that," Reid fired back. "Do ye think I dinnae ken it isnae possible? What the deuce do ye think Alastair and I have been doing in this glaikit wood for the last week? Duncan travels as a cat for a day or two and then evaporates into thin air—no tracks, no scent trail, no naught. Dinnae ask me how he does it."

"Crap!" Betty breathed. "How the heck are we supposed to find him, then?"

"Dinnae ask me. I'm at me wit's end and now this happens." Reid waved at Elliot again and lowered his voice to a broken murmur. "I thought we had him just now. He was so happy to see me and Alastair.... I thought he was finally ready to come home."

Another cruel silence fell over the cave. Echo couldn't turn around to look at Elliot again. He really screwed up. He had ruined their only chance of finding Duncan and bringing him in.

Betty puffed out her cheeks and blew a long breath. "All right. I guess our only option is to go back to the spot where Alastair was killed. We'll search in widening concentric circles until we find some sign. That's the best we can do.... unless someone else has another idea." She turned to Reid. "Is there any chance he would go back to some familiar place....?"

"He hasnae any familiar places on this side of the Boundless. If he isnae going home to Icemeet, he's nowhere. He's running wild with no pattern."

"Okay. We should probably take as many supplies as we can." Betty turned back to Elliot. "Are we allowed to take some of these supplies with us? Will the rebels seek retribution if we take their stuff?"

"Och, lassie, ye take what ye please," he muttered. "I'll replace it for ye. It's the least I can do."

No one said anything for a minute and then Echo and Betty went over to the bundles of supplies. They collected a few things, but Elliot didn't move. He kept his head down. Echo certainly hoped he realized just how badly he ruined their whole mission.

Betty followed Reid outside. Echo was just about to go with them when Elliot stopped her for the second time. "I'm sorry, Echo. Ye're right. I dinnae have any life worth living out here."

"Well, what do you want me to do about it? You chose this life for yourself. You could have been anything you wanted to be in Kald."

"Och, no! The Laird can use his magic to track me down."

Her eyes popped. "He can? How have you managed to live out here without him finding you?"

"I told ye. The rebels have their own wizards protecting the fort. The Laird couldnae send his men out here to fetch me without them falling to the rebels. It's the only protection I have left."

"That's just an excuse," she fired back. "Are you with us or not?"

"How can I be when Reid wants to kill me?"

"Did you ever think you could make it up to him somehow? Did you ever think you could redeem yourself with him—with all of us?"

"How? I cannae bring Alastair back."

She smacked her lips in annoyance. "I don't have time to mess around with this right now. If you want to do the right thing, you have to stop running and hiding like this. If you're with us, you have to be just as committed to finding Duncan and putting him on the throne as the rest of us are. You can't undermine us just when we're on the brink of victory."

"I ken, lass," he murmured. "I ken. Believe me I ken."

"So what do you want me to do?"

"Give me another chance. Give me a chance to make it up to ye....to all of ye."

She pinched her lips shut. She didn't want to give him another chance. She wanted to walk away from him and leave him to figure out his life by himself. That's what he deserved.

"All right," she finally said. "I'll give you another chance, but only one. If you screw up again, I'll kill you myself. I won't let you do anything that could compromise our mission."

"Aye, lassie. Ye have me gratitude."

She looked over her shoulder. Reid and Betty were nowhere in sight. "I can't speak for Reid, though. He said he'd kill you if he ever laid eyes on you again."

"Ye leave him to me, lass."

"Don't do anything to him. Don't retaliate because he threatened to kill you."

"I winnae retaliate, but I cannae make it up to him if I stay here, can I?"

She felt herself softening in spite of herself. "I guess not. Come on."

Chapter 8

Elliot made sure to keep a healthy distance between himself and the other three travelers. Reid went out in front in his tiger form. He kept sniffing the ground, climbing trees, and going off in different directions.

He slowed down several times to make sure Betty stayed with him. He could have streaked away covering much more ground, but he kept stopping and looking back to wait for her. Echo and Elliot wouldn't have been able to keep up with him otherwise.

Echo kept a hundred yards of space between herself and the other two. She always kept them in sight and followed Reid's trail, but she never went near him and Betty.

Elliot lurked at the very end of the line. He really was a sad waste of a man if he'd been reduced to this. Echo was right. Was this any life worth living? Why was he cowering in the forest under the protection of rebels and bandits? This wasn't a life any man would want.

Betty was also right that Elliot could have killed Torran in the forest last night. Elliot could have put up a lot more resistance to Torran's demand that Elliot fire on the Buchanans.

Betty and Echo already told Elliot what Duncan's rise would mean. He should have acted on it. Now he had some serious ground to make up and he didn't feel safe enough to go near the others after Reid's threat.

Reid and Betty pretended that Elliot wasn't there. Reid couldn't fail to smell and even see Elliot following them, but Reid didn't attack Elliot the way he said he would. That was an improvement.

Maybe Echo was also right about Elliot finding a way to make it up to Reid. Elliot couldn't imagine what could possibly make up for accidentally killing Reid's cousin. At least Elliot hadn't killed Duncan. That would have been a catastrophe.

Reid kept going all day. He never once shifted back into a man. He never told the other three if he found any trace of Duncan. Maybe this whole expedition was a giant waste of time.

Elliot considered going back to the rebel fort, but he immediately dismissed the idea. What difference did it make if Reid never found Duncan? At least the party was heading away from Kald. The Laird's magic weakened with every mile they traveled farther away. That would make it harder for the Laird to find them.... or to find Elliot.

The day waned into evening and shadows spread through the forest. The party kept moving until nightfall. Elliot lost sight of the other three in the gloom, but he had nothing else to do with his life but to keep on going.

He stopped in his tracks when he heard footsteps coming toward him. He relaxed when Echo appeared out of the shadows. "There you are. I thought you might have gotten lost. Reid and Betty are making camp over there. Come on."

"Are ye sure I'm welcome with them?" He tried not to grumble too much about it. "I wouldnae want to make anyone uncomfortable with me presence."

She smiled at him with some of the warmth he remembered from yesterday. "I think you'll be the most uncomfortable one. Reid is still furious at you. Just warning you."

"I didnae expect anything less."

"Maybe you should give me your weapons."

He raised his eyebrows. "Whatever for?"

"He'll be less likely to attack you if you're unarmed. He already hesitated to kill you once. Don't give him an excuse."

"Ye're right, lassie."

She gave him the first full, bright smile since his blunder last night. "Keep saying that and you'll be just fine."

He laughed, but he still felt nervous around her. He unbuckled his saber and handed it over along with his dirk. "I'm counting on ye to defend me if he does attack, lassie. I dinnae fancy me chances against one of those cats."

"I'll keep an eye on him for you." She turned away. "Come on. Betty is cooking for us."

She led him to the camp that Reid and Betty had made. They had lit a fire and Betty was roasting some of the cured meat that she took from the cave. She looked up at Elliot, but Reid didn't raise his eyes from the flames.

Echo and Elliot sat down across from them. Betty slid a piece of meat off her skewer, put it on a piece of flat bark, and handed it to Reid.

He started eating it without speaking to her or anyone else. Betty didn't try to engage him in conversation. She put another piece of meat on her skewer and lowered it into the flames.

Echo turned to Elliot. "What were you telling me earlier about the Laird's magic being able to track you into these woods?"

"He has his eyes everywhere. He's the most powerful wizard in the country. He sees all and kens all. There isnae ought hidden from him. He sent his soldiers and wizards after me and Grant and Lily more than once. He laid traps for us and spirited us back to the castle when we tried to run from him."

"Why do you think he hasn't done the same thing to us? If he's that bent on capturing you, he must be able to overcome the rebels' magic, too."

He shrugged and looked away. "I dinnae ken about that."

"Liam says you and Grant grew up in the castle," Echo began.

"Aye. What of it?"

"He says the Laird tried to kill you and your mother hid you with the maid who raised you as her own."

Elliot gaped at her in horror. He didn't want to talk about this, much less think about it. He finally shuddered and looked away again. "I dinnae ken ought about that, either."

"Don't you think it's time you pulled up your socks and started thinking about it?" Betty interjected. "Your brother is the Laird's grandson which means *you're* the Laird's grandson."

Elliot gulped, but he couldn't look at either woman. "Not necessarily."

"Oh, come on, Elliot!" Betty snapped. "What's the use in denying it? Your brother is a dragon shifter which means he's a direct descendent of the Creighton line. Do you realize the odds that you aren't one, too?"

"I think what Betty is trying to say," Echo added, "is that you could help us a lot more if you *were* the Laird's grandson. Even if you didn't share both parents with Grant—which is unlikely—you might share at least one."

"Liam says Lady Ilisa was the Laird's daughter," Betty began again.

Reid startled everyone by speaking up, but he addressed himself only to Betty. He continued to pretend that Echo and Elliot weren't there. "Aye. Jaimee says the same thing."

"What did she say?" Echo asked.

He allowed him to glance at her and immediately averted his eyes. "She says Lady Ilisa was Laird Balfour's daughter and had two sons at Tyrekirk before she fled to Icemeet."

"Yes!" Echo pointed at him. "Now I remember. She had Grant and Elliot and then...."

"Hold yer noise right there, lassie," Elliot cut in. "Dinnae say ought else. I dinnae want to hear it."

"Be quiet, Elliot," Betty snapped. "You're going to hear it whether you want to or not." She turned back to Reid. "What else did Jaimee say? Let's see if it matches up with what Liam told us."

"She says Lady Ilisa was married to Camdyn Carmichael at Tyrekirk and the Laird threatened to kill her two sons, so she used magic to hide them."

"That's what Liam said," Echo added. "He also says that Lady Ilisa had Duncan when she was married to your father, Neill Buchanan—or pretended to be married to him."

"Aye," Reid snarled. "She couldnae be married to him as she was already married to another man. Then she went home to Tyrekirk and had another son with her husband."

"Ness," Elliot blurted out and immediately realized his mistake. Reid glared at him and then went back to ignoring him.

Betty turned to Elliot. "Which means that you're the Laird's grandson just like Grant is. You're a dragon shifter...."

"I am NOT!!" He shot to his feet and strode away into the dark.

He couldn't be a dragon shifter. He couldn't be. He would rather be dead than one of those monsters. The thought made him sick.

The whole memory came crashing into his mind no matter how hard he tried to push it away. He saw Grant transforming into the biggest, blackest, deadliest dragon that Elliot had ever seen—and he'd seen plenty hanging around Tyrekirk all his life.

He couldn't be that. He would have to destroy himself if he was. That was the best way he could rid the world of the Creightons. He couldn't be one of them. They were evil. They slaughtered innocent people and the Laird himself ruled the country with an iron fist. He was the reason the rebels deserted to the forest in the first place.

Elliot buried himself in the darkness trying to get himself under control. The rebels would hunt him down without mercy if they found out he was the Laird's grandson.

He wasn't the Laird's grandson. That story Echo and Betty told him back at the fire must be wrong. He couldn't stand it if it was true. Jaimee and Liam must have mixed something up.

Maybe Elliot really was the son of a maid. Maybe the woman who raised him had a son before Lady Ilisa hid Grant with them. Maybe Grant and Elliot grew up as brothers but they weren't really related. Maybe only Grant had royal blood after all.

Footsteps behind him made him jump and spin around. His hand flew to his saber and his blood ran cold when he remembered that he didn't have it anymore.

"Are you okay?" Echo murmured. "We didn't mean to upset you."

He growled under his breath. "I'm certain *they* did."

"Well, I didn't. We're just trying to get to the bottom of this. Reid was just talking about Grant a minute ago."

"I dinnae want to hear ought about Grant," Elliot snapped. "He's dead to me."

"Well, you have to hear about it, Elliot," she breathed. "You can't keep running away from this."

Elliot looked away into the darkness. He tried to block her voice out of his mind, but she had a way of worming her way into his heart and soul. He found it impossible to ignore her.

"Reid says Grant saved Colton Buchanan's life and helped him escape from Tyrekirk. Colton says Grant is trying to help the Buchanans end the war. Reid says Grant stays in Tyrekirk because he's trying to find a way to undermine the Laird's campaign against the Buchanans."

Elliot tried one last time to clamp his mouth shut, but the words forced their way out. "Aye. Grant's a muckle fine man."

He regretted saying it as soon as he said the words, but she only smiled at him. She took a step nearer and slipped her hand into his. "You could be like that, too. You could be using this power to help people. You could be making the world a better place instead of always running and hiding from what you are."

"I cannae," he choked. "How can being *that* make the world a better place? It's disgusting."

"You aren't disgusting. You're just a man the same as Grant is. Do you think he changed who he is when he realized he could become a dragon? It doesn't sound like it."

"Och, no! He didnae change. Grant never changes. I'm the one who changed."

"You could change again. You could become a muckle fine man like he is. He's taking a massive risk doing what he's doing right under the Laird's nose. The Laird could have killed him for saving Colton, but Grant did it anyway. You could be like that."

Elliot turned to face her. Her eyes gleamed in the night. They shone up at him with a haunted light. Could he be like that? Could he become something fine and strong and worth something.... like Grant?

He tried to turn away, but her eyes held him captive. What if he could? What if he could become something worthy of her? What if he could become a man she would admire and compliment as much as she was complimenting Grant? Was it even possible for a man to change that much?

He suffered another pang of agony when he remembered the moment when he walked away from Grant. He thought at the time that he would never lay eyes on Grant ever again. That was the worst part. Elliot lost a part of himself that day.

He spent his life looking up to Grant. Elliot always wanted to be Grant. Grant offered Elliot a living example of what Elliot always thought a man should be.

Elliot lost that when he parted from Grant. Could he ever get it back?

Elliot didn't think so. He could never face Grant again, but Elliot found a little bit of it in Echo's eyes. She wanted him to be that kind of man again. She actually believed he could be. Wasn't that something worth striving for?

She wouldn't look sideways at him the way he was, and yet, here she was clasping his hand. Maybe he wasn't as completely irretrievable as he thought.

If he thought for a second that he stood a chance to be the man she deserved, he would spend the rest of his life trying to make it up to her. He would spend every waking hour striving to be a man she could respect that way.

Chapter 9

E lliot woke up first the next morning. He made up his mind lying awake last night that he would find a way to make up for his mistake. He would find a way to help this party. He owed it to Echo....and to Reid. Elliot couldn't bring Alastair back, but maybe Elliot could make it up to all the Buchanans by doing something even better.

He sat by the fire until Echo and Betty woke up. Echo smiled at him, but Betty kept her expression flat while she started to prepare some food for breakfast.

A Highland tiger lay curled in a ball at the base of a nearby tree. He uncurled himself, stretched, and strutted over to the others. He meowed at Betty and ran his furry body along her side. She laughed and scratched him....and then Reid came around the other side of her and saw Elliot.

Elliot stiffened when he came face to face with the tiger. Elliot was unarmed and defenseless sitting here on the ground. If Reid attacked him now, Elliot was finished.

Reid flicked his tail back and forth, but he didn't shift. He sat down next to Betty and started licking his paws with elaborate dignity.

"I still can't get used to the fact that he's a guy," Echo exclaimed. "He's so...."

"Cat-like?" Betty laughed again and rubbed Reid's head. "It's funny, isn't it?"

Elliot didn't think it was funny, but he didn't say that. He sat perfectly still, especially when Reid eyed him across the fire several times during breakfast. Elliot seriously considered walking away to get out from under the tiger's penetrating stare. Elliot never felt more like prey than now.

The party finished eating and set off with Reid in the lead as before. Elliot followed the other three much more closely today. He wanted to be on hand in case any opportunity presented itself to further their mission.

He didn't ask Echo for his weapons back and she didn't offer. He could live with that. He didn't want to give Reid any reason to feel threatened by Elliot—as if Elliot could threaten him.

Elliot felt much more settled in himself, now that he'd made the decision to join this party. He'd been wandering around aimlessly with no direction for so long. This must be how Lily and Jaimee felt. They'd been imprisoned in their self-imposed withdrawal. Now they joined their respective Clans and threw their weight and energy into their causes.

Elliot had been doing the same thing and now he came back to life in new ways. He just had to find something he could do to regain his old fire.

Echo stopped among some trees and he drew level with her to see what she was looking at. Reid squatted next to a water hole a few feet beyond where the trees ended. He was back in his human form. "Duncan stopped here. He drank from this pool."

"Did you pick up his scent trail?" Betty asked.

"Aye." Reid turned around and pointed up a nearby hill. "He went up there."

The two of them set off back through the trees. Echo and Elliot fell in behind them. He saw himself and Echo walking side by side just like they might be a real couple. Did he dare to hope?

Reid climbed the hill and paused at the top. All four of them halted and Elliot's heart clenched. This hill gave a view all the way across the Boundless to Icemeet perched on the mountaintop.

The estuary ran down to the coastline with Kald sprawled not far away. The city looked so close and yet so far away.

The Creighton army charged across the planes trying to force the Buchanans to fall back. The two armies clashed with a deafening roar of steel and voices.

Dragons wheeled in the air over the planes and over Icemeet. They bombarded the Buchanan fighting force and blasted fire at the fortress walls.

Siege engines unleashed from the parapet and from positions higher up the mountain. They hurled balls of burning tar skyward. Some collided with the dragons and smashed them screeching to earth. The projectiles that missed landed on the Creighton army and sprayed fire and destruction through the ranks.

Giant crossbows fired massive iron spears at the dragons. The engines could aim remarkably well considering how fast and agile the dragons were. They could maneuver anywhere, but the Buchanans still managed to hit several and knock them out of the sky.

"He came up here," Reid murmured. "He came up here to watch the battle."

"My God!" Betty whispered. "This is so much worse than I imagined. I mean.... the destruction....! How do they keep fighting this war with so many people dying?"

"I should be over there with them," Reid growled. "I shouldnae be here when they're over there fighting and dying to defend our land."

"You're doing something much more important," Betty told him. "If you find Duncan, he can stop all this."

"I dinnae ken about that. What if it's all a tale and he cannae do ought? This could all be for naught."

"Then one more person fighting over there won't change anything. Come on. You found his scent trail. If we find him, you can take him home regardless of the outcome. That will be better for him than running around out here lost and alone."

"Aye. Ye're right, lass." He turned away with a heavy sigh and went back to the spring where he picked up Duncan's scent trail. "I'm going to scout the area. Ye lassies head off that way." He pointed deeper into the forest. "His scent trail goes that way, but he may have broken off again. I want to see if he reappeared somewhere else."

"Okay," Betty agreed. "Come on, Echo."

The two women left and Reid turned to his right to circle the spring. He ignored Elliot the way he had been for the last two days. Reid vanished into the trees and Elliot started to relax, now that Reid wasn't around anymore.

Elliot wasn't sure what to do with himself so he decided to go back to the hilltop. He wanted to see more of the battle, but when he stepped into the trees, Echo came back smiling at him.

She handed him his saber and dirk. "I think you better take these. I don't think Reid will go after you ....as long as you don't cross him again."

"Thank ye, lass. I dinnae feel meself without them."

She left to catch up with her friend and he stopped there to buckle on his weapons. He felt naked without them. Now he would be able to defend himself if anything happened.... or if Reid changed his mind about leaving Elliot alive.

He turned back to the hill when he heard a twig snap to his left. It came from the opposite direction that Reid and the two women had gone. Reid wouldn't make a sound like that while he was walking in the woods. He would have shifted back into a tiger by now. Who was over there?

Elliot shrugged it off and turned his steps toward the hill when he heard it again. A soft footstep crunched in something at a distance and then he heard whispering. Someone was definitely over there. Were they sneaking up on him and his companions?

He tiptoed through the woods much more quietly than before. He learned a long time ago how to move around without giving away his position.

He circled the spring and found a rivulet winding into the trees. He followed it, but five yards later, he heard more whispering.

He hid behind a tree and then advanced to a hollow in the forest floor. He darted behind another trunk and peeked out at ten men crouching there. They held a whispered conversation and pointed farther down the stream.

Elliot frowned when he recognized Evan with them, but he wasn't in charge. Torran wasn't with the group, either. Three of Torran's rebels put their heads together listening to what Evan was saying. The other three were Fyfe, Errol, and Gowan.

Elliot recognized the whole situation laid out before his eyes. Torran must have sent these men out to track the Buchanans. Duncan might be able to vanish without a trace, but Reid, Elliot, and the two women couldn't.

Gowan was a great tracker. He would be able to track Reid and Alastair in their cat forms. Gowan must have realized by now that Elliot and the two women were traveling with at least one Buchanan.

Evan pointed over the edge of the hollow and Elliot tensed every muscle when he saw Reid in the distance. Reid was in his cat form the way Elliot expected, but the wind was against him and he was facing the other way. He didn't see or smell these rebels sneaking up on him.

He coiled his legs under him to press his body to the ground. He slunk along on silent paws like he might be stalking something. Had he found his brother after all?

A wave of mental confusion staggered Elliot's mind. He could stand here and do nothing. The rebels would attack Reid and maybe even kill him. That would solve the problem of Reid threatening Elliot.

How could Elliot ever face Echo if he did that? If he ever hoped to go any further with her, he would always have Reid's death hanging over his head.

Didn't Elliot just pledge to do better—to be a better man? If the rebels killed Reid, they would go after Duncan next. Would Elliot stand by and watch them kill Duncan, too?

He only had to think about Echo's eyes looking up at him and he made up his mind. His hand flew to his dirk and he surveyed the terrain beyond the hollow. Every moment took Reid farther from the rebels, but they were still close enough to spring on him unawares.

Elliot turned away and set off at a fast run. He only checked his stride to make sure he didn't give himself away.

He skimmed back up to the spring, dodged left, and charged down the hill on a dead sprint for Reid's position. Elliot didn't even try to quiet his footsteps now. He snapped as many branches and made as much noise as he could.

He exploded into the open brandishing his saber on high. Reid whipped around to glare up at Elliot, flattened his ears against his head, and hissed in a rage. He didn't see Gowan and Fyfe breaking cover and the rebels pouring out of the hollow.

The rebels didn't see Elliot until the last possible moment. Fyfe and Errol raised their sabers to attack Reid while his back was turned.

Elliot lunged between them and smashed Errol's blade down with a punishing clang. The weapon hit the dirt and Elliot attacked the rebels with everything he had. He plunged his dirk at Errol's chest only to get cut across the shoulder by Fyfe moving in to attack.

More rebels surrounded Elliot and half of them went after Reid. The cat erupted off the ground and sprang for his nearest attackers, but Elliot didn't see any of that.

Gowan recognized Elliot and charged swiping his saber. He blocked Elliot's next parry and Fyfe joined Gowan to hem Elliot in.

Elliot's mind dissolved in battle fury. He whirled one way and then the other as five men attacked him at once. He dove forward and managed to impale Errol, but that meant nothing. Errol was always the weakest of the bunch.

Elliot still had to deal with Gowan and Fyfe. Elliot wasn't looking forward to facing Gowan on his own, much less with four other men helping him out.

Fyfe sprang forward and tried to duck under Elliot's saber arm while Elliot was still stabbing Errol. Fyfe's blade sliced the muscle connecting Elliot's arm to his back and Elliot roared in pain and rage.

He spun around to face Fyfe and Gowan struck. He hacked down with his saber, and when Elliot blocked the stroke, Gowan slashed his dirk point across Elliot's cheek.

Elliot wheeled the other way to defend himself against Gowan when he spotted Evan. Evan hadn't run more than ten feet from the hollow. He stood back there with a bow drawn to his cheek. He was aiming at Reid.

Reid had shifted back into a man and taken weapons from rebels he'd slashed to ribbons with his claws. He defended himself against four men and drove them back toward Elliot. Reid didn't see Evan, and even if he did, Reid wouldn't be able to stop what was about to happen. He was too far away.

Fyfe and Gowan both surged to attack Elliot again. Gowan sliced once across Elliot's thigh and Fyfe hit him in the stomach, but Elliot barely felt their cuts. He had to stop Evan at all costs.

Chapter 10

E lliot made a split-second decision and rounded on Fyfe. He wasn't as strong or as skilled as Gowan. Elliot concentrated all his power on slashing Fyfe to smithereens. Gowan landed another brutal chop across Elliot's back, but the blade hit his shoulder blade and glanced off without knocking him down.

Adrenaline fueled Elliot to something close to madness. He batted Fyfe's saber aside and Elliot brought his own blade down in a ferocious cut at Fyfe's head. Fyfe blocked the stroke exactly the way Elliot anticipated and Elliot drove in with his dirk. He feinted for Fyfe's chest and Fyfe defended with his own dirk.

Elliot reacted instantly and drove his dirk point first into Fyfe's eye. The crack of fracturing bone vibrated up the blade, but Elliot let go of the weapon instantly. He leapt past Fyfe's falling body and charged Evan.

Elliot couldn't waste time running. He jumped, soared through the air, and smashed his saber down through the bow and arrow. He hit Evan's wrists and one of his hands dropped away.

Elliot was so far out of his mind that he hardly registered when he swiped his saber back the other way and gashed Evan across the neck.

A deafening crash made Elliot spin around fast. He blinked in dazed astonishment at Gowan standing over him with his saber raised to chop Elliot's head off. Gowan's insane eyes drilled down at Elliot in murderous fury, but Gowan couldn't bring his blade any lower. Another saber blocked it and Reid stood over Elliot eyeing Gowan with deadly intent.

Gowan looked up and Reid gave him a cruel grin before he forced Gowan's saber back. He flung Gowan off and Reid stepped in front of Elliot.

Elliot couldn't stand that. He spun around and sprang to Reid's side facing the last five rebel attackers. Elliot advanced shoulder to shoulder with Reid as they drove the rebels deeper into the woods.

Reid dropped one of them and then Elliot downed a second, but the other three held their own. They started to push the two men back when shouting female voices distracted everyone.

The three rebels glanced behind them to see Echo and Betty running into the fight. Echo must have given Betty Barclay's saber because they were both armed.

Elliot's nerves snapped and he swiped out with his blade. He stabbed one of the rebels in the face before the other two knew what they were doing. Reid pounced next and hacked the fourth across the chest before running him through the middle.

The last remaining rebel whipped around to face the two men and Elliot finished him off. The guy buckled at Elliot's feet....and then the devouring pain of Elliot's injuries hit him full force. Every part of him hurt.

He buckled to his knees trembling. "Elliot!" Echo gasped. "Jesus!"

Reid rested his hand on Elliot's shoulder. "Easy, lad. Hold tight and we'll fix ye up right proper."

"What happened?" Betty glanced to one side and spotted Evan. "The rebels.... How did they......?"

Reid spun the other way tensing every muscle. "Duncan's over there!"

"He is?" Echo asked.

Reid didn't answer. He dropped his weapons, took off running, and shifted before he vanished into the trees.

"We should go after him," Betty suggested. "We can help him corner Duncan."

She raced away to catch up with Reid. Echo hesitated and her eyes searched Elliot's. "Go, lassie," he panted. "This is more important."

She bolted into the trees, but a second later, Elliot heard a scuffle breaking out behind the foliage. It was moving to his left. Whatever they were doing in there, it sounded like Duncan was getting away from them.

He forced himself to his feet and his leg screamed in pain, but he drove himself forward. He staggered to his left into the trees. Whatever was in there was moving incredibly fast. Echo and Betty wouldn't be able to keep up with it and Reid couldn't catch Duncan alone.

Elliot picked up speed and his adrenaline masked the pain. He had to cut off Duncan's escape—if Duncan really was there.

The noise came closer nearing his position. He charged to intercept it....and had to check himself when two Highland tigers streaked out of the undergrowth.

The first one led by at least fifty feet. Elliot was the only thing standing between Duncan and freedom.

Duncan ran so impossibly fast that Elliot almost missed him. Duncan spotted Elliot and dodged. He would have skimmed around Elliot and escaped, but Elliot veered back the way he came, adjusted his course twice more, and dove on top of the cat in a flying tackle.

Duncan weighed a lot more than Elliot thought and the cat proved mind-blowingly strong. He bowled Elliot over and over, and in a split second, the tiger turned all his claws and teeth on Elliot.

The cat let out a hair-raising screech, twisted in Elliot's grasp, and unleashed all his ferocity on Elliot's already injured body. The cat slashed wicked scratches down Elliot's chest and tried to lash out at his face.

Elliot reared back to protect himself and almost lost his hold on the cat. He had to rip his own skin to yank the cat far enough away to stop Duncan from attacking him.

The tiger vented his insane energy on Elliot's arms and hands. Duncan sank his fangs into Elliot's wrist and ripped back with all his might. He shredded the flesh and laid Elliot's arm open in a gory flayed mess.

Elliot roared in pain and, without thinking, he slammed Duncan down hard on the ground. The cat let out another spine-chilling screech and Elliot followed up his advantage. He lunged off the ground, pounded the cat down hard one more time, and punched at the cat's face.

He pinned the cat in the dirt and punched three more times before Echo caught his arm. "Don't hurt him, Elliot! We have to capture him unharmed."

Elliot didn't want to capture this creature alive. He wanted to kill it once and for all, but a second later, Reid showed up. He was back in his human form and he knelt over the cat still struggling in Elliot's grasp.

The cat shrieked and hissed and spat something awful. Elliot had to strain every muscle just to hold it. He already felt the strength draining from his wounded arm, but the blood and exposed flesh didn't seem to belong to him.

Reid brought out a piece of rope, but when he tried to tie up the cat, it shifted into a young man with black hair and deep, black eyes. He was unshaven and he wore a black kilt and tartan like Reid's with no other clothes.

He struggled and raved so furiously that he would have broken Elliot's grip. Elliot's blood made his hands slippery on Duncan's skin. Elliot couldn't hold onto bare skin as well as fur.

Duncan started to wriggle away until Echo and Betty jumped in to help. "Take it easy, Duncan!" Echo called. "We're trying to help you!"

"Settle down, laddie!" Reid told him. "It's me! It's yer brother, Reid!"

Duncan didn't seem to understand what anyone was saying. Reid dropped the rope and dove in to help the other three restrain Duncan. Reid brought his face right up close to Duncan's eyes. "Laddie! It's me! Do ye ken me? I'm yer brother. Duncan! Look at me!"

Duncan looked right at him, but his eyes registered not a flicker of recognition. He started thrashing again.

"I cannae hold him...." Elliot choked.

"Just a wee moment longer...." Reid seized the rope and got busy wrapping it around Duncan's wrists. Reid bound Duncan's wrists behind his back only for Duncan to shift again.

He slithered out of their hold and rocketed away in a flash. He covered the ground impossibly fast and would have escaped all over again. Elliot lunged for him, landed on top of the cat, and got into another deadly wrestling match against the creature.

Reid, Echo, and Betty got there much quicker this time. Reid floundered to bind the cat to stop him from getting away again, but Duncan shifted again before Reid could finish the job. This was going nowhere. No matter how they bound him, he could get out of it in an instant by shifting.

Duncan reared off the ground and tackled Reid onto his back. The two men wrestled and fought each other, but Elliot couldn't get up. That last tackle drained what was left of his strength. He sprawled on the ground where he was.

Duncan kept screaming and roaring in mindless insanity. Elliot didn't see how Reid, Betty, and Echo could stop Duncan from getting away and Elliot couldn't help them.

Elliot collapsed back on the ground and felt himself starting to black out. Pain electrified his arm and radiated into his chest. He rallied just enough to raise his head to see Betty storm across the clearing.

She clubbed Duncan hard across the back of the head with the butt handle of Barclay's saber. Duncan buckled on top of Reid and lay still at last.

Chapter 11

Reid heaved Duncan's unconscious body off himself and Duncan flopped into the dust. He was out cold but otherwise unharmed which was more than anyone could say for Elliot.

Betty went over to Reid and held out her arm to help him up. "Are you all right?"

He nodded breathing fast and glanced down at his brother. "Aye, I'm right enough. Now what do we do with this lug? He's stronger than I realized."

Echo crossed the clearing, put her weapon on the ground, and knelt down next to Elliot. "We need to make camp and treat Elliot's injuries. We can decide what to do about Duncan at the same time."

"Aye, lass." Reid pulled Duncan up and slung his brother over his shoulder. "Lead the way."

Echo inspected Elliot's arm. "You go back the spring and make camp there. I need to stop the bleeding before we move him."

Reid and Betty limped away. Echo caught Elliot looking at her, but his eyes didn't seem to be focusing right. "Lassie...."

"Lie quietly. I need to fix up your arm. This might hurt."

"Lassie...." He struggled to drag his eyes into focus. "Do ye think...I made it up to him....?"

She had to smile at him. "Yeah. You did that and then some. You proved yourself today."

He sank back and shut his eyes. He didn't respond when she repositioned the torn flesh of his arm, but a peaceful smile curved up his lips. He was happy and he deserved to be.

That left her with one job and she didn't have any bandages or antiseptic to disinfect his arm. The wound Duncan inflicted on Elliot really needed sutures. It needed more than sutures. It needed surgery, but she wouldn't be able to do that here. She'd be lucky to keep him alive once the infection set in.

She had no extra cloth to bandage his arm so she used her saber to cut his shirt into strips. He didn't open his eyes through the whole process so he must not have cared.

She wrapped up his arm, but when she removed the last scrap of his shirt, she discovered all the other wounds on his stomach, sides, chest, and back. The blood on his cheek had dried, but it still looked awful.

The slash on his thigh was still bleeding, but she'd used all her resources on his arm. Maybe the others know some way that she could help Elliot.

She touched his shoulder. "I need you to wake up now, Elliot. I could carry you up to the camp or you can help me by walking."

"Dinnae carry me, lass," he husked. "Let me walk back as a man."

She had to bite back another grin. He still had his eyes shut so he didn't see her blush. He was such a man if he cared about that.

She hauled him upright, but he couldn't support his own weight. His knees kept buckling. She supported him on her shoulder and staggered up the hill to the spring.

Reid and Betty had started a fire even though it was only late afternoon. Echo and Elliot lowered Elliot onto the ground just as Duncan was coming around.

He glanced around at the party with suspicious, wary eyes. Then he saw Reid and started scrambling backward to get away from his brother.

Reid squatted down in front of Duncan. "Laddie! Dinnae ye ken me? I'm Reid. I'm yer brother. Colton sent me to bring ye home to Icemeet. Ye'd like that, wouldnae ye?"

Duncan glanced over at Echo and Elliot and then looked toward the trees. He obviously didn't understand a word his brother said.

He backed up until he bumped into a tree trunk. He jerked around trying to see what was stopping him from getting away. He didn't recognize the tree, either.

Without warning, he lunged sideways, shifted, and would have bolted into the forest again, but Reid was ready for this. He scooped up a large rock from the bank, slammed it down on Duncan's skull, and knocked his brother out again.

"So much for bringing him in unharmed," Betty remarked.

Reid heaved a massive sigh, sank down on the ground next to Duncan's body, and let the rock fall out of his hand. "I dinnae ken how else to get him anywhere, much less all the way to Icemeet with the whole muckle Creighton army standing in the way." He passed his hand across his eyes. "What I wouldnae give for Connell about now."

"Who's Connell?" Betty asked.

"He's me cousin and he's a wizard. He could bind Duncan and stop him from shifting. Connell could make Duncan as light as a feather and float him all the way up the blasted mountain." Reid tried to shake off the colossal task in front of him. "Never ye mind. I'll manage it somehow. Colton is counting on me. The whole blimming country is counting on me."

"We'll come with you," Betty offered. "I have no idea how we'll do it, but it will be easier with three people. We won't let you do it alone."

He looked up and smiled at her. "Thanks, lassie. I'm grateful."

Echo tried not to notice that look passing between them. She bent over Elliot to take her mind off Betty and Reid. "Turn on your side so I can take a look at your back."

Elliot obeyed her and groaned when she wiped the blood off his shoulder blade.

"How bad is it?" Betty asked.

"We really need some bandages and something to stop the infection. We won't be taking Elliot anywhere in this condition."

Reid stood up. "I'll fetch yer supplies, lassie."

Betty spun around to stare at him. "You have medical supplies—out here?"

"Aye. Stay here and dinnae let Duncan get away. I dinnae fancy going through all that a second time if I can help it."

He shifted and rocketed away into the bushes. "What's that all about?" Echo asked. "How can he have bandages and antiseptic *here*?"

"I have no idea," Betty replied. "He can't even carry weapons when he's in his tiger form."

Echo glanced over at Duncan. "What are we going to do about *him*?"

"God only knows." Betty started unpacking the last of the food supplies the party had brought from the Serpent Cave. "How is he supposed to rule the country when he doesn't even recognize his own brother?"

Echo concentrated on Elliot, but he batted her hand away when she tried to clean up his face. "Dinnae, lassie. It hurts too much."

She left him alone. She couldn't do anything more from him out here in the middle of nowhere.

"Maybe one of us could go up to Icemeet, talk to Snowflake, and get her to send their wizard down here to deal with Duncan," Betty suggested. "That sounds a sight easier than transporting him up the mountain the way he is."

Echo was just about to answer when Reid came back. The tiger zoomed into camp carrying a bundle in his mouth. He strutted over to Echo and dropped it in her lap.

Reid shifted and squatted down next to her. He started untying the knotted fabric. "What is this?" she asked.

"Bandages....and ointment from me Clan. It will stop the infection and kill the pain. It speeds up healing." He laid the open bundle on her lap, took out a small glass jar, and held it up. "Put this on his wounds. It seals them and kills all infection."

"Wow!" Echo exclaimed. "That's amazing."

"It's naught but we've been using for centuries. Snowflake used it on Alastair's burns. It's the only thing that eases the pain." Reid turned to see Elliot listening with his eyes open. "How are ye, laddie?"

Elliot gulped. "I'm no good, lad. I'm sorry I didnae...."

"Och, hush! Ye captured Duncan yer own self. Ye were in yer rights to hurt him, but ye didnae." Reid gripped Elliot's shoulder. "I'm grateful for me life, laddie. We're square for Alastair."

Elliot shut his eyes and turned his face away. "Thank ye, lad. I didnae mean to kill him."

"I ken ye didnae. Just.... dinnae do it again for me own sake."

He returned to the other side of the fire, sat down next to Betty, and left Echo and Elliot alone. She took the lid off the jar. "Let's see how this stuff works. Which one would you like to try it on first?"

He didn't open his eyes. "Me back, lass. It hurts something awful."

"Okay. Turn over."

He whimpered under his breath when he rolled onto his side again and she smeared the ointment on his shoulder. It dissolved some of the crusted blood, but Reid was right. It sealed the wound and stopped it from bleeding anymore.

She waited for a second. "How's that?"

"It's fine," he replied. "It works. The pain is going away."

"Stay there while I bandage it up."

She went through the supplies Reid had brought. She spent the next two hours treating and bandaging all of Elliot's many wounds, but when he finally sank back on the ground, he let out a relieved sigh. "Thank ye, lass. It's much better."

"We should put the ointment on your arm."

He opened his eyes and looked up at her so plaintively that her heart twisted. "Can it wait until morning, lassie? I dinnae think I can take it right now."

She beamed at him. "Sure. No problem."

She sat back, tied up what was left of Reid's bundle, and settled down by the fire. Reid was just coming back holding a bunch of other stuff. Echo had been so engrossed in helping Elliot that she didn't realize until now that Reid had left a second time.

He laid a bunch of weapons in a pile under the trees and started unfolding a large square of black plaid. "What is that?" Betty asked.

"It's Alastair's tartan." Reid folded the fabric in half and draped it over Elliot. "It will keep ye warm tonight, lad."

Elliot shut his eyes and gulped again, but he didn't thank Reid. He didn't have to and Reid only smiled at him. No words could express his gratitude and relief at Reid's forgiveness.

Reid squatted down and Betty started handing out the food she had prepared. "This is the last of the food. Whatever we're going to do, we need to do it now."

"It's obvious, isn't it?" Echo replied. "We have to get Duncan back to Icemeet."

"I dinnae ken about that any longer," Reid remarked. "He'd only run off again."

Elliot hoisted himself onto one elbow to join the conversation. "Ye must take him. He cannae stay out here if he's to bring peace to the land."

"I dinnae see how he can do that at any rate," Reid replied. "He's in no condition to do ought and we'd all be taking our lives in our hands if we tried to take him across the Boundless now."

"Here's what I don't understand," Echo chimed in. "If the Laird can use magic to find out where anyone is, how has he not located Duncan before now? I understand why the Laird wouldn't have been able to get to Duncan as long as he was at Icemeet, but this forest is the Laird's territory. He should have killed Duncan a long time ago."

"Who can say why the Laird does and doesnae do ought?" Reid returned.

"The thing is," she went on, "if Duncan survived this long running around at random in the forest, maybe he's safer here than if we tried to take him across the Boundless with the war on."

Reid looked away and didn't answer. Betty turned to Elliot. "What about asking your brother for help? If he's really trying to end the war, he might be able to do something."

"I dinnae think so, lassie, and not because I dinnae fancy seeing me brother again. We'd have to take Duncan into Kald and I dinnae like to take him anywhere near the Laird. He's safer here as Echo says."

"Anyway," Echo added, "Duncan can't do anything against the Laird until we find Lady Rhona Armstrong. He's supposed to marry her."

"There is no Lady Rhona Armstrong," Reid countered. "We've been over this a thousand times with Jaimee. She came to Icemeet with Liam looking for Lady Rhona. We've searched high and low and there is no Lady Rhona anywhere, either in Kald or in Icemeet."

"Then Duncan can't take the throne until we find her," Echo replied.

Chapter 12

E cho woke up in the middle of the night again. She sat up right away and put more wood on the fire. This was the last batch so she would have to go out into the forest to get more before morning.

She glanced around the circle. Betty lay asleep across the fire. Reid was gone. He had slipped away to go curl up and sleep in the woods as a tiger.

Echo looked over at Elliot to find his eyes open. He was watching her.

"Are you okay?" she whispered.

"Aye, lass."

"Are you in pain at all?"

"Not a bit. That ointment of Reid's did the trick—all but me arm. That throbs something awful."

"Are you ready for me to put the ointment on it now? I should probably do that before any infection sets in."

He heaved a shaky sigh. "I suppose ye'd better. There willnae be any better time."

He dragged himself up into a sitting position, but not without several gasps of pain. He groaned when he straightened his leg to rest it in front of him.

She started unwinding the bandages on his arm. "I've been thinking."

"I wondered what that grinding noise might be."

She smirked at him and he grinned back. It was wonderful to see him so relieved after reconciling with Reid. "I was thinking we won't be able to take you to Icemeet the way you are. It wouldn't be safe for you or for us."

"Och, ye dinnae need to say it, lass. I'd only slow ye down."

"It isn't that. You need to hole up somewhere until these heal." She laid aside the bandages and looked at his mangled arm. "I mean, how exactly do you think you're going to travel with *this*? You can hardly walk on your leg."

He lowered his gaze and watched her peel the last bandages off his arm. "Ye're right, lassie. Ye're always right."

She looked up to smile at him. He returned it and sent another thrill rushing to her heart....and then he glanced down at her mouth. Was he thinking about kissing her?

She really wanted to kiss him. She felt so close to him right now, but her nerves made her deflect the tension by turning the moment into a joke. "I wouldn't go that far. I have been known to be wrong.... once or twice."

He laughed again and instantly winced when she touched his wrist.

"I'll need to open it up again to put the ointment inside," she told him. "It's the only way to completely prevent infection."

"Ye do what ye must, lass. I'm in yer capable hands."

She didn't turn that into a joke. His arm was nothing to joke about. He swallowed hard and turned his head away while she peeled back the flaps of torn muscle and skin. She got busy smearing the ointment on every surface.

His breathing caught, and by the time she finished, he was gasping every few seconds and dripping with sweat holding back the pain.

"I'm really sorry about this," she murmured. "I'm almost done."

"Dinnae ye bother yerself," he choked. "It feels better already."

She laid all the flesh back in the right place and wrapped it all up with the bandages again. When she finished, he collapsed onto the ground, threw his good arm over his eyes, and trembled for several minutes.

She rested her hand on his good knee and a shiver of excitement went up her arm. There was so little of him undamaged, but every wound and cut shone like a badge of honor.

He wasn't a waste of a man the way she thought. He was noble and good. He proved that today. He only needed the right circumstances to bring it to the surface.

She studied him while he lay there with his eyes covered. What would he be like if and when he changed into a dragon? She couldn't imagine that even after seeing Duncan and Reid shifting into tigers.

Then she remembered and glanced away. Duncan was still where the group had left him. Reid had tied him to a tree while Duncan was unconscious. Duncan's eyes were open and he watched Echo and Elliot with deep, black, suspicious eyes, but at least he wasn't trying to get away anymore.

Echo tapped her finger on Elliot's leg. He took his arm down, and when he looked at her, she nodded toward Duncan.

Elliot hefted himself onto his elbow and peered at the young man across the fire. "Duncan? Do ye ken where ye are?"

"Aye." Duncan looked around. "Where's Reid?"

"He went out to sleep in the forest," Echo replied. "Would you like me to go get him for you? I'm sure he'd be delighted that you remember who he is." She frowned at him. "Do you remember....?"

"I remember all." Duncan looked over at Elliot. "How's yer hand, lad?"

Elliot snorted and lurched back into a sitting position. "It's been better. Thank ye for asking, laddie."

"I'm...." Duncan broke off when Betty started to stir. She screwed up her face and looked around before she realized that Duncan was looking at her.

She furrowed her brow even more that he wasn't trying to get away. "Duncan?"

"Aye, lass?"

She squinted into the trees. "Where's Reid?"

"I'm guessing he's still asleep," Echo replied. "I was going to get him when...."

Footsteps broke the stillness as Reid stumbled into the firelight. He frowned down at his brother. "Laddie?"

Duncan split in a huge grin. "Aye?"

"Ye're...awake," Reid stammered. "I mean.... ye're lucid."

Duncan blushed. "Aye. I'm sorry about earlier."

"What happened? Ye were out of yer head."

Duncan laughed and lowered his eyelashes. "I suppose I was."

"How did ye.... Ye're all right now. What happened?"

"I dinnae ken. I cannae say what's happening to me at any time. I cannae control it."

"Then we have no way of knowing when or if it will happen again," Betty remarked.

"We need to get ye home to Icemeet, lad," Reid told him. "Ye cannae stay in the Laird's country."

Duncan's smile evaporated and his eyes darted to the shadows again. "I cannae go home—not now."

"Why not now?" Reid asked. "Is it the Clan ye're worried about? They may not like it, but they winnae raise a hand to ye as long as Colton, Jaimee, and I are with ye."

"It isnae the Clan." Duncan stiffened against the ropes holding him. He no longer made eye contact with anyone. He kept searching the darkness for hidden enemies.

"Are you afraid of something, Duncan?" Echo asked. "Is that why you fought us earlier—because you were afraid someone would come after you?"

He didn't answer. He gave the ropes one more tug, and when they didn't give, he erupted in panicked struggling.

"Easy, lad!" Reid squatted down and extended a hand to calm Duncan, but he never got there.

Duncan wrenched once, shifted, and twisted out of the ropes in a heartbeat. He sprang for the trees and Reid pounced on him. Reid seized the cat in both hands and flattened Duncan to the ground.

Echo sat rooted to the spot as Duncan exploded in a fit of screeching trying to contort himself out of his brother's grip. She tensed to go help Reid, but Betty materialized out of thin air at Reid's side and smashed her saber hilt down hard on the back of Duncan's head.

He collapsed in a pile of fur. He didn't shift back.

Reid hauled himself to his feet and passed his hand across his eyes. "Christ on the cross!"

"We have to do something," Betty murmured. "This can't go on."

"What happens if you tie him up really tight like this?" Echo asked.

Reid turned around and scowled at her. "Huh?"

She waved at Duncan. "What would happen if you tied him up when he's in his tiger form like this? The ropes would be too tight for him to shift back into a man. Would they kill him if he shifted? Would they cut him in half? Would they stop him from shifting at all?"

"I.... uh...." Reid rubbed his head. "I dinnae ken, lass. I dinnae think anyone has ever tried it before."

"What do we have to lose?" Elliot asked. "It's better than knocking him out so many times."

"Aye. Ye're right." Reid studied his brother's body. Duncan still hadn't shifted.

"Do you want me to help you?" Echo started to get up.

"I'll see to him, lassie. Thank ye for suggesting it. I dinnae ken what I'd do without ye lassies helping me." He bent down and started untying all the knots he used to bind his brother in his human form.

Then he got busy trussing up the cat like a Christmas turkey. He tied the cat much more tightly and more thoroughly than he did before. If Duncan ever came to, he wouldn't be able to move.

Echo didn't mention a second time that, if Duncan shifted, the ropes might kill him. Reid didn't need to hear that, but from the way Reid was acting, Echo guessed that he was past the point of caring.

Reid wrapped the cat in miles of rope and then lashed the bound cat to the same tree Duncan had been sitting under a moment before.

Reid tied every knot three or four times just to make sure before he collapsed by the fire. He buried his head in his hands. "I cannae go back out to the forest. I dinnae dare to leave him alone."

Betty touched his shoulder. "You'll just have to sleep here."

"We should break it up into watches," Echo suggested. "We'll take turns sleeping and keeping an eye on Duncan."

"I'll take the first watch," Elliot volunteered. "I cannae sleep with the pain anyway. I can yell loud enough to wake ye even if I cannae move meself."

"Ye're a brick, lad." Reid shifted, curled into a ball with his tail over his face, and shut his eyes. A second later, he cracked one eye open, glanced at Duncan, and shut his eyes a second time.

Betty smiled down at him and then turned to Echo and Elliot. "Thank you for today, Elliot. I'm sorry I was so hard on you at the cave. I can see now that I was wrong about you."

"Ye werenae wrong about me, lass," he murmured back. "Ye were right. Ye were all dead right. I was a coward and now I cannae bring Alastair back no matter what Reid says."

Chapter 13

Elliot gazed into the flames. He kept waiting for Echo to lie down and go to sleep, but she didn't.

Silence fell over the camp. After a long time of staring into the flames, Betty stretched out, curled into a fetal ball, and shut her eyes, too. Echo watched her for a long time. In a little while, Betty's breathing lengthened and she fell asleep.

"Ye should go to sleep, too, lassie," Elliot murmured in Echo's ear. "Ye havenae slept hardly at all. Ye've been so busy tending to everyone else."

"I'm not tired anymore. I don't think I could sleep, now that I know Duncan might go off again at any moment."

"Aye. It's a rub." He studied Duncan across the fire. "I dinnae ken how he can be so sane one moment and raving the next."

"We'll probably never know." She turned to scrutinize Elliot in the firelight.

Her intense stare made him squirm so he tried to make a joke. "What's on yer mind, lass? Did I grow another head just now?"

She didn't laugh. "We forgot to put the ointment on your face."

She picked up the pot, dabbed some of the goo on her fingertip, and started drawing it across the gash on his cheek. He flinched and then gazed deep into her eyes right in front of him.

She was so close, so inviting, so beautiful glowing in the flames. He longed to kiss her and he glanced down at her mouth.

The pressure of her touch made him flinch and then the ointment started to ease the pain. Her hand stroking his face felt immaculately wonderful. He wanted her to touch him everywhere else. He wanted to take her in his arms, but he couldn't do that.

She put her hand down and put the lid on the jar. "That's done. It isn't bleeding anymore so I don't think we should bandage it."

"Ye could wrap bandages all round me head and turn me into a corpse."

She burst out laughing and lowered her eyelashes. "Don't joke about that."

His heart burst with happiness to see her laughing at his joke. "It's worth it to see ye smile. Ye're a beautiful lass and I never had a nicer nurse tending to me."

She looked up and then turned away blushing. "You're a charmer, aren't you?"

"Only with ye. There arenae any lassies at the fort that arenae already married to someone or other. The lads get to looking a might ragged after so many years."

She studied him a second time and she didn't look away. "Don't you think it's time you left the fort and accepted your destiny? You don't really plan to hide in the forest for the rest of your life, do you? You were obviously made for something greater."

He wanted to avert his gaze, but he found it impossible. Her eyes held him there where he had to let her see him for who he really was.

"I dinnae ken what me destiny is, lass. Even if I'm the Laird's grandson, I dinnae belong at Tyrekirk the way Grant is. I couldnae. I'm not made for that."

"What are you made for?"

"I dinnae ken. I dinnae ken me own self."

"That's not good."

He finally broke away and stared into the flames. "I cannae be a dragon like him. I couldnae stand it."

"What would be so bad about that?"

"I couldnae be a Creighton. They're devils and I should ken. Grant and I worked for the Laird for years. No one kens his devil work so well as Grant and I."

"But Grant is working against him. He's only in the castle at all to try to defeat the Laird."

"Then I must be outside it. Two of us under the Laird's roof would only cause trouble. Didnae ye say...." He broke off. He didn't want to talk about what she said.

He had nothing but good memories of the woman he thought was his mother. He didn't want anything to tarnish those memories by making him believe she wasn't his mother after all. That would be terrible.

"Have you ever tested yourself to see if you could shift the way Grant does?" Echo asked.

"Och, no! Never! I couldnae do that!"

"Why not?"

"If I was a dragon, I wouldnae ken who I am. I dinnae ken who I am either way. If Grant is.... Och, I dinnae ken what I'm saying. Everything I ken about meself is coming apart at the seams."

The words tore his soul as they left him. He'd never articulated this much to anyone, not even to himself. He never wanted to think of himself as anything other than the same as whatever Grant was.

If Grant was a dragon, then he and Elliot couldn't be the same. That was the worst of it.

Without warning, her warm hand materialized on his bare knee. It made him shiver with excitement, and when he looked up to meet her gaze, she smiled at him.

She leaned in, cradled his cheek in her palm, and kissed him. Her lips felt impossibly soft, majestically sweet, and lusciously enticing. His whole body caved to that sensation and he couldn't stop himself from kissing her back.

She leaned into him. Her fingers threaded into his hair and she pulled him closer. She exhaled and her sweet breath went up his nose. Her smell flooded his brain with fevered desire and he felt his blood start to boil for her.

He snatched a fistful of her hair and crushed her into his mouth. He gnawed her lips in ravenous madness. Her tongue ignited so much volcanic craven need in him that he didn't try to stop himself. He had to have her....and then he remembered what they'd just been talking about.

He wrenched her off him and pushed her away. He saw himself shoving her away too hard and he hated himself for it, but the memory repelled him.

"Dinnae, lassie." He forced himself to turn aside. He turned all the way in the other direction so she could only see the back of his head. He couldn't stand to look at her or to have her look at him. "Ye dinnae ken what you're doing."

"I know exactly what I'm doing," she growled in a deadly undertone. "It's you that doesn't know what you're doing. You know you want to, Elliot."

"Of course I want to! What I want...." He choked on the words and clamped his eyes shut. "Ye dinnae want to get with any dragon."

"What if I did want to get with a dragon?" she half-whispered. "What if that would make you even more attractive to me than you already are? Would that make any difference?"

"Perhaps not to ye, but it would make a difference to me. I cannae do ought with ye if I am one." He shut his eyes even tighter, but the all-consuming agony in his heart wouldn't go away. Every word made it worse. "I wouldnae want to keep living if I am one."

"It doesn't matter to me," she insisted. "Do you see how it is between Reid and Betty? She likes it. It makes him more attractive to her, not less so. It could be like that for us."

He shook his head. "I couldnae. We dinnae ken where we'll be tomorrow. Ye dinnae start something ye cannae finish."

Chapter 14

E cho sat up in the cold grey light of dawn and looked around. Reid was awake, sitting up, and adding wood to the fire. Betty was still asleep.

Duncan was still in his tiger form and tied so securely that he couldn't move. His watchful, wary eyes darted from one face to the other. Elliot was gone, but Echo didn't think anything of it at first. He couldn't go far in his condition.

His condition raised more than a few questions about how he was going to travel anywhere, much less up to Icemeet with everybody else.

She was just thinking about standing up when he came back. He limped on his injured leg and hunched over at the waist. He hugged his bandaged arm against his stomach and his face had swollen up around the gash in his cheek.

He hobbled over to the tree where he'd been sitting last night, but he didn't sit down. He leaned his shoulder against it and took the weight off his leg while he surveyed the other four members of their party.

Echo tried not to look at him. Her feelings about what happened last night were starting to get the better of her. Excitement that something might happen between her and Elliot got all jumbled up with dread that he would reject her and anger that he already had.

What was wrong with him? Why did he have such an aversion to being a dragon shifter? Didn't he see how captivating that made him to her? Didn't he see what an asset it was?

If he just embraced it, he could fly Duncan up to Icemeet in a matter of minutes. Elliot could incinerate all his enemies. He could have torched those rebels and avoided getting injured in the first place.

She tried to tell herself to be patient with him. He had his reasons for not wanting to be a dragon, though she couldn't help but feel he was being cowardly about that, too. It wasn't like he could run away from it if he was one. He'd obviously been trying to do exactly that ever since he parted ways with Grant.

Mostly, she felt hurt that he didn't welcome her the way she welcomed him. He must not want anything to develop between them—not badly, at least.

She pushed those thoughts away when Betty woke up. Betty went off to the spring and came back with the hair around her face dampened. She squatted down next to Reid. "Well?" she began. "What's the plan?"

"I'm taking Duncan to Icemeet," Reid replied. "I dinnae care what it costs. I'll do it. I *must* do it."

"We're coming with you," Echo told him. "Elliot can stay here or go back to the rebels."

"Och, that's nice!" Elliot blurted out. "Go on and leave me here alone. I should have kenned it would end like this."

Her temper flared and she rounded on him. She told herself not to air their private business in front of Reid and Betty, but a second later, she plowed on ahead. She just didn't care anymore.

"Duncan is our mission and it isn't like you can travel the way you are. You should go back to the fort where you can heal up." He turned his face away and compressed his lips. Her anger died when she saw how upset he was. "Do you really think coming with us is even possible?"

"What if it was? Ye wouldnae have me if I wanted to come."

"How could you come?" she countered. "How would you travel all that way in this condition?"

"I've already crossed that line. I cannae go back to the fort and ye ken it."

"Why not? What's stopping you.... besides the fact that you're injured?"

"I've killed that party yesterday. I've fought alongside the Buchanans. The rebels winnae have me."

"Who would ken?" Reid asked. "Ye took the shot that killed Alastair and ye told us Torran doesnae care for ought else. No one has to ken ye fought alongside the Buchanans yesterday. Those men are all dead."

"I've already thrown me lot in with ye. I've crossed that line and I cannae go back." He rounded on Echo. "It's ye that told me to cross it. Ye cannae ask me to go back on it now."

She softened toward him. "All right. The question is how we're going to get Duncan to Icemeet."

Elliot looked away again. Did he realize what that meant?

"As long as he stays bound up in his cat form, he should be easy to carry, right?" Betty asked. "He doesn't seem like he can shift when he's tied up."

"So will he stay in his cat form while he's ruling the realm, too?" Reid sneered. "I dinnae see how he'll unseat the Laird in this state."

"We have to find a way somehow," Echo replied. "Maybe your wizard can fix whatever is wrong with him."

"And if he can't?" Betty asked. "How is Duncan supposed to unite the Clans if he's out of his mind?"

"Uniting the Clans means unseating the Laird," Echo pointed out. "Why else would the Laird want Duncan dead....and Grant and Elliot dead....and Ness dead? They're all Lady Ilisa's sons which means Duncan is the Laird's heir."

"Grant is the Laird's heir now," Elliot interjected. "Grant is older than all of us. Duncan has no claim on the throne with Grant and me in the way."

She turned to face him. "Maybe if Grant knew the truth about Duncan, he would abdicate in favor of peace."

"Someone should ask him.... *Elliot*." Betty put heavy emphasis on the last word, but he didn't rise to the suggestion.

"We dinnae ken ought but Grant is only playing at peace," Reid argued. "He could kill Duncan himself at the first chance to ensure no one threatens his position."

"How do ye dare to insult me brother to me face?" Elliot spat. "Grant doesnae play at ought and I dinnae suppose he saved yer brother's life for a lark."

"Why don't you prove it to us, Elliot?" Echo countered. "No one is in a better position to get Grant on our side than you are."

He glared at her, but at least he didn't turn away again. She was finished taking it easy on him. He needed someone pushing him. He wouldn't break out of this malaise otherwise.

"Whatever happens," Betty finished, "Duncan isn't getting anywhere near the Seat of Armstrong until someone gets rid of the Laird."

"The Buchanans would be only too happy to destroy the Laird," Reid told her. "Colton and I already support Duncan...though I cannae speak for Duncan himself. Even if he was in his right mind, he'd have to agree to rule the Creighton dynasty.... which is asking a great deal if ye ken me meaning."

"What would it take to unseat the Laird?" Betty asked. "What kind of headwind are we looking at?"

"Ye've seen the war on across the Boundless." Reid waved behind her toward the hill where the party saw the assault on Icemeet. "The Creightons are stronger. That's the truth. No one on the Buchanan side wants to admit it, but it's true. We cannae find any way to throw the advantage of their dragons. Jaimee has been working on that problem alone since she arrived here. The dragons are too strong."

"The Creightons must have some weakness," Echo replied.

"I cannae think what. We dinnae dare to assault Kald itself. The Laird's magic protects Tyrekirk and naught but common folk live elsewhere. Crossing the Boundless to assault Kald would accomplish naught."

Echo turned to face Elliot again. "You're going back to the fort. Why don't you....?"

"Am I?" he countered. "Did we discuss this?"

"Just listen to me for a second, all right? The rebels want to fight the Laird, too. They're a fighting force that's already on this side of the Boundless. Why don't we try to recruit them to help us? Then you'd be helping us while you recuperate."

"I can already tell ye what they'll say," Elliot replied. "The rebels winnae ever consent to putting a Buchanan on the throne—not ever. Ye put that right out of yer mind."

"Who do they think they're going to put in the Laird's place?" Betty asked.

"One of their own, of course."

"Who—Torran?"

Elliot nodded. "Quite likely."

"It's out of the question," Reid countered. "It winnae ever happen."

"They wouldn't have to know who they were putting on the throne," Echo pointed out. "You could tell them they're deposing the Laird, which is true."

"What about contacting Grant and Lily?" Betty suggested. "If they're trying to bring down the Laird from inside the castle, that's three prongs coming together from three directions. We all want to bring down the Laird. We'll have a better chance at this with all of us working together."

"That means sending someone inside Kald to talk to them," Echo pointed out. "I'll go."

"Are ye daft?" Elliot fired back. "They dinnae ken ye from a hole in the ground."

"Lily knows me. Why don't you come with me?"

"Who was it just said I cannae travel?"

"So you can go to the fort. You don't have to go to Kald. You can help us either way."

"One moment more, lassie," Reid countered. "If we're coming together to unseat the Laird, we need a battle plan. The Buchanans can assault from across the water, but it will take planning. We must get word to Colton and Jaimee...."

"You can do that," Echo replied. "I'll go to Kald and Elliot can go to the fort. We can kill two birds with one stone that way."

"So what do we do with Duncan in the meantime?" Betty asked.

"If he stays tied up, you can carry him back to Icemeet like this," Echo replied.

"I'll be in for a thrashing the moment we untie him," Reid remarked. "He'll be spitting mad. I dinnae see him ever forgiving me the indignity."

Betty laughed, but she was the only one who did. "What do we do with him once we unseat the Laird? It isn't like he can function in any meaningful way when he's like this. We can't count on him to regain his sanity in time to take over ruling the country."

"We'll just have to work on unseating the Laird first. We can deal with who's going to take over afterward."

"Grant can take over afterward," Elliot chimed in. "He's already the Laird's heir."

"We winnae unseat the Laird only to put another Creighton on the throne," Reid snapped. "Ye winnae use Clan Buchanan for yer own aims. We're doing this to put our own man on the throne. If it isnae Duncan, it's no one.'

Echo interjected before it could turn into another argument. "When are we calling this assault?"

"It must be a time far enough distant to prepare all three armies," Reid pointed out.

"Two armies," Elliot corrected. "Grant and Lily winnae command the Laird's army. The Laird himself still controls the troops."

"Having Grant and Lily on our side will be better than nothing," Echo replied. "Grant has resources inside Tyrekirk that we don't know about. He might be able to do something."

"And he's a dragon," Betty pointed out. "That's at least one dragon on our side."

She gave Elliot another pointed look, but he didn't reply nor did he turn away. He completely ignored her.

"I say we converge at the next new moon," Reid suggested. "We can all keep track of that."

"Great idea!" Betty exclaimed. "That should give us all time to organize our own forces."

"So.... are all agreed?" Echo turned to each person in turn. "Do we all know what we're doing?"

"So...." Elliot began. "I'm going to the fort and ye're going to Kald?"

"We could be going together if you were willing to set foot inside the city."

Reid turned to the cat still tied to the tree. "Now I suppose it's the time for me to get me eyes scratched out."

"Put on yer plate armor, laddie," Elliot called, and this time, they all laughed.

Duncan hadn't made a sound during the whole conversation. There was no way of knowing if he understood a word they said about him or the lengths to which everyone was going to put him on the Seat of Armstrong.

Reid bent down and started untying the bound cat from the tree. Betty started cleaning up the campsite, raking out the last dying coals, and covering them with dirt.

Echo went over to the pile of weapons. She separated them into three for herself, Betty, and Elliot. Reid wouldn't need anything. He wouldn't be able to carry them in his cat form. Then again, he might decide to travel as a man, now that he and Betty would be carrying Duncan.

She turned around to ask him if he wanted any weapons. Elliot hobbled over to her. He barely put any weight on his injured leg at all.

He swiveled as far away from the others as possible and lowered his voice to a confidential murmur. "I'm thinking ye're right again, lassie. I cannae travel like this. Will ye go on to the fort—just to help me get there? I ken ye're bound for Kald. I dinnae like to slow ye down."

Her head shot up. "Why are you so set against seeing Grant? You could be doing so much more if you went with me to Kald."

"Of course I dinnae want to face Grant, but it's more than that. Look at me. I winnae be able to get to the castle before the new moon anyway. If I travel with ye, ye winnae get there, either. If ye're worried I'll be too slow, ye go on and skip the fort. I'll get there eventually and I'll deal with the rebels."

She gazed into his eyes struggling with conflicting emotions. She didn't want to go off alone—not because she was afraid of what she might encounter. She didn't want to separate from him. She had been looking forward to spending some time alone with him. Maybe then she could get through whatever was bothering him about being a dragon.

Having Grant on Duncan's side was one thing. Having two dragons would be even better. Why did Elliot keep holding himself back? Didn't he see what an advantage this was?

Reid distracted her. He talked to Duncan while he untied the cat from the tree. "It's time to go, laddie. Nice and easy. We'll take ye home to Icemeet and Connell will sort ye out. Then we'll see what's what."

Echo started to go back to arranging the weapons in their piles when, without warning, a blast struck the tree branch above her head. She thought at first that it might be a lightning bolt, but that was impossible. It was a beautiful day with a cloudless blue sky overhead.

She ducked as the branch split away from the trunk with a loud crack. She spun around just in time to see another sizzling jet erupt from the ground next to Reid. It *was* lightning!

Fountains of explosive electricity, flames, and gleaming sparks shot from the tree roots where Reid had just been squatting. He toppled onto his back to get away from them and Echo stared in stark horror at Duncan.

He had shifted back into a man again and all the ropes lay scattered at his feet. He reared off the ground with all the fire, lightning, and sparks rupturing from every part of him. He writhed and bellowed in agony and Echo could no longer deny the truth. He was shooting magic. He had to be.

Betty grabbed Reid and hauled him out of the way just as another fork of lightning smashed into the ground between Reid's legs. It would have annihilated him if Betty moved any slower.

Magical explosions pelted in all directions. A tumbling fireball struck another tree and the entire crown burst in flames. Burning branches rained around their heads and Echo ducked.

Elliot grabbed her and started pulling her into the trees to get away from Duncan. More shots fired from his chest and eyes and fingertips while he convulsed out of control.

Elliot swiveled in front of Echo to block her with his body just as a torch of sparks spat from Duncan's eyes. He twisted and flailed so badly that the sparks first geysered into the air.

Then he turned his head around and the whole stream slashed down into the clearing where the party had spent the night. The sparks sliced through a dozen trees before Duncan whipped his head sideways and the flow struck Elliot square in the chest.

He let out a shriek that set Echo's hair on end. His body hurtled backward, smacked Echo out of the way, and he slammed full force into a different tree trunk.

He folded to the ground......and exploded out of his skin. He reared off the ground, but he wasn't human anymore. His skin turned black and scales erupted all over him. His neck and body stretched to an impossible length and massive wings thumped outward from his shoulder blades. He transformed into an absolutely gargantuan dragon a hundred feet tall.

Echo stared up at him slack-jawed in shock. Nothing prepared her for this. Elliot's scales shimmered blacker than coal with a subtle sheen of gold gleaming beneath each one as the first rays of morning sunshine lit him up. They made him look monstrous and impossibly powerful.

He rose on his hind legs, beat his wings, and thundered to shake the world. His head wove back and forth on his long, sinewy neck and his immense tail whipped and cracked in the forest behind him. He toppled trees and snapped branches without even realizing it.

He arched his neck downward and took one booming step into the camp. Duncan didn't see Elliot's giant form right in front of him. Duncan's magic bombarded Elliot's face, chest, and wings and Duncan's magical attack enraged Elliot.

He archer higher, gave one more terrifying bellow of pain and fury, and lunged for Duncan. Elliot unleashed a catastrophic barrage of fiery breath that smashed Duncan into the tree to which he had just been tied.

The magical explosions coming from Duncan died instantly, but that didn't change the fact that Elliot was now a huge dragon ready to turn his fire on anyone who happened into his path.

Echo couldn't let that happen. She glanced around and spotted the branch that Duncan snapped off. She snatched it and lunged for Elliot. She never understood how she summoned the strength to lift that branch, but she did.

She sprang right next to Elliot's head and brought it down with a brutal swipe on top of his head. His head slammed into the ground full force.

The dragon lay there stunned for a moment and then imploded. The darkness vanished from his skin, he turned back into a man, and Elliot lay crumpled and broken at Echo's feet.

Chapter 15

Reid turned the spit over the flames. Juice burst from the rabbit that he had hunted for the party's evening meal. Fat hissed in the coals and fragrant steam drifted through their camp.

It wasn't dark yet, but no one wanted to leave after what happened in the morning. No one even brought up the prospect of leaving and Echo wasn't about to broach the subject.

She still had difficulty reconciling what she had seen with the man she thought she knew. Knowing Elliot was a dragon shifter did nothing to prepare her for the reality when she finally came face to face with it. Now she understood why he had been so reluctant to find out that he was one.

Reid took a dirk from Betty, sawed off a piece of meat, and handed it to Duncan. Duncan had been subdued and lucid all day after Elliot blasted him with dragon fire. Reid hadn't tied Duncan up, either.... not yet.

"Take some of this, laddie," Reid told his brother. "Ye must be hungry."

"Aye. I havenae hunted in days."

"What can you remember since you left Icemeet?" Betty asked.

Duncan shrugged. "Bits and pieces. I remember everything about meeting ye lot. I wish I didnae."

"Laddie...." Reid began. "Alastair's dead. Do ye remember that?"

Duncan looked down at the meat in his hand, but he didn't eat it. "Aye. I remember."

Echo glanced over her shoulder. Reid, Duncan, and Betty all looked in the same direction, but there was nothing to see over there. Elliot had stumbled out of their camp the moment he regained consciousness after he shifted into a dragon. He wouldn't talk to anyone or even look at them.

Echo could still hear him moving around in the forest over there. He hadn't left even though all his injuries vanished when he shifted. He could move just fine and the bandage had fallen off his arm when he changed into a dragon.

"If ye've magic in ye," Reid remarked, "it follows that ye're losing yer mind."

"Dinnae say that, laddie," Duncan choked. "I cannae be a wizard."

"I'm sorry, laddie, but ye are one. We all saw."

Duncan stared at the ground. He looked miserable and Echo studied him more closely. He couldn't look more different than Reid with his dark hair and eyes. They had different mothers, but Echo would never have known they were brothers.

"What does his magic have to do with him losing his mind?" Betty asked.

"Wizards tend to go a wee bit wild when they first develop their power. Most grow into it when they're young. Others dinnae ken they have it until later. The later it comes to the surface, the more difficult it is for a wizard to harness their power. Duncan must have had magic all his life and never kenned. He's struggling to get control of and it's affecting his mind."

Duncan groaned and turned away. "It's a curse! I wish I hadnae been born."

"Dinnae wish that, laddie. If it's true, ye'll be the saving of us all."

"I dinnae want to be Laird!" he cried. "I just want to go home and run around the mountains with the rest of the lads. I cannae live in Tyrekirk and wear a crown and all. It's me worst nightmare!"

Reid gripped his shoulder. "No one's making ye do ought, lad. We dinnae ken how we'll depose the Laird at any rate."

"Do you think you can make it back to Icemeet without losing control again?" Echo asked. "Do you have any way of knowing when you might snap again?"

Duncan shrugged. "How am I to ken? I dinnae ken what's happening to me nor why."

"The good news is that Elliot can travel now," Betty remarked. "He must have some kind of healing powers. Shifting must have healed his injuries. He's fine now."

"We don't know that," Echo replied. "Maybe Duncan's magic healed Elliot. He did say he was sorry for hurting Elliot the last time he was lucid. Maybe you felt sorry for him and healed him without meaning to."

Duncan looked up. "Do ye think so, lass?"

"Why not?" Reid countered. "This magic of yers could be a blessing. Ye dinnae ken the good ye could do yer Clan with it."

Duncan perked up and started to smile. "Ye're right. I didnae think on all that."

"Heck, you might be able to unseat the Laird without ever setting foot in Kald," Betty remarked. "You might take over the country and rule from Icemeet. Anything could happen."

Duncan laughed. "All right, then, lass. I'll do it."

"Slow down, lad," Reid told him. "Ye must gain control of this power first. Ye're no good to anyone the way ye are."

"I dinnae ken how," Duncan replied. "I dinnae ken ought. Most times I dinnae even remember who I am."

"Is there anything we can do to help you?" Echo asked. "Do you need to train or something?"

"We'll take ye home to Connell," Reid replied. "He'll ken what to do about this."

Echo glanced over her shoulder again. "I should probably go talk to Elliot."

"Ye tell him, lassie," Duncan told her. "Tell him...."

"I will." She got to her feet. "Don't worry."

She headed off in the direction she had last heard Elliot moving around. She couldn't think what she would say to him, but she had to be with him. She couldn't let him suffer by himself anymore. She should have gone after him right away. She shouldn't have left him alone with this.

She found him by the spring. He squatted on the bank and he kept picking up pebbles, tossing them into the water, and watching the ripples.

She went over to him and squatted down next to him. "How ya doing?"

He shot to his feet and strode away from her. "Dinnae come near me, lassie. Dinnae ye bother with me ever again!"

"Elliot, wait!" She hurried after him, but when he saw her following him, he picked up his pace to leave her behind. She had to trot to keep him in sight.

"Come back!" she yelled. "Don't walk away from me!"

"Ye dinnae want to have ought to do with me, lassie. Ye saw for yerself...."

"I'll be the one to decide who I have anything to do with. I saw for myself and I still want you around. Doesn't that tell you how I feel?"

He spun around so that fast that he startled her. "Do ye think I didnae see? Did ye think I had me eyes closed the whole time? I saw."

"What?" she urged. "What did you see?"

"I saw *ye*." He turned away with an agonized grimace. "I saw yer face when ye looked up at me. I winnae ever forget that."

She cringed. She could well imagine the look she had on her face when he first shifted right next to her. He terrified her. He would have terrified anyone.

She pushed that away. "You surprised me, okay? I wasn't expecting you to be so big. It doesn't change how I feel."

"Well, it changes how I feel." He clipped the words over his shoulder. He wouldn't face her, but at least he wasn't walking away. "I cannae ever look at ye again. I cannae ever see ye looking at me like that again—not for anything. I'd do anything to prevent it."

She gulped. Now she understood. He didn't want to scare her. He didn't want to see her scared of him. She didn't blame him. It must be really frightening for him to be like that.

She eased up behind him and dared to slide her hand over his bare shoulder. He no longer had a shirt. "Do it again."

"Never!" he roared. "Do ye think I want to be *that*? It's horrific. I cannae be that. I should rid the world of meself, but I'm too much a coward even for that. I dinnae ken what I'll do. I cannae go anywhere nor be near anyone. I dinnae want to live like this."

"Don't you see? If you don't learn how to shift back and forth at will, you might do it accidentally. Doing it is the only way you're going to learn how to control it."

"I cannae!" He spun around and bellowed in her face. "Do ye think I enjoy nearly killing the only people in the world who care about me? Do ye think I relish being a Creighton? It's the worst curse imaginable."

She didn't answer for a minute. She stared up into his face. He was the man she'd come to know, the man who changed first in one direction and then in the other.

Watching him struggle with himself only drew her to him even more. She didn't blame him for running from his dragon nature, but there had to be a way to reconcile himself to his own being.

He turned away and started walking down the bank, but he didn't move fast enough to leave her behind. He didn't try anymore to stop her from following him.

"Duncan said the same thing just now about his magic," she told him. "He thinks it's a curse. He's sorry for hurting you."

"Ye tell him I'm the one that's sorry."

"Maybe it's a blessing. Maybe you could use this in our favor. You can still do some good in the world. Don't give up hope."

He stopped walking, picked up a stone, and winged it into the water. "Ye dinnae ken ought, lassie. Dinnae pretend ye do."

"Why don't you explain it to me, then? How can I understand if you don't tell me?"

He stood with his back to her for a long time. He picked up another stone, but he didn't throw it. He stood with his head bowed turning the stone over and over in his hands. "It's Grant."

"What about him? He's a dragon, too. I'm sure he cares about you a whole lot more than the four of us do. He would love to see you again."

"Och, no, he wouldnae! He'd thrash me if he didnae kill me himself."

"Why? What happened between you two?"

"He......" He broke off and shuddered.

She eased over to his side and peered up at his twisted face, but he wouldn't look at her. "What did he do?"

"He? He did naught. I pushed him away for being a dragon. I slapped his hand away for trying to touch me and I told him I didnae want to see his face again." He looked away and his cheek spasmed. "I cannae live with that memory....and now I'm one as well. I couldnae ever face him again. I dinnae deserve him. I never did if I could turn me back on him so easily. I should have stood with him as his brother, but I didnae."

Echo's heart twisted and she squeezed his arm without thinking about it first.

He tossed the rock and set off down the shore. "Anyway, what's done is done and I cannae go back to Kald as it is. Ye go on, lassie. Ye find yer friend. Grant and Lily will listen to ye."

"Wait a minute!" she cried. "You can't just walk away! Don't you get it? This is your chance to make up with him."

"I winnae ever make up with him, lass. I winnae ever see him again and that's me own doing."

"You didn't think you could make up with Reid, either, but you did it. What if Grant is as torn up by this as you are? What if he's just waiting for you to come back? Did you ever think of that?"

"He isnae. Believe me."

"I don't believe you. He's your brother. You two love each other...."

"He loves me. I dinnae love him or I couldnae have treated him so cruelly. He's better off with Lily than with me."

"And what about me?" She lunged for him, grabbed his arm, and forced him to turn around and face her. "Are you really going to walk away from me—from what we could have? Do you honestly believe *I'm* better off without you? That's stupid, Elliot. You're ruled by fear."

"Ye dinnae understand that, either, lassie. Ye've yer own path to follow. Ye said so yerself. I cannae go back to the fort as it is...."

"Why not? You're the only one who can get the rebels on board with this plan to converge on Tyrekirk."

He shook his head. "I winnae go back to the fort. If the rebels found out, it would be worse than if I didnae go there at all."

"What are you going to do instead? What's your plan?"

His eyes swiveled to the west. "I'll go off alone. I'll see what's beyond those mountains and.... I dinnae ken. I'll make me own way somewhere else."

The sadness and hopeless resignation in his voice and eyes wrung her heart. Before she knew what she was doing, she grabbed his face in both hands and kissed him.

She expected him to shove her away or protest, but he only kissed her back. He kissed her gently and passionately, but that somehow made it so much worse. Was he savoring this kiss because he knew it would be their last?

When she broke off, he gazed down into her eyes. His expression overflowed with so much tortured emotion that she knew she had guessed right. He was preparing himself to separate from her forever.

"I want you, Elliot," she murmured. "Seeing you like that makes me want you more, not less. You were beautiful like that."

"Dinnae say that, lass." His voice broke in a tormented undertone and he looked down at her mouth again. "Ye dinnae ken what ye're asking."

"I know exactly what I'm asking and I want it. I want to see you like that. I want to know you and touch you like that. I want you to be that. I want to admire you like that and I want you to admire yourself like that."

He gulped and raised his hands. He closed them to cradle her cheeks, stopped himself, and finally summoned the courage to clasp her face in a tender hold. "I dinnae dare to, lass. I might kill ye.... or ye might have to kill me if I lost control again."

"You would learn to control it. I would help you." He shook his head and she plunged onward trying in desperation to convince him. "At least try. At least let me help you. Don't leave. If you leave now, no one will be left who cares about you. Don't go off among strangers. I can't stand that."

"I cannae put ye in danger, lassie," he whispered. "I cannae be the one responsible for ye getting hurt because of me."

He let her go and walked off again. He found another spot farther down the shore and went back to chucking stones into the water. Was he waiting for her to walk away? Was this his way of inviting her to withdraw in good grace and leave him alone?

She watched him for a while. There had to be a way to get through to him.

When she finally made up her mind, she walked up behind him, but she didn't touch him again. She stood off to one side. If he wanted to pretend she wasn't there, she would let him. She wouldn't let him go without trying everything possible to get through to him.

"When I was at Ironforge," she began, "I thought about leaving the Last Division and going off on my own among strangers. I had no one else in the world. The five of us were the only family I had, but I was on the verge of leaving forever. I just hadn't worked up the courage to do it yet and then Liam showed up to call us back into service. I guess I put it off a little too long."

He turned around and stared down at her with wide eyes. "Why, lass? Why would ye leave yer only home and family to go out alone?"

She didn't point out that he was talking about doing the same thing. "I couldn't stand the isolation anymore. It had gotten too lonely. We took an oath to shun society and love. We swore we would never marry or have children and I was really starting to regret that promise. I wanted to go back out into the world and find someone, get married, and have children after all. I wanted a life."

"Lassie!" he breathed. "I didnac ken!"

"How could you? I never told anyone. I never told my closest friends. I didn't want to let them down after everything we went through together. I thought they would push me away or tell me all the reasons I was doing the wrong thing. I thought they would tell me that the poor needed me too much and that having something for myself was selfish. I thought they would tell me that I was throwing my life away by having a family and children when there were already too many families and children in the world as it was." She looked out at the water. "I came up with all kinds of reasons not to tell them."

"Lassie...." he began again.

She turned around and faced him. She came toward him and kissed him even more deeply and powerfully than before.

She pulled off much sooner this time and she straightened up to confront him. "I want you, Elliot. I want everything that you are, especially the part of you that's a dragon, but I can't stand you rejecting me like this."

"I'm not rejecting ye, lassie, I just...."

"Then prove it. If you don't want me, I'll walk away right now and go find someone who does want me. I won't keep hanging around trying to get you to see sense. I've been alone way too long."

She watched the interplay of confused emotions struggling in his features. He kept looking down at her mouth like he wanted to kiss her, but he didn't move in again.

She finally took a step back. "That's what I thought. Have a nice life, Elliot."

She turned away fighting not to dissolve in tears before she got out of his presence. How could he do this to her? He wanted to. She knew he wanted to. If he couldn't overcome this mental block about being a dragon, she was better off without him.

That didn't stop this groundswell of anguish threatening to destroy her. She had to get away from him. He obviously wasn't the man she was looking for.

She marched up the bank toward the trees. Reid, Betty, and Duncan needed her a lot more than Elliot did.

"Lassie!" he called after her.

She spun around smacking her lips in exasperation. She didn't want to drag this out all over again. "What?"

He didn't answer. He regarded her from down by the water's edge, but something in his expression made him look different.

She waited for him to say something, but he didn't. He just stood there.

All at once, he started walking toward her. He strode up the bank much more determinedly, and when he reached the place where she stood, he didn't hesitate.

He slipped his arm around her waist and pulled her in to kiss her. He attacked her mouth in ravenous bites the way he did last night. He pressed her body into his and his manhood swelled between his legs.

He shoved it into her and seized her clothes while he kissed her faster and harder and deeper. He lifted her off the ground mauling her mouth and slithering his tongue around hers. He held nothing back and showed her with all his passion how much he wanted her.

His hand crept down her back and grabbed a big fistful of her ass. He crushed her against him and that intoxicating grip electrified her with scorching desire. She had kept her feelings locked down for so long that they erupted out of control now.

She wrapped her arms around his neck and her body trembled all over. His touch and his presence made her reel in drunken madness. He wanted her and he no longer held himself at a distance from her.

He crawled his hand lower and squeezed between her legs. Her desire overflowed into a torrential avalanche that knew no bounds. He crashed down on his knees on the ground and she wrapped herself around him. She held onto him for dear life as he took her beyond everything she knew to whatever the future held for them both.

Chapter 16

E lliot drew Echo into the shadows outside the campsite. The fire gleamed beyond the trees. Reid, Duncan, and Betty sat around talking. They couldn't see Echo and Elliot in the surrounding darkness.

Elliot squeezed Echo's hand tighter and pulled her in close. He kissed her and whispered low into her gasping mouth. "Dinnae say ought to the others about this, lassie. Wait until we leave and they go their own way."

"Why not?" she whispered back. "Are you ashamed of what we just did?"

"I winnae ever be ashamed of ye, lass. Ye believe in me and that will always be enough for me. I only want to keep this to meself for the time being. Everyone will find out soon enough. I want ye to meself just a little longer before it's all over the countryside."

The firelight lit up her face when she smiled. She rose on her tiptoes and smothered him with her kisses. Her body thrilled him beyond belief. He still could hardly believe his good fortune that she actually wanted him enough to do what they just did down by the spring.

She sank down on her heels and let go of his hand. "Do you want to go first?"

"We can go together. Come along."

He stepped into the light and the other three looked up. Elliot and Echo sat down in the same places across the fire where they had been sitting last night.

Duncan's eyes skimmed down Elliot's body. "Are ye all right, lad? I didnae mean ought about.... all that."

"I'm grand, lad. Are ye?"

Duncan nodded and accepted another piece of meat from Reid. "I'm grateful that ye put me down when ye did. I dinnae ken what I'm doing."

"That makes two of us." Elliot turned to the other two. "I dinnae ken how to say how sorry I am that I put ye lot in danger. I was out of control."

"It's okay," Betty told him. "It wasn't your fault. You probably wouldn't have shifted at all if Duncan hadn't hit you and you were trying to protect Echo."

He looked away until Reid handed him some of the meat. "Duncan agrees for me to tie him up tonight," Reid informed him. "We'll leave in the morning for Icemeet."

"Perhaps ye shouldnae," Elliot suggested. "Ye two would ae be able to subdue him alone if the same thing happened."

"This plan to assemble the armies at the full moon is more important," Betty replied. "We need to go ahead with this plan for us to go to Icemeet, you to go to the rebels, and Echo to go to Tyrekirk. Everything depends on all three coming together at the same time."

Reid got up on his knees. "Are ye ready, lad?"

"Aye." Duncan scooted back from the fire to the base of the tree where he spent the previous night. He shifted, but he didn't fly into a rage or attack anyone.

He stretched out on his side and extended all four paws toward his brother. Duncan lay still and calm while Reid tied him up again. Reid tied him just as securely as before.

"He can break out of that anytime he wants to," Echo pointed out. "You won't be able to hold him if he really wants to get away."

"We'll just have to hope he doesn't try too hard," Betty replied. "Maybe he'll be more cooperative now that he understands what we're trying to do with him."

"Betty and I will return to Icemeet either way," Reid added. "We can still raise the assault even if we lose Duncan."

Echo sighed. "It seems an awful waste after we went to so much trouble to catch him."

"He kens now what's at stake," Elliot remarked. "He'll understand our plan. He may still be able to help us if he regains his sanity in time."

"Here's hoping," Betty chimed in and the conversation came to an end.

Reid trussed up his brother so the cat couldn't move. Then Reid tied the bound cat to the tree with several lengths of the rope. He tied the cat right up against the trunk with the tiger's body and limbs plastered to the bark.

"I guess we better get some sleep." Echo stretched out on the ground by the fire. "We have some miles to cover tomorrow."

Elliot gazed down at her while she folded her elbow under her head and shut her eyes. He still struggled with the revelation that he was a dragon like Grant was. Elliot still burned with shame when he remembered how he treated his brother before walking off and leaving Kald.

Echo believed in him. She still wanted to be with him even after she found out the horrible truth. The last few hours of his life alone with her by the spring seemed like a faraway dream belonging to someone else. He didn't think he had the strength to be that happy.

Did he really plan to stay behind while she went to Kald without him? He didn't want to, but the idea of facing Grant was too painful. He really wished Grant would kill him and put Elliot out of his misery. That was the best that Elliot deserved after the way he acted.

Grant didn't even know where Elliot was. Grant was too honorable to come after Elliot or to seek revenge. Some part of Elliot's being knew that Echo was right. Grant still cared about Elliot. Grant would always be happy to see Elliot and that knowledge drove a white-hot knife into Elliot's guts more than anything. He would much prefer it if Grant hated him as much as Elliot hated himself.

He couldn't stop staring down at Echo. She was too good for him. She deserved someone so much better. She deserved someone like Grant or Reid. She deserved someone strong and steady and reliable, not some loose cannon from the forest.

That story she told him about wanting to leave the Last Division still played over and over in his mind. She was so different from Lily. Echo was the one who insisted that he stand up and take her if he really wanted her.

He never doubted for an instant that, if he didn't prove his feelings for her, that she would walk away and find someone else, someone who could appreciate her. He couldn't let that happen. He had to at least try. He couldn't let her walk out of his life without at least trying to be good enough for her.

She had been challenging him to be good enough for her since he first met her. She wouldn't let him be anything less. His heart cracked when he thought he might not be able to accomplish it. What would he be and what would his life be if she decided he wasn't good enough?

"Are you okay, Elliot?" Betty asked.

"Hmm?" He looked up and then went back to gazing down at Echo. "I'm grand."

He wanted to touch her. He wanted to kiss her and wrap his body around her so they could sleep together tonight, but he didn't want Reid and Betty to see.

He wasn't ashamed of doing it with her. That was one of the few things he'd done since leaving Kald that he was actually proud of—that and saving Reid's life.

He told the truth to her in the trees just now. He wanted to keep their connection all to himself. He didn't want to cheapen it by sharing it with the world. He wanted to cherish it. He wanted to be the only one who knew about what just happened at the spring.

A flash of imagery floated before his mind's eye. He saw himself in his dragon form. He dragged his long, scaly black body around Echo and curled around her. The heat radiating off his scales warmed her while she slept and she snuggled into that scaly nest with a peaceful smile on her face. She even nuzzled her cheek against his scales and reveled in the delicious heat.

He tore his gaze off her and forced himself to look away. He couldn't think of himself that way. He leaned back against the nearest tree and shut his eyes, but he stayed close to her. He wanted to be there to protect her if she needed him.

He stayed awake for a while listening to Reid and Betty talking, but in a little while, they went to sleep, too. Betty stretched on her side and Reid shifted. He wrapped his furry body around her and she giggled when his tail touched her face.

Elliot fought to control himself while he watched them. It wasn't fair that the Buchanans grew up knowing all their lives that they were shifters. They spent their childhoods learning how to be tigers and doing everything with other shifters.

He didn't find out until today that he was a dragon. Now he didn't know how to control when and where he shifted. He wasn't even sure how he could ever shift again. He didn't know how he did it in the first place.

Maybe he couldn't do it at all. Maybe Duncan's magic changed him into a dragon. Maybe Elliot wasn't a shifter at all and this was all a colossal misunderstanding.

He knew that wasn't true. He'd known ever since he first saw Grant shift that day. Elliot had been hiding from the truth, but he couldn't hide from it any longer.

He finally drifted off, but he couldn't sleep. That image of the dragon wrapped up asleep with Echo kept floating into Elliot's dreams. He kept jolting awake and thanking High Heaven that he wasn't a dragon after all.

He shuddered every time he remembered. He *was* a dragon. He couldn't deny it to himself any longer.

Each realization crushed him under a tidal wave of anguish and shame. Only Echo's presence next to him stopped him from leaving and doing something drastic to end this nightmare.

He woke up hours later to grey dawn streaming through the trees. Echo woke up at the same moment and sat up.

They both looked around and Echo frowned. "Where is everyone?"

"Perhaps they went down to the spring." Elliot got to his feet and went over to the tree where Duncan had been tied. "Duncan's gone....and the rope is gone, too."

Echo frowned in all directions and came over to him. "They wouldn't untie him. They wouldn't leave without telling us."

Elliot pointed down at the ground. "Look. There arenae any tracks. They've vanished."

Echo turned in all directions scanning the forest. She returned to facing him, but she wouldn't stop scowling at everything. "You know what this means, don't you? Duncan must have magicked them away."

"Aye. It's just what I was about to say meself."

She whirled away. "We have to find them. We have to help them recapture Duncan...."

He grabbed her arm. "No, lassie. We cannae."

"We can't let him get away! They could be out here searching for him for weeks."

"They winnae do that. Ye heard what Reid and Betty said. Calling this assault for the new moon is more important. We've only two weeks left to rally everyone. Reid and Betty are on their way to Icemeet with Duncan or without him. That leaves me to call the rebels and ye to call Grant and Lily. Ye heard what Betty said. Everything depends on each one coming together at the same time."

Her shoulders slumped, but she didn't stop frowning at the woods. "You're right."

"So that's one to me."

She jerked around to furrow her brow at him. "Huh?"

"I'm right...for once. Ye can put that down as the first time.... possibly in me whole life. I winnae catch up with ye anytime soon, but it's a start."

She burst out laughing. "Keep trying, pal. All right. Let's get out of here."

She went over to the fire and kicked dirt on the dying coals. Then she collected what little was left of their supplies.

She wrapped a few tattered bandages and the healing ointment in Alastair's tartan. She tied it all together to make a bundle she could carry.

She gathered up all the weapons still lying around. "At least Betty is still armed."

"She's with a Highland tiger, lass. Betty will be just grand."

"I guess you're right." She looked up at him and they both laughed. "Here. You take these."

She handed him two more sabers and two dirks. She took two of each and then examined the rest. "We should hide these. We should cover up the fact that we were the ones who killed those guys."

"Ye're right." They both laughed. "Stop that this instant, lass. We cannae go all the way back to the fort this way."

"Okay." She gathered the remaining weapons in her arms. "I'll drop these in the spring. No one will find them there."

He almost told her again that she was right and changed his mind. "Splendid idea."

She read his mind and smirked at him. Then they both walked away together.

She dumped the weapons into the deepest part of the pool and they returned along the route they took to get here. Elliot recognized the landmarks, and by midday, he was the one leading her instead of the other way around.

Chapter 17

Echo and Elliot returned to the Serpent Cave by evening and built a fire. They sat side by side while they shared the food stores and blankets.

"Are you sure you don't want to come to Kald with me?" she asked.

"I cannae go back there in any case. The Laird's magic would detect me the moment I showed me face."

"What kind of reception do you expect from the rebels?"

"I suppose it depends on whether Torran has divined that I killed his men. If he has, I'm dead."

"You could defeat them if you shifted."

"Och, no, lassie! Dinnae even suggest it."

"Why are you so reluctant to use your power? You could do so much with it."

"I couldnae convince them to help Duncan's cause with it. If they find out I'm a Creighton of the Royal Line, they winnae listen to me at all. They'll have naught to do with me. Me only chance is to convince them that I'm still one of them."

She rested her head on his shoulder and gazed into the fire. "You're right. I didn't think of that."

He kissed her on the head and put his arm around her shoulders. He didn't point out that he was right again. He could think of more reasons NOT to shift into a dragon than reasons to do it.

He finally summoned the resolve to voice the nagging doubt that had been plaguing him all day. "I still dinnae trust meself not to lose control and kill someone. Even killing Torran would be too much."

"Why don't you practice?" He started to shake his head. She nodded toward the cave entrance. "It's still light outside and we're all alone. No one will see you except me. I'll help you."

He glanced at her, and when he saw her eyes, he looked away. "Cannae we continue to pretend it never happened?"

She laughed, wrapped her arms around him, and kissed him on the neck. "Would it help if I told you that it excites me?"

"Does it?"

"Yes." She leaned and gave him a full, open-mouthed kiss. Her weight fell against him and he felt her body straining and trembling with barely suppressed passion. Her breathing quickened and caught as she savored his mouth.

She slipped off his lips and whispered in a breathless rush of lust-fueled excitement. "I want to see you like that. I love it."

"If ye put it that way...."

They both laughed and she hopped to her feet. She held out her hand to him. "Come on. Once you've done it a few times, you'll be able to control it. Then you won't have to be so afraid of it."

He didn't want to go. He didn't get up, but she wouldn't leave him alone. She grabbed his hand and dragged him toward the cave entrance.

He hung back until she towed him outside. She parked him under the trees and waved at him while she retreated to a safe distance. "I'm ready when you are."

She halted under the trees and stood there waiting. Elliot stared at her and then down the ground.

"You okay?" she called after a long silence.

"How exactly am I to do this, lassie?" he asked.

"Uh.... I don't know. What did you do last time?"

"I didnae do ought last time. Duncan did it to me."

"That's impossible. Grant is a dragon the same as you. There must be a way."

He screwed up his face concentrating hard, but nothing happened. She finally strode toward him and stopped there studying him. "Hmm. This is weird."

"That doesnae begin to describe it, lass. I dinnae ken ought on how to do it."

"Should I attack you like....?"

"NO!" he roared. "Dinnae do ought."

"Well, what would you like me to do?"

He thought about it for a second. "It's no good. I cannae do it."

She inspected him more closely and then her shoulders dropped. "Oh, well. It was worth a shot. How did it happen with Grant the first time?"

"I dinnae.... We were in a battle. The wizards attacked him with magic. They almost killed him....and it just happened.... a bit like yesterday."

Her shoulders slumped and she nodded. "You're right. We can't do it that way." She started to turn away. "I guess we should go back inside...."

He caught a fleeting glimpse of the disappointed expression on her face....and he knew. She'd been telling the truth about his dragon form exciting her. She wasn't lying to make him feel better.

He wanted to excite her like that. The thought electrified him so much that he felt himself actually starting to harden thinking about it. Without even trying, that smoldering passionate lust blasted out of him with frightening power.

It happened so much faster this time than it did yesterday. Duncan's magic made the dragon skin crawl over him and eat him up from the inside.

This time, it flashed outward with the blinding speed of an erupting starburst. It swallowed him and everything he knew about himself as a man. He *wasn't* a man. He never had been.

He was this ground-shaking monster, this force of nature come to life. He was a torrent of fire spilling across the landscape.

He exploded out of his skin so fast that he knocked Echo flat on her seat, but he couldn't even care about that. She scrambled to get out of his way and raced back to the place she'd been standing a moment before.

She gaped up at him in wide-eyed shock, but she wasn't afraid anymore. She might be stunned and surprised. She might even be a little bit frightened by his size, but he recognized now that she really was excited. Her eyes glowed and danced over his colossal body.

He reared back, spread his wings with a deep resounding thump, and screeched high and long. He thrashed his head against the sky and his tail flattened enormous trees every time he swished it.

He didn't scream in surprise or rage this time. He screamed to hear his own voice and to shout his existence to the four winds. He was alive. He was a dragon and nothing could stop him. This was him. This was the true kernel of his most real self come to life at last.

He lowered his head to scan the ground. He narrowed his eyes at her and her hand instinctively flew to her dirk.

That one quick movement cooled his ardor and he started to shrink back to the ground. He felt himself becoming a man again and his dragon soul exploded beyond all bounds. It revolted against ever becoming a man again.

He reared and beat his wings. The strength and power pumping through his veins thrilled him as never before. He felt unstoppable. He would mow down anyone who stood before him.

He slammed his forelegs down on the ground and looked around again. Echo stood in the same place, but her expression had changed to one of pure delight. She really did like what she saw.

She took a step toward him and he froze. What would happen when she got near him? He didn't trust himself around her.

This volcanic power racing through him wasn't compatible with the way he felt about her. He wanted to shift back into a man, but he'd kept this dragon locked away for too long. It wouldn't go back into its cage willingly.

She took a few more tentative steps nearer. He wanted to take wing and get away from her. He didn't want to hurt her, but she kept getting closer with every step.

She halted in front of him and she didn't retreat when he glared down at her tiny form. She shivered, drew herself upright, and crossed the last few feet to his side. She stood right next to his shoulder now.

He cringed when she raised her hand to touch him. This dragon body magnified every sensation. He didn't know if he could survive her touch or what it would mean. What if he lost control again?

Her hand grazed his scales and he shivered. He shut his eyes and a deep rumble rolled out of his chest. Her hand glided down his neck to his chest. She swiveled around the other side of him touching him all over.

She finally came near his head and stroked the spikes running along the back of his neck. She moved in front of his eyes until she stood right in front of him.

"Would you like to touch me, Elliot?" she breathed. "Would you like to kiss me? You can't do that when you're like this." She leaned in close to his ear. "I would really love to kiss you right now, Elliot. I would so love to feel your arms around me right now."

Her sultry, sex-drunk voice sent another tendril of fire to his brain. He wanted more than anything to touch her and kiss her and to put his arms around her. He wanted to do that as a man.

He straightened up and shifted. He was beginning to understand the connection between these two different states of his being. He still couldn't understand how he did it, but it didn't seem to matter anymore.

He seemed to be able to shift just by wanting to. It came from some subconscious part of himself beyond words or thoughts.

He descended to the ground until he stood right in front of her. She burst into the most brilliant, beautiful smile he'd ever seen. That smile of genuine delight and pride gave him the greatest reward he could ask for.

He smiled back at her and happiness overwhelmed his soul. He was doing it. He was pleasing her and doing what she wanted him to do.

She threw her arms around him and kissed him. He kissed her back, but he broke away long before she finished with him. "Not so fast, lassie."

"What's wrong? You did it. You can do it now."

"Wait a moment." He pushed her away. "Go back over there until I'm sure I can do it."

She beamed at him and retreated back to her place. He shifted back into a dragon—on purpose this time. Once he got like that, he really didn't want to shift back into a man. He wanted to stay like this forever. It felt wonderful. Why did he resist it for so long?

He had to concentrate hard to shift back into a man, but all he had to do was think about being with Echo. He would go back into the cave with her when he finished this exercise. He might be able to do that as a dragon, but he didn't want to. He wanted to be with her as a man.

He shifted five more times and finally returned to his normal form. He grinned at Echo and sighed. "It's done, lassie. I can control it now. Ye were right. It's much better this way."

She smirked when he said she was right, but when she came toward him, her smile faded. Her cheeks glowed and she blushed. "Would you like to.... you know......?"

"What do ye mean, lass? What else is there to do?"

She nodded over her shoulder toward the forest to the west. "Would you like to.... fly around for a while.... with me?"

"You want ....to fly?" He wasn't sure at first what she meant. Then his heart flipped when he realized what flying around would be like.... with her. "Do ye really want to?"

"Yeah!" she breathed. "It will be fun!"

He had to think about it some more before he threw caution to the wind. "Very well. Stand clear, lass."

She wouldn't stop grinning on her way back to her place. She bounced when she walked. She couldn't contain her exhilaration and Elliot felt excitement taking over. Was he really going to do this?

He shifted again and stretched his wings even wider. She was right about that, too. This unstoppable power wanted to vent itself somehow. He wanted to feel the wind rushing over his scales. He wanted to cover the miles and use his strength.

He had to control himself even more to crouch down in front of her. She raced to his side and clambered up his scales to his back.

She straddled his neck and an even more life-changing surge of power gripped his being when he felt her weight settle between his shoulders. She felt as though she belonged there, as if they were made for this.

He extended his wings and he didn't hold back this time. He let the explosive power inside him burst forth and he launched over the treetops.

He caught a glimpse of Kald and Tyrekirk in the distance and banked toward the west. He flexed his wings harder and picked up speed racing over the treetops. He climbed to the clouds relishing the incredible strength and power flowing out of every part of him.

Echo laughed and her voice sparked an insane reaction in him. He rocketed straight up into the atmosphere, gained the highest heights, and tilted toward the ground.

He tucked his wings, narrowed his eyes to slits, and plummeted. He rocketed to earth at impossible speed. Echo flattened herself to his neck, wrapped her arms around him, and shrieked in combined fright and delight.

The wind ripped across his scales. It felt incredible. Every part of him pulsed with life and energy unlike anything he'd ever experienced.

The mountains rushed toward him at mind-numbing speed. He flung out his wings and zoomed up them, down the other side, and far out to sea. Tiny ships floated on the ocean down there. He could fly like this forever and never get tired of it.

Echo sat up, gripped her legs around his neck, and raised her arms into the wind. She whooped and laughed with the wind pelting her face and hair and body. Her reaction made Elliot indescribably happy. She loved this. She embraced all that he was. He didn't have to worry anymore. Everything was okay.

He flew around for hours covering strange continents and circling bubbling volcanoes. He could have gone a lot longer, but when he flew over Scotland again, he saw that it was completely dark down there.

The mission called him back toward the ground. Some things in this world were more important than the joy of flight.

Echo lay down on his neck and pressed her soft cheek to his scales exactly the way he imagined. He didn't try to push that sensation away. It warmed him to the marrow of his bones. He had her heart. He didn't have to wonder anymore.

He set down in the forest, folded his wings, and flattened himself to the ground. Echo slipped off his back and he shifted back into a man.

Her gleaming eyes told him all he needed to know about how she felt. She didn't have to say anything. She put her arms around him, and when she kissed him, he held her close and didn't try to stop her from getting as close to him as she wanted to.

Her body trembled with more delight and energy than ever before and his stomach hurt imagining what tonight would hold for them.

She finally sank down on her heels, took his hand, and burst out in excited laughter. "That was awesome!"

"Ye enjoy yerself while it lasts, lass. We winnae do any of that again for a long time if we keep going the way we are." He nodded to the trees behind her. "Are ye sure ye dinnae fancy running off with me? We could leave all this behind and not come back."

She only smiled at him. "You don't really want that, do you? Just imagine using your power against the Laird. We're going to win with you on our side."

She looked so happy and he felt so close to her that he had to admit that she was right again. He didn't want to leave. Now that he no longer feared his dragon nature, he was looking forward to using his power against.... someone.

He wanted to fight. He wanted to destroy. He wanted to raze the landscape. He couldn't think of anyone he'd rather attack than Laird Balfour Creighton.

She led him back to the cave and they settled down by the fire again. It had burned low and she built it up to a blaze. "You could be doing this with your fire. We'll never have to use a flint or matches again to light fires."

"I dinnae think I could fit in here anyway, lassie." He inspected the cave roof and then pulled the food toward him. "I'll be back at the fort tomorrow. I winnae be shifting anywhere near the rebels for the foreseeable future."

She got serious instantly. "That means tonight's our last night together."

"Aye." He pulled her in for a long kiss and then set the food aside. He wasn't hungry anyway—not for food. He wanted her. He wanted to enjoy the hours left to him before he had to watch her walk away.

Chapter 18

Elliot pulled Echo to a stop among the trees. They'd been walking hand in hand for half the day. Now he drew her close and kissed her.

"This is it, lassie."

"What's it?" she asked.

He nodded behind her. "This is where I split off to the fort."

Her heart spasmed. "So soon?"

"I dinnae want to part from ye just yet," he breathed. "Come with me. We can spend the night here before ye leave in the morning."

"Really?" She looked behind her, but there was nothing there. "What will the rebels think when you show up with a woman?"

"They'll think they've won a prize, but I'll make them understand that ye're mine. They winnae bother about ye."

"Are you sure about that?"

He grinned down at her. "If they dinnae understand it, ye can teach them as well as ye and Betty taught Barclay. Ye can stand on yer on, but they winnae transgress ought if they understand ye're mine."

Another thrill of adrenaline burned her insides when he said it. *Ye're mine.* She loved that feeling of belonging to him. She just wished she didn't have to say goodbye to him, today or any other day.

"All right. I'll come."

He smiled and blushed. "Ye're a mite too easy, lass."

"Should I have said no?"

"I believe ye're a rascal, lassie." He turned away, but he didn't take her hand again.

She scanned the forest ahead searching for the rebel fort, but it took much longer to get there than she expected. She was glad now that he stopped to talk to her out of sight of any rebels.

She spotted movement in the trees before she saw the fort itself. Men armed with crossbows stood guard on the walls of a giant stockade built of logs.

The call went up as soon as Echo and Elliot appeared out of the forest. "Stand off!" one of the men bellowed. "Dinnae approach the gate or we'll shoot!"

"Wait here," Elliot murmured to Echo and he stepped into the open.

He raised his hands and approached the big front gate. "It's me—Elliot Ritchie! Ye ken me, Fraser. I've been gone not more than four days."

The guards went into a frantic scurry of action. Some descended behind the wall while different men climbed up to aim their weapons at Elliot.

"Ritchie!" one of them roared. "We thought ye were dead!"

"What made ye think that? Torran found me in the western forest not three days ago. Ask him if I'm still welcome in this fort."

Another flurry of frantic movement went on behind the wall. Elliot stayed where he was with his hands raised until a big guy climbed up and scowled down at Elliot.

Echo stiffened when she recognized the man who told Elliot to shoot Duncan, but she could see him much more clearly now. Half his head was bald with his long, grey hair tied back in a ponytail. He wore a green kilt that had seen better days.

He was much burlier and more 1powerful than she remembered, but she had only ever seen him in the dark. He glared at Elliot and then glanced over at her, but only for an instant.

She saw in that glance that he didn't recognize her. What would he do if he found out she was the one who attacked him in the dark and punched his lights out? She didn't look forward to that conversation.

"Ritchie!" Torran bellowed. "What the hell are ye doing back here?"

"I was living here the last time I checked."

"I told ye to shoot that Buchanan spy. Ye dinnae dare to show yer face after ye failed in me orders."

"I killed the Buchanan the way ye said. I hit him in the eye. Does that satisfy ye? I checked his body and...." Elliot waved Echo forward. "I brought the man's tartan as proof."

He held up Echo's bundle to show the men on the wall. Torran frowned even more. Why was he so reluctant to let Elliot back inside?

"What is *that*?" Torran snarled.

"That?" Elliot raised his eyebrows at Echo in mock surprise. "Why—it's a woman, man! Havenae ye ever seen one before? I suppose it's been so many years since ye visited the brothels in Kald. Perhaps ye dinnae recall what a woman looks like."

Torran snarled between gritted teeth and Echo had to seriously bite back laughter. "Ye mind yer tongue, lad. I can still best ye when it suits me."

"Ye keep yer distance from her so long as she's inside yer fort, Torran." Elliot's voice dropped a register and betrayed a hint of steel that Echo had never heard before. "She's mine and ye ken the rules as well as I do meself. I'll teach some manners to any man who cannae behave himself about her…. including ye, Torran."

Torran scowled even more dangerously, but he didn't reply. He turned aside and barked down at someone on the ground. "Open the gate!"

A section of the wall slid back. Elliot handed Echo her bundle and they advanced to the entrance. They stepped inside the stockade and the men on the wall started to close the gate again. They all got behind it and pushed to roll it on round logs.

It thumped against its anchor post. Echo and Elliot were inside the rebel fort and she got her first look at the place. Dozens of sturdy log houses had been constructed inside the wall. Nearly everyone present was male, but she spotted two or three women peeking out of windows and doors. At least Echo wasn't the only one.

Torran barged down the stairs leading to the sentry towers on top of the wall. He stormed over to Echo and Elliot and wrinkled his nose at her. "What's the matter with her? She's strange….and she's armed."

"Is there any law against a woman bearing arms?" Elliot asked. "We're all bearing them."

Torran sneered at Echo's clothes. "She's dressed as a man."

"Och, no, man!" Elliot exclaimed. "She's wearing trousers as we were traveling in the forest. That's the only reason, but ye can see she's a woman right enough."

Torran moved over in front of Echo. "Ye're not a Buchanan, lassie?"

"She cannae be," Elliot cut in. "She doesnae have their eyes."

"Did ye come from Kald, lass?" Torran demanded.

"No, I've never been to Kald," she replied. "I was just going there when I bumped into Elliot in the forest."

Torran frowned even more. "Ye've a strange way of speaking. Where did ye come from?"

"She comes from America," Elliot interjected. "Now, if ye've asked enough questions, we'll be off."

"Not so fast, laddie." Torran blocked Elliot's path with his arm. "I've a few questions for ye as well."

Elliot gave an exaggerated sigh. "Very well. What questions?"

"I sent Evan, Gowan, Fyfe, and Errol out to find ye. Our trackers found ye traveling with the Buchanans. Where are they?"

"Who—the Buchanans? I dinnae ken and that's the truth. I havenae seen them since the night ye told me to shoot at them."

"Ye're lying, laddie. Our trackers followed ye and two others in company with one of the tigers. Ye traveled to Spinners Hill and that's where we lost Gowan and the others."

Elliot listened with his head on one side. His bright, curious eyes never left Torran's wrinkled face. "Och, no! I dinnae ken ought about that. I didnae travel with any Buchanans." He laughed a little too loudly. "I would've kenned that. Ye must be mistaken."

He started to leave again and Torran seized Elliot's arm in a death grip. "If ye had ought to do with their disappearance, I'll hear about it."

"I didnae." Elliot shook Torran off. "I didnae even ken ye sent them out."

"So where have ye been for three days?" Fraser demanded from Elliot's left.

"I went hunting as I said. I stayed in the Serpent Cave for a day or two.... That's about the size of it, lads. There's naught more to tell."

Torran didn't buy it at all. "Ye havenae told the lot, lad. Tell us the rest."

Elliot gave another exaggerated sigh. "Very well.... if ye insist. I went hunting with Evan, Barclay, and Graeme....and then we came upon these two strange lassies." He waved at Echo. "But ye already kenned that, I suppose. Evan came running home and spun ye a yarn about them and the Buchanans in the forest."

"Aye." Torran turned to glare at Echo. "Where's your friend, lassie?"

"I really don't know," Echo replied. "I wish I did, but she just vanished in the forest. I have no idea where she is."

Torran must have recognized the truth when he heard it because he didn't ask her any more questions. He turned back to Elliot. "Ye traveled with the Buchanans. Ye camped with them in the Serpent Cave."

"I didnae like to leave the lassies alone with the beasts as ye might imagine."

"Ye didnae have to share our food and all with them as yer guest," Fraser interjected. "Why didnae ye drive them off if ye were so concerned about the lassies?"

Elliot's eyebrows flew up. "Drive them off? Och, no! Me—against two of the tigers? I think not. No, no!"

Some of the listening guardsmen laughed and the tension started to defuse. Then two or three went back to work. Only Torran and Fraser remained to confront Elliot, but he still didn't act threatened by their questions. He gazed at Torran's grizzled face with a benign, indulgent smile plastered across his lips. No one would ever suspect him of the slightest trace of guile.

Torran finally huffed, growled in Elliot's general direction, and stalked off somewhere. Fraser took longer. He compressed his lips like he might be ready to launch into more objections.

Elliot continued to gaze at the man waiting to answer the next question. A second later, Fraser marched off, too.

Elliot smirked at Echo. "There ye go, lassie. We're in."

He took her hand and led her deeper into the stockade which was starting to look more and more like a small town.

She glanced over her shoulder much more warily. His apparently cheery demeanor unnerved her, especially when she saw the way some of the other guardsmen were looking at her.

"Are you sure this is a good idea? These guys.... they look dangerous."

"They are," he murmured back. "Ye'll need to be on yer toes here, lassie, but as ye're only staying one night, I wouldnae worry about it. Ye'll be with me the whole time."

She almost asked him again if he was sure they should even be staying here—or rather, whether *she* should be staying here. She hadn't felt this unsafe in.... well, ever.

She even noticed some of the creepier rebels following her and Elliot between the houses. He completely ignored these men, but she couldn't. She kept her hand on her weapon the whole time.

He turned off into a large roundhouse that had been built into the stockade wall.

The more she saw, the more she understood how this whole rebel group had been structured. The men who had wives—or whatever they were—lived in the houses and cabins dotting the main yard behind the gate.

The roundhouse extended in a curve across the back wall. The roundhouse covered almost the entire wall in a complete semi-circle. The roundhouse ended thirty yards on either side of the entrance gate to leave the gate and wall clear.

Sentry posts dotted the wall all the way around. Some had been built right into the roundhouse roof to guard every side of the stockade. The fort remained under constant watch at all times.

"Did you stand guard up there?" she whispered to Elliot.

"Aye. Everyone does. It's required, but I only did it a handful of times as I just arrived here a few months ago. Come along, lassie, and I'll show ye to me own room."

Chapter 19

Elliot slipped into his bedroom carrying a tray of food. He set it down on the bed next to Echo. The bed was the only place to sit and Elliot used his foot to shut the door behind him. "Well, lassie, ye'll be happy to ken that all the lads are talking of naught but ye down at the canteen."

"They are?" She straightened up to make room for him to sit down on the opposite side of the tray. "That isn't good."

"Aye. Torran is in a right state."

"Let me guess. He didn't believe a word of that pathetic story you told him about Reid and Alastair."

"Not a word of it. I couldnae even tell him I nearly lost me life fighting one of the cats." He held up his arm. "I dinnae even have any scars to prove it."

"So is he out to get you now? Maybe you aren't safe here, either."

"I'll deal to him. Dinnae worry on that." He sat down across from her. "Come and get yer dinner. Ye arenae likely to find anything to eat anywhere else."

"I can't help but worry. What if he tries something after I leave?"

"I'm certain he will."

"Well? What if you wind up dead? Where will that leave me?"

He beamed at her. He cared about her more and more with every passing second. The thought of her walking away tomorrow morning was starting to cause him a lot more distress than he expected.

"I can handle Torran. It's the...."

A loud knock interrupted him in midsentence. He pulled the door open. He didn't have to stand up to reach the latch.

He relaxed when he saw one of the youngest rebels in the whole camp standing in the corridor outside. "Bac! What's the rub?"

"Torran wants to see ye, lad. He's demanding to see ye and yer lassie in his apartment immediately."

"Whatever for?" Elliot asked. "Dinnae tell me he plans to challenge me right now. I'm in the middle of me dinner here."

"I dinnae ken what he wants, but he's calling the captains as well." Bac's eyes darted over to Echo. "Whatever it is, it's big."

Elliot ran his hand across his mouth. "Then we'd best go see what he wants. Ye come along with us, laddie."

Bac shuffled his feet and cast sideways glances up and down the corridor on both sides. "I dinnae think I'd best do that, lad. He hasnae called me."

"I'm calling ye. Even if he challenges me, I'm entitled to a second."

"I cannae be second to ye, lad," Bac muttered. "I couldnae stand against Torran. Ye ken yer own self I couldnae."

"Ye winnae have to stand against him, laddie, for I winnae need a second. Come along. Ye come with us. Come, lass. We'll finish this later."

He pushed the tray away and he was pleased when Echo grabbed her saber and dirk on her way out of the room. He didn't have to explain anything to her.

Bac's eyes widened when he saw her buckling on her saber and sticking her dirk into her belt, but she pretended not to see.

The three of them set off down the corridor. "What's a challenge?" Echo whispered in Elliot's ear.

"If Torran wants to get rid of someone, he challenges them to prove their loyalty."

"Do they have to fight him or something?" she asked.

"Aye. Every change in rank requires a challenge. Every man has to earn promotion by defeating the man he hopes to replace. More times than no, a second steps in to carry out the fight in Torran's place. He's tough enough as it is, but some feel he's too high to fight for himself against the scum he wants to oust. If the man wins, he earns his place."

"And if he loses, he dies, right?" She made a face. "It's barbaric."

"Dinnae concern yerself with it. I can take Torran if it comes to that, but he wouldnae call the captains to his apartment if he planned to challenge me."

"So what does he want?"

"I dinnae care what he wants. It's what I want that matters."

She glanced over at him and his spirits soared at the soft light shining in her eyes. She was still his. "What do you mean?"

"This is me chance to tell him about the assault. We winnae get a better chance to convince him to join the campaign."

"He didn't seem very agreeable to anything connected with you," she remarked.

"I dinnae care about him. It's the captains that matter. He's an incorrigible bastard. The captains are all staunch. They'll join no matter what he says."

She started to say something, but he and Bac drew up to Torran's apartment before she got the chance. Bac opened the door for Elliot and he stepped inside followed by Echo. Bac remained outside in the corridor like he wanted to bolt.

Elliot gave him a sharp look and Bac ducked his head, looked at the floor, and finally entered last. He left the door open. Elliot had to dive past him and pull it closed himself.

The three of them entered an office where Torran sat behind a huge desk. Five other men stood around him, including Fraser.

"Ye arenae welcome in this, Bac," Torran snapped. "Be off with ye."

"He's here as me second," Elliot replied.

"Second!" Torran barked. "Ye're here to talk, not to fight."

"That's as ye say. I brought a second nonetheless." Elliot cast a significant glance over the assembled captains, but he already knew none of them would challenge him. Fraser was the only man here that Elliot didn't count as a friend ....and Torran himself, of course.

Torran huffed with his usual scowl and turned to the papers on his desk. "I've had reports on ye, lad. Some of the lads down in the guard room are accusing ye of...."

"I'm right glad ye called us in, man," Elliot interrupted. "I've had word from a few of me own sources that a combined assault is scheduled for the new moon. Three other armies are converging on Kald to assault Tyrekirk trying to unseat Laird Balfour."

One of the other captains spoke up right away exactly the way Elliot anticipated. The man was named Forbes and he was another deserter from Creighton service. "Ye dinnae say! Which armies are they?"

"Well, as ye ask, the Buchanans are attacking from across the water...."

"We winnae join any assault with the Buchanans in it," Torran snarled.

"Will ye listen to reason, man?" Elliot turned back to the captains and concentrated all his persuasive power on them. "We'd be daft not to coordinate our strike at the same time. The Buchanans can weaken the Creighton army and distract the bulk of their forces on the planes while we slip into Kald on the back foot. It's the perfect solution."

"Who are the other three armies?" Fraser demanded.

Echo turned to Elliot and her eyes widened while she waited for him to answer. Who *were* the other three armies?

He couldn't exactly tell the captains that their only other ally was the Laird's own dragon shifter grandson that no one had spoken to and whom Elliot hadn't seen in months.

Instead, he invented wildly. "We have a force inside Tyrekirk working to undermine the Laird from the inside. They're ready to strike when our armies converge."

"Who is it?" asked a thick-set, greying man everyone called Athol. Elliot didn't know the rest of the man's name. "Who is on this force?"

"Obviously I cannae tell ye that," Elliot explained. "I might compromise their safety and they must keep it quiet so the Laird doesnae find out."

The other captains nodded their agreement. So far, Elliot hadn't lied to them. He just didn't tell them that the force working inside the Laird's castle consisted of two people who still didn't even know about the offensive.

"Who else?" Frasier snapped.

"It doesnae matter one jot who else," Torran interrupted. "It winnae ever happen on me own watch. This assault is doomed to failure...."

"It's doomed to failure if ye dinnae join it," Elliot countered. "Ye've been blowing hot air out of yer arse for twenty years about deposing the Laird. Now ye've a chance to actually accomplish it and ye'd balk because the Buchanans are involved? Ye arenae ought but a mouthpiece, Torran."

Torran pushed back his chair with a tooth-grinding screech, drew himself up, and towered over everyone in the room. "Ye dare....!"

"Aye, I do. Let's see ye put yer mouth to work by organizing these rebels to actually rebel against the Laird they claim to be rebelling against." Elliot took his attention off of Torran with deliberate insolence and returned to addressing the captains. "The assault is scheduled for the next new moon. Ye'll need to arm and organize yer troops by then and ensure ye attack Kald from the west side. Ye dinnae want to run afoul of the other forces."

"That's easy enough," Athol replied. "We'll need to assign another captain to take Gowan's place..."

"What about Bac?" Elliot waved to the young man who had flattened himself to the wall through the whole interview. He cowered in a corner to keep as far away from Torran as possible.

"Bac? Ye're barmy!" Fraser spat. "He's naught but a lad."

"He's a fighter and he can best near anyone on Gowan's squadron," Elliot pointed out. "Ye winnae find anyone better suited to take Gowan's place."

Forbes scratched his chin. "I dinnae ken about that."

"Let me put it ye another way," Elliot replied. "Ye winnae find anyone better suited to take Gowan's place before the next new moon. Ye must appoint a captain immediately who can step in and begin the preparations. Bac is here and he's heard our whole conference. He's yer man."

All eyes turned to Bac who trembled even more violently under their scrutiny than he would have under Torran's. The other captains started nodding in agreement. Only Fraser and Torran glared at Bac as though this was all his idea.

"We could do...." Forbes began.

"We winnae do ought of the kind!" Torran boomed. "I'm still the leader of this band and I say...."

"This is yer chance to be a hero of the rebellion, Torran," Elliot cut in. "Ye can take credit for unseating the Laird the way ye've always wanted to. Ye dinnae fancy being known throughout history as the man who stood in the way of the rebels overthrowing the Laird as ye've been talking about doing for twenty years."

Elliot let the words sink in. Torran didn't stop glaring at him and fuming in suppressed rage, but he didn't dare to contradict in front of the captains.

Fraser glanced over at Torran and Elliot knew he'd won. Torran wouldn't go against the captains now. He wouldn't want word to get out to the rebel faction that he actually tried to stop the group from overthrowing the Laird.

"At any rate," Elliot chirped, "the lassie and I were just in the middle of our dinner so we'll toddle off and get back at it. Ye'll all let me ken if I can help in any way, but I suppose ye lads have it all in hand."

He nodded to Athol and Forbes and turned away. He didn't make eye contact with Torran or Fraser.

Elliot's heart pounded when he took Echo's elbow and steered her out of Torran's office. Bac darted out after them and hurried to catch up with them on their way back to Elliot's room.

"You're insane!" Echo whispered in Elliot's ear. "You know that, right?"

Elliot chuckled. "Dinnae assign me to me grave just yet, lassie. The deed is done. They'll be there with bells on."

"Are ye mad, ye glaikit muckle dobber?" Bac moaned. "What the devil did ye have to go and offer me up as a captain for?"

Elliot clapped both hands on the boy's shoulders. "Ye'll be brilliant, lad."

"I'll be dead is what I'll be! Do ye have any notion what Torran will do to me?"

"He winnae do ought to ye but follow ye into battle. Athol and Forbes will see that Torran keeps his place. Ye mark me words."

Bac's eyes darted right and left. "He'll kill me!"

"Lad!" Elliot barked. "We need ye. Do ye hear? We need staunch men who care to unseat the Laird instead of playing the great leader. We need captains who ken how to fight and that's ye. Ye're wasted in the squadron. Ye can look after yer men and see they're properly equipped. That's more than Fraser can do. Believe me."

Bac rallied, nodded, and shook himself. "Right. I can do all that."

"I ken ye can. Ye're more than ye think ye are." Elliot squeezed Bac's shoulders one more time and pushed him away. "On ye go, laddie. We've work to do." He watched the young man out of sight.

He turned back to Echo and found her inspecting him with her head on one side.

"Go on with ye, lass. Go on and tell me I'm off me head."

"I wasn't going to say that."

"What were ye going to say, then?"

"Nothing."

She turned away and they walked back to his room in silence. He saw her dwelling on something, but he didn't pry. She would just have to tell him when she was ready.

They returned to his room and he shut the door. They sat down on either side of the tray and started sharing the food, but she still didn't break the silence. What was going through her mind? She wouldn't even look at him.

He put the empty tray on the floor when they finished, stretched out on the mattress, and held his arms out to her. "Come to me, lass."

She lay down next to him, cuddled into his side, and rested her head on his shoulder. He kissed her forehead and smoothed her hair, but he didn't say anything. Was now the time when she would finally tell him what had been bothering her since the meeting?

She rolled her head back to look up at him, and when he turned to meet her gaze, he couldn't help but kiss her. His heart ached from all the emotion eating him up inside.

He couldn't walk away from her.... or let her walk away from him. That would be the end of the world. It would be the end of *him*—the him that she had so carefully constructed with her help and support.

Her mouth never tasted sweeter than now. It ignited his passion for her, but this secret concern stopped him from taking it any further. He pulled off her mouth to find her eyes boring into him with that same searching, probing stare.

He tried to make it into a joke. "This isnae like the cave, is it, lassie?"

"No, it isn't."

He waited, but she still didn't broach the subject. Now her silence was really started to bother him.

At last, he gave it up, kissed her on the forehead again, and settled back on the bed. "Ye should get some sleep, lass. Ye've a long march back to Kald in the morning."

She pressed her body even tighter to his and murmured into his shoulder. "Are you sure you don't want to come with me?"

"I cannae. I must stay here and ensure the rebels do their part."

"All right."

Neither of them said any more, but those words weighed heavily on Elliot's mind. Why did he get Bac assigned to take Gowan's place as a captain if Elliot was going to stay in the rebel camp? He should have assigned himself.

He told Bac he needed someone he could trust in Gowan's place. Who was more trustworthy than Elliot himself?

He could have challenged Torran and won. Elliot had known since his first days in the forest that Torran was a stuffed-shirted peacock with more bark than bite. Elliot had been measuring the man from the beginning and Elliot knew he could defeat Torran in a fight.

So why didn't he? What better way to get the rebels to do what he wanted than to take over completely?

Some lingering trace of doubt still blocked him from conquering. He knew and saw it all when he was in his dragon form. That explosive power wiped out all doubt and made him unstoppable.

Now he was a man again and the same old questions and uncertainties plagued him at every turn. They held him back from going to Kald with Echo and confronting Grant the way Elliot knew he should. The same uncertainty checked him from defeating Torran and taking control of the rebels.

A few seconds as a dragon would dispel those doubts, but he couldn't shift into a dragon here. He had to use subtlety and keep his true nature hidden until the time came to let the monster out of its cage.

Chapter 20

Echo woke up with Elliot's arms wrapped around her from behind. His body blasted heat into her and almost burned her back. He had been getting hotter and hotter even since he started shifting. That fire burned him up from the inside. It burned away the man he had been when she met him.

She quivered all over with excitement when she thought about the dragon she touched and rode in the forest. Was that really Elliot? It didn't seem to be the same person because it wasn't.

The man and the dragon represented two sides of the same being. An invisible gossamer veil separated them, but the slightest breath could blow that veil aside to reveal the other part of his nature.

He stirred when he felt her moving. He nuzzled deeper into her neck from behind and her body stretched taut with longing. His arms tightened around her and all his muscles flexed. He crushed her into him and she felt him stiffening.

He raised his head, buried his mouth in her neck, and bit down. He let out a low, brutal growl that set her hair on end. He was a monster, a deadly creature from some forgotten realm of folklore. He was so far beyond human that she couldn't even understand him.

She understood this, though. She understood his teeth and his muscles pulling her to him. She understood his growl that was equal parts threat, command, and invitation.

He unwound his arms just enough for his rough hands to explore her body. One hand scooped up to her neck and he pried her head back onto his shoulder. His iron chest and stomach undulated against her. She knew where this was going and her body matched him stroke for stroke.

He pulled back and rolled her over to face him. Her eyes met his....and the veil evaporated. A man's eyes looked down into hers. She knew everything she needed to know about him.... but something still lingered deep inside him.

She saw it yesterday when he organized the captains to invade Kald. She saw it when he assigned Bac to take Gowan's place as captain.

Why would he do that if he planned to stay here himself? Was he really going to let her walk away from him while he stayed behind? Could he be that cowardly that he would let her walk out of his life rather than face his brother?

She didn't want to believe it. She couldn't believe it. He wouldn't. He couldn't.... but that was exactly what he planned to do.

He rose on his elbow to look down into her eyes. His hair cascaded around his face and framed his features.

She clasped his face in her hands drinking in what might be her last view of him. Her heart ached at the thought, but what else could him staying behind mean? In the best possible scenario, he would be fighting on a different front in a war against impossible odds. When would she ever see him again? Maybe never.

"What is it, lassie?" he whispered. "What do ye see when ye look at me?"

She gulped and shut her eyes, but she had to open them again and look at him. She couldn't hide from this. She had to see exactly what she was walking away from.

He kissed her deeply and his weight came to rest on her. His body impressed his nature on her mind and being, but when he rose up to meet her gaze, the same old questions and realities stared down at her out of his eyes.

She barely spoke above a cracked whisper. "I just feel like.... like I'm never going to see you again. I have a terrible feeling about walking away and leaving you here.... like.... if I walk away, I'm walking away from you forever."

She swallowed hard and shut her eyes. The agony that tore her heart to pieces squeezed out of her eyes and a tear streaked sideways into her hair.

He buried her under so many mindlessly devouring kisses that she almost lost the thread of that feeling. She could forget as long as their bodies merged and flowed in this seamless river of heat.... like lava.... like dragon fire.

Her eyes snapped open to find him looking down at her again. His eyes looked the same.... but not the same. His cheek spasmed once and then it was gone.

"What's wrong?" she asked.

He caressed her cheek so gently, so tenderly, but he didn't kiss her again. "I dinnae ken except.... I feel the same way as ye." He rolled off her and supported himself on his elbow while he searched her innermost heart. "I feel as though I'll never see ye again if ye walk out that gate now."

"Come with me!" she croaked. "Please! Don't let this be the end. It can't be—not after everything that's happened. Do you really want to take that chance? I don't."

He collapsed back on the bed, raked his hair away with his fingernails, and looked up at the ceiling. "All right."

She gave a squeal of delight and pounced on him. Those words skyrocketed her into the stratosphere of hope and happiness. He was coming with her! She didn't have to walk away from everything that promised to be good and great between them.

She landed on top of him trying to kiss every part of him at once. He grunted in pain and flinched. "Och—lass! Are ye trying to kill me?"

She couldn't touch him fast enough. "Thank you! Oh, this is going to be wonderful! What should we do first when we get to Kald? How do we get into the castle? Do we have to send a message ahead of time or what?" She kissed his chest. "Yay! I can't wait!"

"Slow yerself down a moment, lass. Ye'll destroy us both running on at the mouth that way. Settle down and let me think."

She relaxed with her body draped over his, but she couldn't settle down. Excitement and delight fizzed and bubbled in her heart. She wanted to jump up, get dressed, and rush off to Kald right now.

She couldn't do that. He was right. They needed to think this through.

"The castle is surrounded by magical spells and defenses," he told her. "We cannae just walk in the door. We must find another way in."

"What is it?"

"I ken a few ways. The trick will be finding Grant and Lily without tipping off any of the Laird's people."

"Won't everyone in there be the Laird's people?" she asked.

"Now ye're beginning to think a bit straighter." He kissed her, but she could already see his mind turning on how to get into the castle.

Seeing him deep in thought brought her back to Earth. Getting into the castle sounded easy from here. Getting out of it alive wouldn't be so easy. The place would be crawling with enemies—soldiers, wizards—God only knew what the Laird had in there.

She studied Elliot while he thought about it....and then she remembered. He would be facing something much worse in the castle than wizards or soldiers. He would be facing Grant.

She kissed him much more passionately than before. She.... loved him......Yes, she loved him. She could admit that to herself now. She loved him for facing his fears and overcoming them. She loved him for doing the right thing. He just needed the right combination of motivations, but in his heart, he was pure and brave.

Facing Grant would be the ultimate test of Elliot's resolve. It would prove once and for all that he would do whatever it took. He would use his resources and his strength to fix this—everything that was wrong—even the parts of this world that were not technically his to fix.

He stared into space for a long time. She could see the wheels turning in his head. He wasn't thinking about getting into the castle. He was thinking about Grant. Elliot was imagining the moment when he had to face his mistakes and clear the air.

Echo didn't worry about Grant. If he was half the man everyone said he was, he would be too happy to get his brother back.

She thought for a split second and realized that she wasn't worried about Elliot, either. He would do it. He would overcome this the way he'd overcome every other obstacle so far.

She laid her hand against his cheek and turned his head to face her. Only then did she see the deep well of misery in his eyes. "It will be all right."

"If ye say so, lass."

He let her kiss him, but he didn't come back from that distant place. The dark cloud of his past still hung over his head.

"You'll do it," she told him. "You'll finish this and then you can move on."

"Aye. I owe it to him if nothing else."

She kissed him again, but there didn't seem to be anything left to say. They both turned away at the same moment.

Echo sat up first and started getting dressed. He followed a minute later and started folding his tartan to buckle on his kilt. "I cannae go to Kald like this. I must find some clothes for meself."

"Why not?" she asked. "You look fine to me."

"Ye've spent too much time around the Buchanans, lass. I cannae go about with no shirt nor socks nor shoes. It's bad enough I'm going without a sporran."

"Can you get that stuff here?"

"I'll borrow them." He belted his kilt on and pulled the door open. "Dinnae go anywhere without me, lassie. I'll be back in a moment."

He left and she finished tying her shoes. She was just strapping on her weapons when he came back carrying an armload of jumbled goods.

He dumped everything on the bed and she picked up a dusty loaf of bread. "Are you going to wear this to Kald?"

He snorted. "Dinnae give me yer cheek, lassie. We'll need to eat, I suppose."

She laughed and sat down to wait for him to get dressed. "Will anyone try to stop you from leaving?"

"Torran might, but I dinnae think we have ought to worry about from him."

"So you say," she muttered. "I don't like that guy."

"There's naught to like. He's a tyrant as bad as the Laird. I've often thought to find a way to make him disappear in the fighting so there isnae any chance he might take charge in the Laird's place."

"Good idea, but you won't do that if you're in Kald and he's out here."

"There might be a way for all that." He sat down next to her and started pulling on the socks that he'd brought. "Give me something to eat before we leave, lassie."

She got busy cutting up the bread. He had also brought the usual hard cheese and some extremely hard dried meat. She had to saw it off with her saber blade.

He straightened up in front of her fully dressed and started finger-combing his hair into some semblance of order. "Why are ye looking at me like that, lassie?"

"You look different like this—all presentable. You're right. I'm not used to it."

"Ye may not believe me, lassie, but I used to cut quite a figure when I worked in the Laird's service. I'm still too ragged now, but there isnae ought to do about it. Perhaps if Grant doesnae bloody me nose too badly, he'll let me clean meself up a bit."

"He won't do that—bloody your nose, I mean. He'll be over the moon when he sees you."

"*He* may be," he muttered, "but I winnae be to see him."

Chapter 21

The journey to Kald went much quicker than Echo expected. She and Elliot passed through the woods, but he stopped her when they came to the edge of the forest.

"What's wrong?" she asked. "Aren't we going in?"

"Aye." He squinted at the skies and then at the buildings not far away. A high wall surrounded the city with a few random houses dotting the countryside between Kald and the land outside it. "The dragons are aloft."

"Where?"

He pointed to the north. "They're across the Boundless. They must be attacking Icemeet again."

She had to strain her eyes to see what he was looking at, but she still didn't see anything more than dark specks in the distance. "You can see that?"

"Aye. There must be twenty of them up there. The Laird has been bringing in reinforcements from the south."

"I thought only the Royal Family could shift."

"We can, but the Laird has other relatives in other parts of the country. He calls on them when he needs them. Come along, lassie. We havenae a moment to lose, but I warn ye. Things may get sticky once we get into the city."

"What do you mean by sticky?"

"The Laird is a wizard. He has spells all over the country. I'd be very surprised if he didnae have some tracking spell to turn up me location if I ever came back here. We must be on our guard at all times. He might send wizards to capture me the moment I set foot beyond that wall."

"What do we do if he does?"

"I dinnae ken as we can do much of anything. If he captures me, he'll take me to Tyrekirk which is where I'm trying to go at any rate."

"What about me?"

"That's what I'm saying, lass. He might spirit me away from ye in which case ye'll be on yer on."

"What do you want me to do?"

"Carry on with yer mission. Try to get into the castle and see Grant and Lily. Grant may ken a way to help me if he doesnae already ken I'm there."

"How am I supposed to get into the castle if it's all bewitched?"

"I cannae tell ye now without showing ye and I cannae show ye without going into the city."

She puffed out her cheeks. "Okay. I understand. I guess we just have to play it by ear. If you get taken, I'll handle it."

"I ken ye will, lassie. That's why I'm telling you." He kissed her and they set off for the entrance gate into the city.

Elliot followed the road toward the wall. Echo hesitated and kept checking the surroundings, but she didn't see anything to threaten them here.

A pair of guards stood on either side of the entrance, but she saw right away that they really didn't care about doing their jobs. They slouched against the wall and barely looked at Echo and Elliot. "State yer business," one of them drawled.

"We're visiting relatives," Elliot replied.

"Ye may pass." The guards shuffled aside to let the pair through and Echo and Elliot entered the shabby streets of Kald.

She looked back over her shoulder. "They weren't very enthusiastic."

"Aye. The Laird doesnae exactly inspire fervent devotion if ye get me meaning. He uses fear to get what he wants."

They entered the city, but nothing happened. No wizards came out to ambush Elliot and he kept on going past neighborhoods, intersections, and avenues.

He broke off when heavy feet tramped out of the nearby neighborhoods. He pulled Echo behind a building and they hid there holding their breath as a squad of soldiers trooped past.

"What are they doing here?" Echo whispered.

"They're patrolling the city streets." Elliot rubbed his chin and frowned. "It's strange...."

"Why is it strange? If the Laird uses fear to control everybody, he must be using his soldiers as stormtroopers to make his presence felt."

"Aye, but he didnae ever do it this far out before. When I was in his service, he kept his troops closer to Tyrekirk and left the outer neighborhoods alone." He scowled even more darkly. "I dinnae like this."

He moved into the open now that the coast was clear. He headed deeper into the city, but both he and Echo kept a much closer watch on the surroundings.

"This place is a dump," Echo remarked.

"Dump?" Elliot repeated. "What does that mean?"

"It means the city is in disrepair....and the people are living in squalor. He doesn't do much to maintain the place, does he?" She paused on a corner to watch a handful of street children. They crouched against a wall and huddled together.

The oldest didn't look more than seven and all of them wore filthy rags. Their matted, grimy hair hung in dreadlocks and their faces hadn't been washed in years.

The oldest boy tore a baseball-sized piece of bread into fragments and passed them to his friends. The children wolfed down the food. They cast furtive glances around as though they feared someone would come and take the food away before they got a chance to eat it.

The sight drove a knife into Echo's heart. She dedicated her life to helping people like this, but all the food in the world wouldn't fix what was wrong with this city.

Elliot touched her elbow and they kept going, but now that she saw, she couldn't unsee. The evidence of crushing poverty slapped her in the face everywhere she turned. It demanded her attention until she couldn't look away, no matter how painful the sight.

She and Elliot ventured deeper into the city and she kept seeing more and more poverty and hopelessness everywhere. They turned a corner and almost collided with another platoon of soldiers, but the soldiers marched on without paying any attention to Echo and Elliot.

Echo and Elliot froze in the middle of the thoroughfare. Neither of them dared to move, but nothing happened. The same thing happened twice more before the pair completely relaxed and stopped jumping and hiding every time a mob of armed men appeared.

"Why are there so many soldiers around?" Echo asked the last time this happened.

"I dinnae understand it any better than ye, lass." Elliot scowled over his shoulder at the retreating soldiers. "It wasnae ever like this when I was here before."

"The Laird must be worried about people starting an insurgency.... because they *are* starting an insurgency."

"Dinnae say that too loud." Another commotion interrupted them.

Echo spotted another bunch of soldiers, but these men weren't just walking by. They were in the act of driving another group of street children down the avenue. The soldiers attacked the children with clubs and herded them away from a shop on the corner where more soldiers were trying to force their way inside.

Four kilted men stood across the threshold doing their best to bar the entrance. They put up a good fight until the soldiers stepped back and drew their sabers. More townsfolk rushed to the spot from all over. Each wore a different tartan and more people came out of their houses to either watch the ruckus or join in.

The new arrivals attacked the soldiers from behind. The soldiers split to defend themselves. Half had to deal with the men in the shop while the rest did their best to drive off the neighbors coming to help the shopkeepers out.

The soldiers who had been harassing the children spun around and came rushing back. A woman holding a baby and clutching two more small children against her legs tried to scurry out of the soldiers' path, but they raised their clubs and struck her and her children anyway.

"Wow!" Echo breathed. "This is terrible!"

Elliot scowled at the scene and then took Echo's arm to pull her away. "Revolution is in the air, lassie. We may havenae as much trouble taking Kald as we think."

"How do you mean?"

He looked back toward the shop where the situation was disintegrating into a knock-down-dragout battle. "These people have had enough of the Laird's nonsense. They're ready to fight. They just need a reason....and perhaps a leader to follow."

"Do you mean Duncan?"

He gave her a quick shake of his head to silence her. She wanted to question him more about what he knew about the people of Kald, but when he pulled her around the next corner, all her questions died in a heartbeat.

She looked up at huge stone walls rising to pointed turrets. Flags waved from the highest steeples. More walls surrounded the enormous castle with armed guards on the parapet and more guards standing sentry outside the walls.

This had to be Tyrekirk. It looked exactly like a castle out of a fairytale, but this was no fairytale. The Laird was in there. He was waiting to squash anyone who stood up to him.

Elliot pulled Echo into an alley in sight of the walls. "We've made it this far, lass. The Laird doesnae seem to ken I'm here."

"What if he does know? What if he wants you to get into the castle so he can ambush you there?"

"Then it's up to us to find Grant first."

"Are we really going in *that* way?" She glanced past his shoulder toward the sentries. "They're bound to know who you are."

"Aye. They ken who I am and we arenae going that way."

"How, then?"

"Follow me."

He skirted the wall to the south. He came to a stretch of wall with no doorways, no sentries, and no vulnerabilities that Echo could see.

The wall towered hundreds of feet overhead. Nothing interrupted it all the way to the high turrets. "How do we get in here? There's no way in."

"Watch, lassie."

He pulled her against a building across the street as a horse and cart trundled into view. It halted there and the horse adjusted its weight on different legs while it waited.

The fat driver climbed down, went to the back of the cart, adjusted something, and peered up at the wall. Then he came around to the front, unhitched his horse, and led the animal off into the city. He left the cart where it was.

"I don't get it," Echo murmured. "Are we looking at something?"

Elliot chuckled. "Every castle has a weakness, lassie. Come on."

He took her hand and led her across the street. She still didn't understand what she was supposed to see here. She didn't see any way inside the castle.

He led her to the cart and stopped her by its back end. The wooden bed was empty. Elliot circled her waist and lifted her into it. The cart wobbled under her weight and then he climbed up next to her.

"Now what?"

A pile of smelly fabric hit her in the face. Elliot burst out laughing when the stack covered her head and then fell off.

"Ugh!" she exclaimed. "It stinks! It smells like I man who hasn't bathed in a month."

She tossed the stuff away and stared down at the bare wooden boards under her feet. The bundle had come undone to reveal six or seven white shirts. The next second, a ball of sheets plummeted from overhead and thumped down next to Elliot.

"Ye see, lass? It's the laundry chute. Up ye go."

She had to dodge another wad of dirty linen, but when she followed Elliot's gaze, she realized he was right—again. She and Elliot were standing right under a chute constructed in the wall. She looked straight up it at a courtyard higher in the castle.

He bent down and laced his fingers together. She stepped into his hands and he boosted her up. She climbed into the courtyard and crouched there looking around for any threat.

He clambered up after her. He didn't need anyone to boost him. He used hand and footholds in the wall, and when he joined her, he dusted off his clothes and smiled at the surroundings. "Och! It's good to be back."

"Are you sure? Won't the Laird know you're here?"

His smile vanished. "Och, aye. Ye didnae need to spoil me homecoming by reminding me."

She couldn't enjoy the joke. The tension spiked off the charts, now that they were going right inside the lion's den.

He led the way to a high doorway leading into a dark tunnel. It wound deep inside Tyrekirk and Echo had no idea where they were going.

Elliot climbed down some cold stone steps to a dungeon. It looked as much like the setting for a horror film as Tyrekirk looked like a fairytale from the outside.

Elliot paused in the dungeon and looked around with the most curious smile on his face. It was such an inappropriate reaction to the setting that Echo almost asked him what about the place could possibly make him like it so much.

He opened his mouth to say something to her when they heard more footsteps coming closer. Elliot jumped a foot in the air and stiffened. His eyes flashed and his hand flew to his weapon.

"In here, lassie!" he whispered.

He steered her into an empty cell. A heavy wooden door with massive iron hinges stood open not far away. The two of them crowded into a corner as more doors crashed open out of sight.

Men's shouting voices came closer all the time. They echoed off the walls and sounded much louder than they were in this cold, harsh place. The men crashed into the dungeon until they halted right outside the cells.

Elliot put his arm across Echo's chest and flattened her against the wall—as if she really wanted to go anywhere right now.

The men kept bellowing, "Keep quiet! Ye havenae ought to complain of. Ye betrayed the Laird and now ye'll pay the price."

"I didnae!" another man cried. "I wouldnae ever betray the...."

Blows cut the man off and then a devastating explosion rocked the dungeon. Echo and Elliot huddled silent and breathless in their hiding place as a nearby cell slammed open. The soldiers thumped their hapless prisoner and then threw him into the cell right next door.

The prisoner whimpered a few more times and then the heavy door boomed shut. The soldiers trooped away and silence fell once again.

Echo trembled all over. That was close.

Chapter 22

Elliot held his finger to his lips and pulled Echo out of the dungeon cell. She hung onto his hand for dear life. If they got caught, they could be trapped in the dungeon under Tyrekirk forever.

He led her back upstairs. They didn't dare to talk until they reached a long tunnel deep underground. "We must go upstairs," Elliot whispered. "It's the only way we'll find Grant and Lily."

Echo wasn't sure she wanted to find Grant and Lily anymore. She wanted to run for it, but getting out of Tyrekirk was likely to be as dangerous as getting into it if not more so.

Elliot kept going, though. Echo followed him through an endless warren of passageways. She was just about to ask Elliot where they were going when they heard footsteps again. That sound was really starting to work on Echo's nerves.

Elliot pulled her back against the wall. Another posse of soldiers passed an intersection up ahead, but they didn't see the intruders.

Echo and Elliot stayed where they were until the soldiers' footsteps faded out of earshot. Why hadn't the Laird's magic detected Elliot inside the castle yet? Echo couldn't hold out much hope that their luck would last.

Everyone said the Laird's magic could detect anybody anywhere. Elliot himself said the Laird had been on the lookout for him all along. Did the Laird let Elliot enter the castle to trap him?

Elliot took her hand and they tiptoed to the intersection. He looked back and forth in all directions. The whole area was deserted.

He turned off to the left when a shout cracked down the tunnel. "Stop where ye are! Dinnae move!"

Echo and Elliot spun around fast. Echo's hands flew to her weapons as the same troop of soldiers came thundering back around another corner. How did they find the intruders? She didn't even have to ask.

The soldiers definitely saw the pair now and the soldiers plunged in for the attack. They brandished their weapons and spread out to box Echo and Elliot in.

Elliot pulled his saber and Echo sidestepped to put more space between herself and Elliot. The soldiers divided into two prongs and they outnumbered Echo and Elliot at least six to one.

Half the soldiers charged Echo and she met them with a weapon in each hand. She slashed, hacked, and stabbed in all directions. She killed three of them, but she still wound up backing against the wall to defend herself against the rest.

She couldn't stand against so many even fighting to her utmost. More soldiers rushed to the spot from all over until she couldn't see the end of their numbers. The Laird's magic must have triggered an alarm somewhere.

Five soldiers surrounded her. One on her right thrust out with his saber. She blocked the stroke, but another on her left caught her off guard. His blade sliced her arm and she yelped in pain.

The reaction came so fast that she never saw it coming. A blazing torch of flame erupted from somewhere across the passage. It flashed out with mind-blowing speed and set dozens of soldiers alight.

The men attacking Echo turned away and came face to face with Elliot in his dragon form. He was so big that he had to crouch under the ceiling and flatten his wings against his back. He couldn't stand upright and he flattened his belly to the floor.

His smoldering slit eyes fixed on the soldiers, and as soon as they staggered away from Echo, he unleashed another brutal cascade of fire. He incinerated twenty men in one breath.

The soldiers writhed in their death throes and then their charred remains crumbled to the floor. Elliot growled deep in his chest and looked down his scaly nose at them. Smoke billowed from his nostrils and his growls made the floor vibrate under Echo's feet.

She blinked at the ash and charred corpses. She fought to breathe and her knees trembled. He acted so fast that she still had difficulty comprehending what just happened.

She lunged off the wall and staggered over to Elliot. She put her arms around his head and rested her cheek against his scales. "Thank you!" she panted.

He growled again and the sound translated through her body. It excited her, but it also made her feel safe in ways she couldn't explain. He protected her.

She kissed his scales and the words that had been burning in her mind and heart came out of their own accord. "I love you, Elliot."

He nuzzled his big head against her body and growled again. Then he collapsed back into a man—the man she loved.

He put his arms around her and his mouth smothered her. He buried his face in her hair and his hot breath seared her ear. "And I love ye, lass. I wouldnae let anyone harm ye."

She collapsed into that kiss, but a second later, he pushed her off. "We must hide these bodies before someone finds them. Come and help me, lassie."

"Where will we put them?"

"Down in the dungeon. We'll lock them in the cells."

He went over to the bodies. The soldiers that Echo and Elliot killed before he torched the others with his fire were still untouched and intact. Elliot picked up one of them and slung the body over his shoulder. "Ye get those, lassie."

He nodded toward some of the burned remains. They didn't even look human anymore. She picked up two in each arm and followed him downstairs. He got to the dungeon first, deposited his body in the cell that Echo and Elliot had been hiding in a few minutes ago, and went back for more.

She did the same thing, and when she returned to the passage, he was already on his way downstairs again with a second body.

She returned to the tunnel, but when she bent down to pick up another two, she froze when she heard footsteps approaching again.

This wasn't a troop of armed men, though. She heard a light step hurrying from the left. It approached fast, paused, and then dashed on as though someone wanted to hide that they were here at all. Could it be that Echo and Elliot weren't the only people down here trying to evade the Laird?

Echo tightened her grip on her dirk and crept forward to see who it was. She turned at several intersections and held her breath to listen. Whoever was scurrying around down here sounded small and light—almost like a woman.

Echo picked up the pace and held her weapons in front of her in case the mystery person attacked her. She hesitated at another intersection and heard the footsteps coming closer. The person would pass right in front of Echo and she would finally see who it was.

She pressed her eye to the corner and her heart stopped when she saw Lily running toward her. Lily wore black leather pants and a leather jacket over her white shirt. Other than that, she looked exactly the way Echo remembered her.

Lily didn't see Echo. Lily glanced over her shoulder like she might be afraid of something or someone following her. If she kept going in the same direction, she would race out of sight and Echo would never see her again.

Echo stepped out without thinking and planted herself in Lily's path. "Lily!"

Lily reared back in surprise, saw Echo's weapons, and Lily's hand flew to a dirk at her belt before she recognized her friend.

Lily froze and her jaw dropped. "Echo! What are you doing here?"

Echo dove for her and grabbed Lily's hand. "Come on! You have to hurry!"

"What's going on?" Lily gasped. "How did you get into the castle? This place is crawling with soldiers and the Laird has the whole place boobytrapped with spells."

"I know! Just come on. It's important."

Echo dragged Lily past the few remaining bodies and down the stairs into the dungeon. Echo heard Elliot moving around in the cell. He had no idea what was coming.

Echo exploded into the dungeon just as he came out of the cell. Lily stopped dead in her tracks and gaped at him in shock.

The next minute, she charged him and threw her arms around him. "Elliot! You're here!"

He laughed and put his arms around her. "Lassie!"

She jumped back still gaping at him in amazement. "How did you...." She looked over at Echo, shut her eyes, and shook her head. "Never mind. I don't want to know."

Elliot laughed again. "It's good to see ye again, lass. I missed ye."

"Forget that. Come on. You have to see Grant."

She grabbed his hand and started hauling him out of the dungeon.

"Lassie...." he began. "Perhaps I hadnae better...."

"No way! You have to! He's going to be thrilled to see you."

He tried to drag his feet, but she wouldn't let him. She towed him back upstairs and wouldn't let him stop to dispose of the rest of the bodies. Echo hesitated, but in the end, she figured the Laird would find out sooner or later anyway if he didn't already know.

Lily led Elliot into a different stairwell. She didn't seem too concerned about hiding Echo and Elliot from whatever trigger spells and booby traps the Laird had set up in this castle.

She finally emerged in a huge, sweeping gallery that towered to an arched, decorated ceiling. It looked like a cathedral built inside the castle.

She pushed open a side door and she, Echo, and Elliot entered a massive room with an almost equally impressive ceiling. The furnishings could only be described as royal, but Echo didn't have time to admire all the carpets, furniture, statues, paintings, and tapestries everywhere.

A giant wooden desk stood under towering windows to one side. A kilted man bent over stacks of papers and the sun shone on his curly brown hair. He furrowed his brow at whatever he was working on. He looked so much like Elliot that Echo knew exactly who he was.

Elliot froze on the threshold and stared down the long room.

"I told ye not to interrupt me while I'm working," Grant snapped over his shoulder.

"It's me, darling," Lily murmured in a shaky undertone.

He still didn't look up. "Och, lassie! Did ye find the Eighteenth Platoon yet?"

"Yeah," Lily breathed. "I found them."

"Well?" Grant straightened up and turned around.

He froze and Echo's stomach clenched when his expression changed. He blinked once as though he didn't believe what he was seeing.

All at once, he burst into the biggest, happiest smile Echo had ever seen. His eyes glistened with moisture and he barged down the room. "Laddie!" He grabbed Elliot and crushed him in a huge hug.

Grant gripped Elliot's shoulders and sniffed into Elliot's neck before he straightened up to look at his brother. "Lad! Ye dinnae ken how I've dreamed of this moment."

Elliot tried to lower his eyes and failed. "I'm sorry......"

"Stop!" Grant clapped him on both shoulders and burst out laughing. His eyes sparkled with tears, but he laughed like a little boy. "So ye found one of these lassies, did ye? I should have kenned!"

"Two of them, actually," Echo told him.

"Aye?" Grant ran his wrist across his nose, but his face shone with so much happiness that Echo's eyes hurt to look at him. He patted Elliot's cheek and laughed again. "Me laddie. Me own wee laddie."

Echo saw his affection making Elliot uncomfortable so she spoke up again. "Betty is here, too—or she was. She's.... somewhere."

"Are ye here to stay, then?" Grant elbowed his brother. "Ye'd like to think that through before ye agree. This is no place for any sane person. Ye can take me word on that."

"Actually, we only came to give you a message," Echo replied. "We're organizing an offensive against the Laird."

Lily turned to face her. "Who's we?"

"It's a long story."

"We've met up with Reid Buchanan in the forest west of Kald," Elliot added. "The Buchanans will assault Tyrekirk at the next new moon. The rebel deserters will come from the western forest at the same time. Can ye help us, lad? Can ye do ought from in here?"

Grant frowned for the first time. "It willnae be easy. Come along here and let's discuss it."

He led the way back to his desk. His manner put Echo completely at ease. He was so easy-going and down to earth. She suspected he would be like this, but she didn't expect the effect he would have on her.

He struck her as a natural leader, but he dealt with everyone on such personable terms that she couldn't help but like him.

He returned to his desk, pushed a bunch of papers out of the way, and pulled out a large map of the countryside. It showed Kald and Tyrekirk on one side of the Boundless and Icemeet on the other.

"Now then." He pointed to the forest. "Where are the rebels hiding?"

"I cannae tell ye that," Elliot replied. "I'm sorry, lad. I dinnae mean ought against ye, but I cannae take the chance the Laird might find out. The rebels are preparing this assault. They'll be here. That's all I can say."

Grant only beamed at him. "I understand."

"That's not all," Echo added. "It turns out that Lady Ilisa had a son with Neill Buchanan."

"You mean.... Colton is a...." Lily stammered.

"It isn't Colton. Colton, his brother Reid, and their sister Edeena were born before Lady Ilisa ever went to Icemeet. Their mother is Caitrin Buchanan. She died right after Edeena was born. Ilisa's son is Duncan Buchanan, Neill's youngest son. He's a hybrid between dragon and Highland tiger....and he's Grant and Elliot's brother."

Grant and Lily stared at her exactly the way Echo knew they would. "This is incredible!" Grant murmured. "A hybrid between both Clans could unite Buchanan and Creighton. He could end the war and take the Seat of Armstrong!"

"Exactly," Echo replied. "We have to unseat the Laird so Duncan can take the throne. The only problem is...."

"The problem is we dinnae ken where the blighter is," Elliot growled.

"And the fact that Duncan is half out of his mind," Echo finished. "Or all the way out of his mind—one or the other."

"Out of his mind!" Lily gasped. "How do you mean?"

"He's a wizard," Elliot told her. "He's lived his whole life among the Buchanans with no idea what he is. His magic is coming to the surface and he's out of control."

"He's running wild in the western forests," Echo went on. "He uses his magic to erase any trace of his whereabouts so it's almost impossible to find him."

"How do ye ken all this if he's so elusive?" Grant asked. "Have ye seen him yerselves?"

"Och, aye!" Elliot snorted. "We've seen him. We've seen more of him than we liked."

"Oh, and Elliot is a dragon, too." Echo waved back and forth between the brothers. "Just in case you weren't sure."

Grant laughed again and squeezed the back of his brother's neck. "Ye're in good company, lad."

Elliot turned bright red, but he didn't resist his brother's affections.

"How do you know the Buchanans will do what you want them to do?" Lily asked. "We tried to reason with Colton when he was here. It didn't work out very well."

"Reid is on his way to Icemeet and Betty is with him," Echo told her. "They'll bring the Buchanans. I'm certain of it."

"What do ye say, lad?" Elliot asked Grant. "Can ye do ought from in here or......?"

At that moment, a sickening, low purr of a voice interrupted from the other end of the room. It floated on the airwaves and weaseled into Echo's guts. She wasn't even sure she heard it with her ears. It seemed to come through her mind.

"Well, this is a charming wee family reunion if I've ever seen one."

Echo and Elliot whipped around fast. Grant and Lily froze and all four of the friends stared at a shriveled old man with long, lanky grey hair. His robes brushed the floor and he was so old that he didn't look capable of hurting anyone.

Deep wrinkles creased his face, but the disgusting smirk of triumph showing his broken crooked teeth made Echo's blood run cold. She knew the instant she laid eyes on him that this had to be Laird Balfour Creighton, the greatest wizard alive.

Chapter 23

E lliot's fury erupted at the sight of Laird Balfour Creighton. Elliot always hated this old viper. Now an even more murderous desire exploded out of Elliot to kill the bastard once and for all.

Elliot rocketed off the ground and hurtled down the room. His human skin stripped away and his wings shattered the stone walls on either side when he extended them.

He streaked toward the Laird and opened his mouth to burn the old fool to the ground.

The Laird waved one gnarled hand in Elliot's direction and Elliot smashed down hard on the floor. His own momentum kept him skidding across the stones until he tumbled to a halt in the middle of the room.

He huddled there trying to clear his head. He wasn't a dragon anymore. He was just a man and he couldn't move any of his limbs. He could still turn his head on his neck. That was all.

"Elliot!" Echo screamed, but he couldn't reach her.

The Laird took one menacing step forward and raised his hand. Elliot caught a glimpse of Grant charging forward.

He crashed into an invisible magical field blocking him from advancing. It trapped him and Lily behind it.

Echo yelled and wrenched her body in all directions, but she couldn't move her arms away from her sides. She was still standing up, but she couldn't take a step.

She jerked trying to free herself from magical lines coiling from the Laird's fingertips. They twined around her and held her captive the same way they immobilized Elliot.

He struggled to reach her, but it was no good. His rage threatened to consume him again when the Laird walked over to her. Elliot didn't want that bastard anywhere near Echo, but Elliot couldn't stop him.

Elliot felt the dragon fighting to break out. He wanted to burn the Laird for even looking at Echo, but the Laird's magic snuffed out the dragon's power. Elliot couldn't shift as long as the Laird bound him in these magical filaments.

"Ye're under arrest, lassie," the Laird snarled at Echo, "ye and me delightful grandson here. I must thank ye for bringing him back to me. He'd have languished in that infernal forest for the rest of his life if ye hadnae woke his dragon soul for me. No one could have done it better."

He chuckled and strolled down the room to where Grant and Lily still stood. Elliot could see Grant's mouth moving and he was furious. He pounded the magical field with his fists and yelled at the Laird, but no sound came through from the other side.

The Laird waved his hand once. "Be silent! Ye've done enough to hamstring me forces and now ye'll do as I say. Ye'll cooperate with me plan or ye'll stand by while I execute yer lovely Lady Lily here before ye go to the gallows yer own self."

Grant stopped hitting the field and he stopped yelling, but he didn't stop glaring at the Laird. He fumed in silent rage, but he couldn't do anything, either.

The Laird heaved an almighty sigh and paced back the other way while he eyed Grant, Lily, and Echo with small, shrewd eyes. He completely ignored Elliot.

Elliot seethed in helpless rage. He had to find a way to stop this man. Echo and Elliot had been seeing evidence all day of the Laird's oppression. Elliot couldn't let this man ruin the country any longer, but the dragon in his soul was Elliot's only power to stop the Laird. What could Elliot do without that?

"Now then," the Laird went on, "we'll continue with our campaign to finish off the Buchanans and end the war. Once we accomplish that, we'll hunt down Duncan Buchanan and finish him off, too, along with anyone who tries to put him on the throne."

"NO!!" Echo shrieked. "You can't! Don't you dare harm Duncan!"

He turned his flinty, cruel eyes on her. "*Anyone* who tries to put him on the throne, lassie, starting with ye. Defy me at yer peril. Ye will fail and Duncan will fail. No one will challenge my reign...." He dragged his gaze over Elliot, Lily, and finally Grant. "Anyone who stands against me will die, beginning with ye four."

He waved his hand once and the floor underneath Elliot collapsed. It didn't break and crumble the way stone would have. Instead, it softened and then evaporated.

He plummeted down, down, down and slammed down hard on the cold, mossy floor in the dungeon cell in which he and Echo had just been hiding.

The bodies were gone, the door was shut, and his weapons had vanished. He was alone and he didn't even have to ask where Echo was.

He groaned in pain from the fall and rolled onto his knees. He shut his eyes and gulped down rising despair. How did he know that returning to Tyrekirk would end in disaster? At least Grant didn't hold any grudges against him.

The sight of his brother laughing in delight at seeing Elliot again warmed Elliot's heart....and then the sight of Echo in the Laird's power wiped all that happiness away.

Elliot propped his hand against the wall and heaved himself to his feet. He stumbled over to the door, but of course it was locked. He was trapped in here and he couldn't shift.

He blundered to the hard wooden bench against the wall and collapsed on it. He hung his head and shut his eyes.

So many memories crowded his mind. He remembered sitting around the fire with Reid, Betty, Echo, and Duncan. Duncan seemed so level-headed and friendly then. He seemed like the kind of man Elliot might want to be friends with....as long as Duncan wasn't shooting spells, shifting into a tiger, and mauling Elliot within an inch of his life.

Elliot remembered flying around with Echo on his back. What a wonderful time that was. He wouldn't even mind facing execution as long as he could think about that evening in his last moments. Was she thinking about it somewhere?

He also remembered the moment when she kissed his scaly nose and murmured the words that made his world complete. *I love you, Elliot.*

She loved him. He had known for days, but the words still flooded him with so much excruciating desire and happiness that he didn't know how to cope with it all.

Then there was that torturous moment when Grant embraced him and called Elliot his own wee laddie. Elliot would cherish that moment for the rest of his life—for as long as it lasted.

He rested his head back against the stone wall and let himself float away on the picture of Grant laughing with tears standing in his eyes.

Elliot would gladly die right now, now that he had that memory to sustain him. It made all the painful memories worth the trouble. He had his brother back.

That memory was almost as good as the one where Reid forgave Elliot for killing Alastair.... or the time when Reid gave Elliot Alastair's tartan as a blanket.

So many good memories.... Elliot had had a good life. He had people in his life that he could love, but none of them came close to his love for Echo.

He drifted in a world of memory. He replayed memories from his childhood and from his adventures with Grant in Kald before Elliot fled to the forest. Those memories gave him the relief he needed from the reality of his situation.

After several hours, he stretched out on the bench and went to sleep. He had no way of knowing how long the Laird would keep him locked up in here, but it wouldn't be long.

The Laird wanted something from him or the Laird would have killed Elliot by now.

The outer dungeon door slammed and woke him from his doze. The slam didn't sound as loud now with Elliot's cell door closed to block the noise. A key scraped in a lock. Now at least Elliot would find out what the Laird had in mind.

Elliot didn't sit up when his cell door opened. The guards would yank him off the bench. They would drag him upstairs to face the Laird whether Elliot wanted to go or not.

He almost didn't believe it when Grant ducked into the cell, shut the door behind him, and relocked it with himself and Elliot alone inside.

"Laddie!" Elliot started to sit up.

Grant dove for him and held Elliot down on the bench so he couldn't rise. Grant brought his face close to Elliot's and whispered fast. "Listen to me, lad. I dinnae have much time. I have a wizard friend in the castle. He's arranged to give me a moment with ye so the Laird doesnae overhear."

"Why? What's amiss?"

"What *isnae* amiss, ye mean!" Grant hissed. "Everything's amiss! Now listen, lad. I cannae help ye out of here without risking Lily and me. Do ye understand? We're stuck. I havenae any choice but to help the Laird in this campaign."

"What campaign?"

Grant grimaced. "It's always the same. He's building up another assault on the Buchanans, but ye must listen to me, lad. He's had me all this time and now he has ye as well. He plans to make ye cooperate in this war as well."

Elliot snorted and relaxed back down on the bench. "He winnae have any luck with that. I winnae raise me hand against the Buchanans. Ye can be sure of...."

"Will ye only listen for one second, lad?!" Grant snapped. "Would ye stand by and let him kill Echo while ye protect the Buchanans? Of course no! Ye'll do it and be thankful. Do ye think I'm in this glaikit castle helping him for a lark?"

Elliot froze staring at his brother's shadowy face. "Is that it, then?"

"Aye," Grant breathed. "He'll call ye up to his audience hall and he'll tell ye straight. Ye help him in this campaign or he'll kill Echo."

Elliot let out a shaky sign. This was so much worse than he expected.

Grant jumped and spun around to look behind him toward the door. Then he whispered fast to Elliot. "I must be going. Me time's up. Dinnae underestimate him, lad. He's more a devil than any of us imagined."

He started to stand up, but Elliot shot out a hand, seized his brother's wrist, and yanked Grant down. "Laddie...."

Elliot couldn't get the words out. He lunged for his brother and crushed Grant in his arms. There were no words for how he felt right now. The next instant, Grant tore out of his embrace, unlocked the door, and raced away without another word.

Elliot sank back down on the bench. He would give anything to call his brother back, but that wouldn't work. No amount of time would be enough to spend with Grant.

What a fool Elliot was to ever leave Kald. He should have stayed with Grant no matter what.... but then Elliot wouldn't have met Echo—or maybe he would have. He didn't know. How could he know anything for certain?

Chapter 24

E lliot woke up for the second time to hear the outer dungeon door slam open again. He knew right away that it wasn't Grant this time. No such luck. Tramping soldiers' feet resounded on the stairs outside and the key scraped in the lock.

Elliot got to his feet. No one was going to drag him kicking and screaming to the Laird's audience hall. Elliot had been there often enough. He always entered it on his feet like a soldier and a man. He would do it now even if he couldn't fight the Laird.

He remembered on his way upstairs. The Laird was his grandfather. That fact only made Elliot hate him even more.

The Laird threatened to kill Grant and Elliot. That was the only reason Lady Ilisa hid the two baby boys with a castle maid. None of this would have happened if the Laird didn't threaten to kill his own grandsons.

Then he threatened his own daughter. He would have killed Ilisa for not revealing where the boys were. That was the only reason she ran away to Icemeet.

Another puzzle piece snapped into place in Elliot's mind. Duncan was his brother. Elliot flashed back to that night sitting around the fire with Reid, Betty, Echo, and Duncan.

Why did Elliot let that night go by without facing the truth? He could have shared that evening with Duncan—his brother. He could have shown Duncan…. what?

A surge of affection cracked Elliot's heart in half. Grant had always been all Elliot ever had. They had never had anyone but each other. Now they had another brother—a younger brother. Duncan.

Elliot couldn't let the Laird hurt Duncan or even threaten him. A fresh wave of hatred and determination consumed Elliot's being. He would stop the Laird from doing anything to Duncan. No one was going to raise a finger against Elliot's brother. Elliot didn't care if that person was a wizard or anything else.

By the time the guards halted outside the Laird's audience hall, Elliot had made up his mind. He would find a way out of this. He would find a way to save Echo and get himself and Echo out of Tyrekirk. He had to.

He had to find a way to bring Duncan to the throne. Duncan would gain control over his magic and then he would regain his sanity. He had to. He was the only person powerful enough to drive the Laird off the Seat of Armstrong.

Pride and affection gave Elliot superhuman strength. His brother. He would put his brother on the throne of Armstrong. Elliot didn't give a damn if Duncan was a Buchanan. Him being a Buchanan only made him the better candidate.

The soldiers opened the big doors and Elliot strode into the hall. He didn't need an escort.

He approached the dais to find Grant, Lily, and Echo already there. Elliot saw Echo struggling against more magical bonds holding her immobile. She must have been laying into the Laird because he had cast another spell over her face so she couldn't move her mouth.

She struggled to speak and muffled noises came from behind the spell. Elliot didn't need to hear her to know what she was trying to say to him. Her eyes said it all.

The Laird had his back to the hall according to his custom. He looked out through the tall windows toward the Boundless and Buchanan country beyond.

He started talking the moment Elliot showed up. The Laird didn't turn around, but his satiny voice filled the hall so everyone could hear him.

"Do ye see the pathetic wee mites fighting to defend their land? They're naught but dust in our path. We'll wipe them out of the country and be done with them. Then no one will stand in our way."

He kept saying 'we' and 'our', but he didn't fool Elliot. This man was out for himself. He didn't care who he destroyed in the process.

"Ye'll fly out over the Buchanan force and assault Icemeet...." the Laird began again.

"Fly!" Elliot blurted out. "Ye want me to...."

"Aye." The Laird finally turned around and his eyes flashed dangerously at Elliot. The old man's lips turned up in a nauseating smile, but his eyes betrayed enough menace to make that smile hideous and deadly. "Ye and Grant are the most powerful dragons in the country—much more powerful than our relatives to the south. Ye'll fly over there and destroy Icemeet. As soon as ye bring down the fortress, ye can finish off all the Clansmen trapped outside. Ye should be able to clear them up with no trouble."

He paused to leer at Elliot's surprised countenance. This was the worst yet. Elliot wouldn't mind organizing the logistics of this disastrous war the way Grant and Lily had been. He could handle that.

Now he saw the whole plan laid out in all its bloodthirsty horror. The Laird wanted Elliot to use his dragon form—that part of his soul that gave him so much power and energy.

How could Elliot turn that power on defenseless people? How could he do that to Duncan's people—Reid's people? Killing Alastair was bad enough, but this?

His heart revolted against it. The dragon part of his being was good and noble and worthy. Echo convinced him that he could use his dragon self to make the world a better place.

Without warning, the Laird shot out a hand toward Echo. He didn't even look at her before he released a trail of sparks that twined through the air.

It snatched Echo off her feet, tossed her into the air, and flung her down hard on the floor. The spell covering her mouth vanished and she screamed out in such torturous pain that Elliot couldn't stand it.

He lunged for her, but the Laird slapped his other hand and invisible magic hit Elliot flat against his chest. An unseen force stopped him dead in his tracks. He had no choice but to stand there and watch Echo twitching and contorting in agony on the floor.

She screamed loud and long. That scream went on and on without end. She flipped onto her back still spasming in torment. She finally twisted onto her other side and her frenzied eyes locked on Elliot.

"Don't do this, Elliot!" she shrieked. "You can't do this! You can't go along with this! Don't......!"

The Laird flicked one finger and silenced her. She collapsed on the floor, unconscious, but the magic still kept her body wrapped in whatever spell stopped her from moving.

Grant stood off to one side with his arm around Lily's shoulders. Tears poured down her cheeks and she covered her mouth with one hand, but neither of them could intervene.

Elliot stared down at Echo while he fought down murderous rage. Threatening Duncan was bad enough, but this broke the last tie holding him to any form of sanity. He couldn't let anyone hurt Echo, much less threaten to kill her.

"Well, laddie?" the Laird asked with mock cheerfulness. "Give me yer word that ye'll carry out the campaign and I'll release ye and Echo. Ye can spend yer time in luxury and comfort.... until tomorrow morning when ye go out against the Buchanans."

Echo's eyes opened just enough to focus on him. He could almost hear her urging him to hold the line against the Laird's wickedness. If she could speak right now, she would tell Elliot not to give in. She would tell him to protect Duncan and the Buchanans at all costs.

He couldn't do that. He couldn't be responsible for putting her in danger.

He locked his eyes on the Laird, and when Elliot said the words, he absolutely meant them with all his heart. "I give ye me word I'll do it."

The Laird laughed out loud, turned away, and walked back to the window still chuckling. The bonds holding Echo disintegrated. She twisted over on her side and tried to push herself up on her arms, but she couldn't rise any higher than that.

She retched on the floor and coughed and gagged, but Elliot couldn't look at her. He stared at the back of the Laird's head.

Lily sprang forward and grabbed Echo by the shoulders. "Oh, my God, Echo!"

She started to lift Echo off the floor, helped Echo to her feet, and supported Echo out of the audience hall, but Elliot still couldn't move. He'd given his word that he would attack the Buchanans and do everything in his power to destroy them. He would never be able to go back on that now. He had no choice but to do it.

Grant strode over to him, but Elliot couldn't look at his brother. The Laird occupied Elliot's whole attention. Elliot felt some secret clue hovering in the air between himself and his grandfather.

Elliot couldn't think of this man as his grandfather. This was some fiend from Hell, some shade sent to Earth to tempt Elliot into betraying himself.

The Laird wanted to corrupt Elliot's dragon nature. The Laird wanted to poison everything good and right and true in Elliot's being. This decision came down to that alone.

Elliot had to find some way to defeat this man. Elliot had to find the hidden key that would unlock the secret. That was the only way the Laird would fall.

Elliot didn't know the moment when the pall hanging over him snapped and freed him from his trance. He glanced over to find Grant looking at him with a strange expression. Elliot couldn't read his brother. That on its own was a first, but being apart for a few months didn't stop them from understanding each other. It came from somewhere else.

Elliot turned away and Grant accompanied him out of the room. They followed the corridors.... somewhere.

Some other mysterious trigger unlocked Elliot from his thoughts. He looked around and jumped out of his skin. "What are ye.... This is the.... Fourth Tower."

"Aye. Did ye think ye were going back to the dungeon after ye gave him exactly what he wanted?"

Elliot rounded on his brother. "Dinnae tell me ye'd have done any differently. Ye wouldnae let him threaten Lily if ye could avoid it."

Grant clapped him on the shoulder and squeezed. "I'm saying naught against ye, lad. Ye did what ye had to do and I dinnae blame ye. He said he'd free ye and he did." Grant went over to a nearby doorway. "Echo's in here. She'll be right glad to see ye."

He threw the door open and stood back. Elliot studied his brother for a second. How did the Laird sow the seeds of doubt in Elliot's mind so easily?

He couldn't deal with Grant right now, not after what Echo just suffered. He walked into the room to find Lily and Echo sitting on a couch under the window.

Lily had her arm around Echo's shoulder and murmured fast into Echo's ear. Lily's face drained of all color when Elliot walked in.

Elliot stopped in front of them. How could he face Echo after what just happened? Would she ever forgive him for agreeing to help the Laird hunt down Duncan?

Lily squeezed Echo's hand, got to her feet, and came over to Elliot. He prepared himself to take a tongue-lashing from her, but she only hugged him and then kissed him on the cheek before she left the room.

The door latch sounded too loud in the silence. Echo looked up at him and he didn't recognize her mad, furious eyes. She looked like a demon about to attack him.

She stood up to confront him and he realized that she was shaking all over. Her eyes had gone bloodshot and her usually sunny countenance radiated some kind of vicious insanity that frightened him down to the bone. Was she about to throw him out.... or worse?

She took one last shuddering step toward him, and before he knew what was happening, she wrapped her arms around his waist, buried her face in his chest, and burst into tears.

He had never seen her cry before. She handled every situation so steadily. Feeling her shaking against him and clutching at him in agonized misery scared him even more than thinking she might attack him, but it also destroyed the last shred of reserve holding her apart from him.

He folded his arms around her and buried his face in her hair. He shut his eyes. He didn't want to think about what would happen tomorrow morning, but it didn't matter anymore. He was here now and she needed him more than the Buchanans, more than Duncan, more than the whole country.

He pulled her down on the couch, leaned back on the cushions, and pulled her down on top of his chest. She dissolved into even more racking sobs. She cried loudly and her tears soaked his shirt, but he didn't care. Those tears meant more to him than all the honor in the world. Her tears meant even more to him than his word.

He held her close and stroked her hair. He didn't have to do anything except be here. He didn't have to be anything but a chest for her to cry on. He might not have any answers to any other problem in the world, but he could be that.

He didn't even have to ask why she was crying. He didn't need to know. She would tell him if he did need to know.

How long had it been since she let her feelings out like this? She sounded like she was crying out decades of suffering. She cried for people long dead, promises broken, opportunities missed, years wasted. It was all in there wrapped up in one wave of misery.

He kissed her on top of the head every now and then, but mostly he just kept running his hand down her hair and rubbing her back. He clasped her head into his heart. She had become so precious to him and now he couldn't imagine living without her.

He could even imagine living in this castle as the Laird's pampered slave if he could only stay here with Echo. He didn't blame Grant for doing it. Anything would be better than losing this woman.

She cried for a long, long time. Just when he thought she would pull herself together, she fell apart again, but he didn't mind. He would gladly lie here with her forever if she needed him to. What difference did it make as long as he made himself what she needed?

The sun started to slide down toward the horizon by the time she finally finished, sat up, and rubbed her face against her shoulder. She shook her hair back, sniffed, and looked around at the room with her bloodshot eyes. They were twice as red as before.

Elliot sat up next to her, put his arm around her shoulders, and squeezed. He kissed the side of her head, but he still didn't speak. He waited for her to start.

She shot him a glance on the side. She looked awful, but what difference did it make? His shirt clung to his chest with the dampness of her tears. He wore them as a badge of honor.

Honor. His word of honor.

She was the one who brought his dragon self to the surface. She was the one who made him think his dragon nature could be good and beautiful and somehow holy. Was his word of honor worth sacrificing that? Was he really going to foul the dragon's sacred power to keep his word to Laird Balfour Creighton?

He didn't realize he had slipped into another state of mind until she spoke to him. "Are you all right?"

He jerked around to stare at her. "Hmm? Of course. I'm grand."

She snorted. "How can you be? How can you destroy the Buchanans when the fate of the country depends on Duncan taking the throne?"

"I dinnae ken how we'll do it, but I cannae stand by and see anything happen to ye. If we're to bring Duncan to the throne, it willnae be bought with yer blood nor any other innocent blood. That's no victory I want to take part in."

She looked down at her hands and didn't answer.

"Besides, Duncan isnae in his right mind as it is. He isnae fit to rule. There's no sense throwing yer life away until he is."

She raised her head to look at him when someone knocked on the door. Echo stiffened and looked around. Was she looking for her weapons?

Elliot called out, "Aye?" and Grant walked in.

Elliot got to his feet to meet his brother. Elliot could face his brother, now that he understood. He no longer questioned any of Grant's choices. Elliot knew now that he would make exactly the same choices if their positions were reversed.

Grant glanced down at Echo. Elliot couldn't read anything in his brother's expression except pity and compassion.

"Is everything all right?" Elliot prompted.

"Och! Right." Grant shook himself. "Listen, laddie. The Laird plans to finish the pair of ye off as soon as ye carry out this business in the morning."

Elliot snorted. "It isnae any more than I expected."

"Aye," Grant replied. "Lily and I will do what we can to get ye out of the castle as soon as possible afterwards, but it may take time."

"I'm grateful," Elliot told him.

Grant compressed his lips. Then he opened it to say something and stopped himself. Elliot waited, but Grant seemed to come to some decision within himself. He only nodded and walked out of the room

Chapter 25

E lliot swung his feet to the floor and ran the fingers of both hands through his hair. He looked down at the old clothes he'd taken off last night. He had dropped them on the floor. They were so dirty already that throwing them on the floor couldn't possibly make them any dirtier.

He could still remember telling Echo when he left the rebel camp that he needed to find some new clothes. Now a clean shirt, spotless white socks, brand new shoes, a beautiful fur-lined sporran, and a new belt lay spread out for him on the chair by his bed.

An immaculate new tartan lay on top of the pile of neatly folded clothes. That tartan had never been worn by anyone before. Not one wrinkle marred its perfectly smooth surface.

It was Armstrong tartan. That had to be the ultimate insult from the Laird to Elliot. The Laird didn't even have the decency to give him a Ritchie tartan to wear today—today, the day Elliot was supposed to carry out this slaughter against Clan Buchanan.

The Laird even ensured that the windows of this room looked northward over the Boundless. Elliot saw more than he wanted to of the battle raging over there.

The Buchanans battled the Creighton army on the planes. The Buchanans launched massive spears and flaming balls of burning tar from siege engines mounted on the high peaks over Icemeet. The Buchanans could bombard the battlefield from a distance without any interference from the Creightons.

Only the dragons could reach those positions, but as soon as any dragon got near them, the Buchanans launched their missiles to shoot the dragons down.

Only five smaller blue dragons remained to assault Icemeet. None of them had the firepower to damage the fortress and the Buchanans shot two of those dragons out of the sky while Elliot watched.

The creatures fell shrieking into the middle of the battle where the ferocious Buchanans hacked the dragons to pieces.

Elliot measured the battle while Echo slept to recover from her ordeal in the Laird's audience hall. The Buchanans were using different tactics than the ones they had used when Grant and Elliot had been foot soldiers in the Laird's service.

The Buchanans always fought as cats then. Horror stories went through the Laird's troops about soldiers getting shredded to death by wild tigers, but the Buchanans weren't doing that now.

In some ways, they had become even more dangerous, more determined, and more destructive than they were even in their tiger forms. They could do much more damage with their weapons and they could think much more clearly.

They planned every strike and maneuver with deadly precision, and as he watched, Elliot realized they had one other advantage over their Creighton adversaries. The Buchanans were much more disciplined and better trained.

Something had happened to them while Elliot's back was turned. They had become a concentrated fighting force that moved and adjusted on the battlefield.

The Creighton soldiers recoiled whenever they saw one of their dragons shot down. Everyone knew Clan Creighton didn't stand a chance without their dragons and every dragon's death drove that point home more clearly than anything else.

Clan Buchanan exploited every single one of these horrible reversals. They attacked the Creighton army with frightening power and drove the Creightons back even further. They succeeded more than once in driving the enemy into the Boundless itself.

The Creightons only recovered from these surges when their dragons turned away from Icemeet to assault the Buchanans on the ground. No wonder the Laird wanted to use Elliot to attack the Buchanans. He needed something to turn the tide. His dragons weren't enough anymore.

Elliot only had to think for a second to figure out why the Laird hadn't used Grant for this before now. The Laird still needed an heir. Grant was the only heir the Laird had until Elliot came along.

It also explained why the Laird planned to kill Elliot the moment he got what he wanted. The Laird already had one grandson powerful enough to dethrone him. He didn't need two of them.

The Laird had already killed off Ness Creighton, the crown prince everyone thought would take the Laird's place after the Laird died—if that ghastly shade ever did die. He might live forever and continue to plague the country with this madness.

The Laird couldn't be too pleased that Elliot finally came out of the woodwork with his dragon self all ready to rain hellfire on the world. The Laird would get rid of Elliot and then Duncan. That would leave only Grant to take the throne.... whenever that happened.

Echo rolled over under the covers behind his back. She kissed his side and ran her satin hand up and down his spine. She caressed his shoulders. Her touch felt so intoxicatingly beautiful. He wanted nothing but to turn around, kiss her, and crawl into bed with her for the rest of his life.

That would only happen after he got through this morning's nightmare. He had to put on his Armstrong colors, go out there, and kill as many Buchanans as he could.

Watching them fight only made him admire them more than he already did. Was Reid over there with them? He must have told Colton and Jaimee and everyone else that Elliot had killed Alastair. How could Elliot ever face them?

He didn't have to face them. He only had to fight them, destroy them, and smash Icemeet to rubble. Then he never had to deal with Clan Buchanan again.... until the Laird called on him to hunt down Duncan and kill him, too.

Duncan. How could Elliot do this to Duncan? How could Elliot even think of destroying Duncan's Clan?

Echo sighed and turned back the other way. "I guess we better get going. We don't want the Laird's men dragging us out of bed like this."

Elliot barely heard her. He kept gazing at the Armstrong tartan sitting there waiting for him. Was he really going to wear that? It looked revolting to him. Everything about it repelled him. He didn't think he could even touch it.

She climbed out of bed on the other side and started getting dressed. That was his signal. He stood up and pulled on the clean shirt the servants had left for him. He combed his hair and tied it back.

Then he picked up his filthy old Ritchie tartan, folded it, and used the brand-new belt to buckle his kilt on. He felt better once he finally did it. The Laird could suck on his Armstrong tartan.

Echo raised her eyebrows at his kilt, but he only smiled at her while he arranged his tartan on his shoulder. Then he put on his socks and shoes. He was as ready as he was ever going to be.

They left their room together. The servants had provided Echo with fresh clothes, too. They gave her leather trousers and a leather jacket like Lily's, but these were brown instead of black. They looked much nicer and much less flashy than Lily's expensive attire.

Elliot liked Echo better like this. She didn't look as much like a lady who belonged in a castle. She looked like a rebel from the forest which was how he liked her.

They stepped outside to find a squad of soldiers waiting for them. Echo snorted and shot Elliot a knowing look. Of course the Laird wouldn't give them the option of complying of their own accord. That wasn't the point.

They had to understand that they were prisoners living under the threat of death. That was the point. The Laird wouldn't waste a chance to send them a message impressing them with the fact.

The soldiers escorted the pair to a little-used stairway at the far end of the Fourth Tower. Elliot had never used it or even seen it in all his time at Tyrekirk, but then again, he'd never stayed in the Fourth Tower as a guest before, either.

The stairs wound up and up and up until they emerged on top of the highest turret. The wind whipped Elliot's hair out of his eyes. He could see the whole battle going on far below.

The landscape reminded him of a tiny chess set. The miniature people moving back and forth on the planes didn't seem real from up here. That must make them a lot easier to send to their deaths, but Elliot wouldn't be killing them from up here.

Ten dragons soared over the battlefield following the same routine as before. They tried to hit Icemeet and had to retreat from the crossbows and siege engines. They turned their fire on the ground forces only to get drawn back by more projectiles from the mountains.

Grant and Lily were already there along with the Laird and at least thirty soldiers. They crowded the roof and Elliot saw at first glance that the soldiers were the only people present carrying weapons. Grant and Lily were unarmed and they both looked extremely nervous.

The Laird turned his menacing eyes to Elliot. "Well, laddie! Here ye are. Are ye ready to fulfill yer word?"

"Aye." Elliot let his eye track over the battlefield and up to Icemeet. "I'm ready."

Echo took a step nearer. She started to slip her hand into his. Her eyes tormented him with all the things he knew she was about to say, but she never got a chance.

Three guards jumped out of line, grabbed her, and yanked her away from him. She stumbled, started to struggle to free herself, and in a flash, one of them had a dirk at her throat.

She froze as the cruel steel bit into her neck, the neck Elliot had just been enjoying...was it only a few hours ago? His time with her might be a lifetime in the past. He could hardly remember it with the Buchanan forces staring him in the face.

The Laird gave another grotesque smile of approval when Elliot didn't react. The Laird stepped closer to the parapet and pointed down at the ground. "Do ye see that man there—the big one with the black hair? That's Colton Buchanan, their Clan Chief......and that...." He pointed up at Icemeet.

Another body of Highlanders erupted from a hidden place between the fortress and the mountains' steep cliffs. A tall figure led the charge holding an unsheathed saber on high. The noise coming from the onrushing Buchanans drifted on the breeze all the way up to Tyrekirk's highest turrets.

"That's Jaimee Abernathy, Colton's wife," the Laird snarled. "Finish them off. If ye can kill Reid and Duncan Buchanan, so much the better...." His sharp eyes traced the battle. "But I dinnae see either of them. Never mind." He went back to pointing at Icemeet. "There's a weak spot in the northern wall behind the gate. All ye have to do is fly over there and hit it. Once ye do that, ye can bring down the rest of the fortress with the whole lot of them inside."

Silence fell except for the wind in Elliot's ears. Everyone on the turret watched him and waited, but he couldn't move.

"Well?" the Laird demanded. "Go do it. Fulfill yer word or else."

Elliot didn't understand the moment when he did it. He hardly felt himself leave the ground. His body moved on its own.

He took a running step, planted his foot on the turret's edge, and launched himself into space. He spread his arms and soared across the Boundless. His wings caught him and his neck and tail stretched out as he picked up speed.

His spirit broke free at the same time. All his power erupted as gold-black scales spread over his body. Fire unlike anything he'd ever known kindled in his soul.

He could shoot that fire anywhere, but his heart and mind wouldn't let him. He couldn't unleash his fire on innocent people, not to keep a promise that would devastate the country and destroy everything he believed in. He couldn't bring himself to do it.

He swooped over Icemeet and the siege engines fired at him. A ball of burning tar hit him in the shoulder, glanced off, and fell harmlessly to the rocks below. Three spears struck the scales on his chest and abdomen, but they only bounced off. Their points sparked on his iron scales and did no damage.

The Highlanders on the rocks stared at him in horror. None of their weaponry worked against him. Of course not. The Laird was depending on it.

He wheeled over the fortress and back toward the plane. Dozens of archers loosed from hidden spots along the cliffs, but their arrows only pattered like raindrops on his scales. He barely felt them.

He dove down the mountainside zooming low over the Buchanan forces. Colton and Jaimee both spun around to glare at him. Colton was Reid's brother—Duncan's brother. Elliot couldn't bring himself to kill Colton—not for anything.

Jaimee was Echo's friend, one of the very few friends Echo had left in the world. He couldn't take that away from her. Jaimee was also a Buchanan. She was Reid's sister-in-law. He spoke so highly of her and so did Alastair. Elliot couldn't be the cause of her death, not when the whole Clan depended on her.

He saw it all in a few seconds. He could do it. He could destroy this Clan with a few well-aimed puffs of his breath. He could bring down Icemeet and then wipe Clan Buchanan off the face of the Earth.

He never doubted for an instant that he had the power and the strength. From the terrified looks on the Buchanans' faces, they all knew it, too. He just had to carry out his promise.

He banked and climbed back up to the cliffs over Icemeet. He gave his word he would attack the Buchanans. How could he fulfill his promise without destroying them? He spotted the weak spot on the northern wall. One strong blow would bring it down, but he couldn't do it.

He aimed for the siege engines and belched a massive wave of fire at them. He set all the siege engines aflame, but he timed it so that the Highlanders manning them had a few seconds to duck behind the rocks.

They sprang up to find all their engines and crossbows burned to a crisp, but he didn't harm anyone.

He shot another wave of fire and hit the gate itself. His fire bounced off the massive granite block and did no damage. Could the Laird see Elliot waffling up here? Was the Laird giving the order for his men to kill Echo?

Elliot tilted downward toward the planes. He no longer had any choice. He had to make a stand one way or the other—stand by his promise or break it.

He angled his wings to drop on top of the Buchanan fighting force. All the dragons fell in line with him. They spat fire at the Buchanans to lay the Clan to waste when, at that moment, a flash of movement caught his eye.

He glanced westward and spotted a man stepping out from behind the rocks farther up the Boundless. He looked so small and weak from up here. He was on the Creighton side of the estuary—far enough away from the battle that he couldn't do anyone any harm.

Elliot blinked in blank astonishment as the man came into view, raised his arms, and fired a volley of magical spells into the air. Explosions burst among the Creighton dragons and pelted three of them out of the air.

Vaporous tendrils wrapped around two more, tangled their wings, and brought the dragons crashing to earth. Their screeches snapped Elliot out of his trance and he veered hard to the west. He hurtled up the Boundless and his dragon heart burst when he recognized the man on the ground. It was Duncan.

Chapter 26

E cho caught one of the guards by the wrist, yanked him hard against her back, and elbowed him in the face with all her strength. She ripped the dirk out of his hand and plunged the blade into another man's ribs.

She kicked out and toppled another three guards, but she had nowhere to run. She charged the parapet before the rest of the Laird's forces caught her. "Duncan!" she screeched down the turret. "Duncan!"

The sight of Duncan using his magic against the Creighton dragons electrified her, but he was too far away to hear her. He strode down to the Boundless, but he didn't come any closer.

He kept bombarding the dragons with dozens of spells, most of which she didn't recognize. She had no idea what he was doing to them, but he could fight them so much better than any other Buchanan.

He blasted them with light and fire, tied them in knots, and even caused a few of them to shift back into men while they were still airborne.

Duncan's appearance had an equally explosive effect on Elliot. He wheeled back toward the east, tucked his wings, and plunged toward the Creighton army. He unleashed his fire on them and started driving the survivors back toward the Boundless.

"Traitor!" the Laird bellowed. "Faithless, worthless liar!"

He stepped right to the edge of the parapet and fired more spells down at Elliot, but Elliot was flying too fast.

He zoomed past the turret so fast that the noise of wind howling off his wings drowned the clash of battle and the explosions of spells behind him.

Echo jumped up and down pumping her fists in the air. "Yeah! Go, Elliot, go!"

He pretended not to hear. He pivoted right and left to herd the Creightons away from the Buchanans. Colton reacted in a heartbeat and all the Buchanans charged forward to push the Creightons into the estuary.

Elliot came wheeling in for another pass. He spread his enormous wings and they thumped the air. He kicked up a tempest wind that flattened the Creightons and sent them somersaulting over each other. They didn't stand a chance.

He hovered on high pounding the enemy with all his power when, without warning, the Laird released a giant net woven of golden light. It whisked over the battlefield and surrounded Elliot.

"Elliot!" Echo shrieked. "Elliot—NO!!"

It was too late. The net wrapped him in its gleaming threads and the whole tangled web collapsed in on itself. It compressed the dragon and he gave an excruciating, broken roar of agony.

He contorted as his gargantuan body imploded. The net shrank more and more until a tiny pinprick of pink skin hung suspended over the battlefield. The dragon was gone and Elliot had returned to his human form.

Time ground to a halt and Echo's heart plunged into her shoes as his body started to fall. He flapped in the air as the wind tossed his limp arms and legs in all directions. He was unconscious if he wasn't dead already.

She snapped out of her horrified stupor and lunged for the parapet. "ELLIOT!!" she screeched. "ELLIOT!!" She tried to scramble over the ramparts. She would have thrown herself off a three-hundred-foot drop, but she didn't care.

The soldiers hauled her back and Elliot slammed into the ground with impossible force. She heard the Laird chuckling in the background, but she couldn't see anything but the tiny figure lying smashed and destroyed on the ground. This couldn't be happening. He couldn't be dead down there.

"He was a useless waste of flesh anyway," the Laird snarled. "I kenned he hadnae a shred of honor in him."

Echo turned her burning eyes on him. Hate and murderous fury unlike any she'd ever known consumed her from the inside. She would kill this man if it was the last thing she ever did.

She dedicated her whole life, her whole being to helping other people. She hated killing and she swore when she left Afghanistan that she would never take another human life as long as she lived.

That oath meant exactly nothing to her now. This man deserved to die. He deserved to die the most painful death she could dream up. She wanted to see him suffer. She wanted to watch him moan in torment while he begged for death.

A devastating smash brought Echo's attention back to the battle. The Creightons and the Buchanans struggled against each other right at the water's edge. The dragons that survived Duncan's assault had taken advantage of Elliot's attack on the siege engines.

They streaked up the mountain and surrounded Icemeet. The archers showered the dragons with arrows, but they couldn't drive them off, now that the siege machines no longer held the dragons at bay.

Fifteen dragons surrounded Icemeet. Where did they all come from? Did the Laird have reinforcements in reserve just in case something like this happened? He must have because Echo didn't recognize these dragons. They hadn't been flying around out here before, but she didn't see where they came from.

Duncan fired continuous spells and incantations, but he couldn't do as much damage from all the way down by the Boundless. Icemeet was defenseless and the dragons started pounding the walls with crushing fire.

They swung around to the northeast and angled low toward the gate where the Laird said the walls were weakest. The dragons unloaded on it one after the other. They teamed up in gangs to combine their firepower. They would bring down the fortress any second now.

Echo glanced toward Elliot and swallowed hard. She couldn't reach him from up here. She would have run all the way down the stairs and across the estuary to reach him, but the soldiers held her fast and stopped her from going anywhere.

She looked around in helpless confusion. There had to be some way to stop the slaughter. She couldn't see Colton or Jaimee anymore under the combined forces fighting over a few feet of gravel beach along the Boundless. There must be a thousand people down there all fighting for their lives.

A flash caught Echo's peripheral vision, and like something out of a forgotten dream, another dragon erupted out of nowhere. She spotted the shift just in time to see Duncan transform into a dragon and launch into the air.

He was every bit as colossal and deadly as Grant and Elliot and his scales were blacker than black. Duncan's skin swallowed all light until he flew like a streak of invisible death come to life.

He rocketed up the mountain at mind-numbing speed and collided with the dragons assaulting Icemeet. He dwarfed them by many times and his attack scattered them away from the fortress, but only for a second.

They fled from him shrieking in fright....and then they all came rushing back to attack him as one. Their fire only bounced off his scales so they changed their tactics.

They picked up speed and slammed into him with bone-crushing force. A few of them climbed high into the atmosphere and dove for him. They picked up speed while he was preoccupied with defending himself against the others.

These dragons dive-bombed him, collided with him, and sent him reeling. His bellows rumbled over the landscape and Echo winced at the sound. He was in pain. He couldn't beat them. He was only one dragon against many and he was their enemy.

He tried to retreat over the planes and they hounded him all the way. They hurtled past him, slashed him with their talons, smashed into his wings, and tossed him in all directions. He couldn't survive this.

Echo commanded herself to look away. She couldn't watch Duncan go down like this. He was their only hope of victory and he couldn't even protect himself from these much smaller dragons.

The Laird chuckled again. That sound couldn't be heard beyond the turret, but it seemed to radiate his menacing power outward to the ends of the Earth.

Duncan reacted like he heard it, too. He turned tail to flee from the Creighton dragons, but he didn't fly toward the west.

He pumped his wings picking up speed. He could fly much faster than his smaller relatives and he outstripped them soon enough. He zoomed eastward, angled low over the battlefield, and plunged.

He snapped his wings out, swung his feet forward, and picked up Elliot's unconscious body without slowing down or stopping. The Creighton dragons started to catch up with him, but he was already gaining altitude and climbing into the clouds.

Echo burst into a fresh outburst of screaming. She fought the guards with all she had and screamed for Elliot, Duncan—anybody!

Duncan didn't turn around until he climbed miles into the sky. He dwindled to a black speck against the clouds and then soared around to the west before he vanished entirely.

Chapter 27

Echo buried her face in her hands and shuddered. She didn't want to take her hands down. She didn't want to see the room surrounding her. She didn't want to remember that she just spent last night in this room with Elliot.

He couldn't be gone. Duncan wouldn't have bothered to pick Elliot up if Elliot was already dead. Right?

She told herself that over and over again, but she couldn't shake this lingering dread that Elliot's fall had killed him. If she could only see him again, she could face anything the future held.

How did she come to care about him so much in such a short time? How did he become the center of her world?

He conducted himself beyond her wildest dreams during the battle. Some part of her soul knew he wouldn't be able to destroy the Buchanans. He couldn't do that to Duncan. Elliot couldn't be the one responsible for crushing the whole country under the Laird's heel. Elliot was too good for that.

Thinking that only made her anguish more excruciating. She found him. She fell in love with him....and now she had lost him. This was a thousand times worse than leaving him at the rebel camp would have been. At least then she would have known where he was. He would have been alive somewhere waiting for her to return to him.

She let out one more shuddering breath and took her hands away from her eyes. The moment she looked around the room, she knew she couldn't stay here. She had to get out of Tyrekirk somehow, but she was still the Laird's prisoner. He would certainly carry out his threat to kill her, now that Elliot had turned against him.

She stalked out of the room. She had no idea where she would go or even if the Laird's magic would let her go anywhere. She might run into one of his spells when she tried to open the door.

She didn't. It opened easily and she stepped out into the corridor. She was just deciding what to do next when a young man walked past. He wasn't wearing a Creighton tartan and he didn't look evil and corrupt like the Laird.

"Excuse me," she began. "I was wondering if you could tell me where I can find Lady Lily Armstrong."

"I'll take ye to her, Miss. Follow me."

He set off down the corridor like this was the most normal thing in the world, but he kept casting curious glances at her on the side.

She finally noticed and asked him. "What? Am I not supposed to be walking around the castle?"

"I dinnae ken ought about any orders that ye arenae allowed to walk about as ye wish....so long as ye stay inside.... but then again, if ye werenae allowed, ye wouldnae be."

She nodded. "I thought so."

He hesitated and then blurted out, "Ye're one of these lassies from the future, am I right?"

"Yeah. That's right."

"I wish I could question ye about it. I'd love to ken what it's like."

"It isn't much better than here. There are still madmen trying to rule the world and destroying it in the process. There are still good people trying to stop them and getting hurt and killed. I don't think that kind of thing will ever change."

He shrugged and faced front. "Ye may be right, lassie."

He acted so familiar that she glanced at him curiously. "Are you sure you're supposed to be talking to me?"

He laughed. "I can talk to anyone I please, lass."

His eyes twinkled and his face lit up when he smiled. He didn't act at all dangerous.

"Who are you?" she asked. "You aren't one of the Laird's men, are you?"

"Me name's Tristan." He extended his hand to her. "I'm in the Laird's service as ye might say, but I answer to His Lairdship Grant Ritchie Armstrong. I've done what I can to help his mission.... which I must admit isnae very much.... but we can all keep trying. We havenae ought else to do, have we?"

"Doesn't the Laird know you're working for the other side? I didn't think he would tolerate someone staying in the castle who is openly hostile to his plans."

"Och, he's tried to kill me a few times. I dinnae suppose he'll ever stop trying, but as I'm a wizard, too, he finds it a mite more difficult to oust me than he might do another man." He halted in the middle of the corridor. "This is it, lassie."

"What's it?"

"Lady Lily's room." He nodded to the nearest door. "This is where ye wanted to go. She's inside there."

"Oh!" Echo jumped. "I forgot. Thank you, Tristan."

He nodded and turned away still smiling at her. "Think naught of it, Miss."

He walked off and she watched him go. So a few good people were still working behind the scenes.

That short but meaningful conversation hardened Echo's resolve. If Tristan, Grant, and Lily could keep going in the face of disaster, Echo could do it, too.

She pushed open the door and walked into Lily's room. The room had been laid out the same way as Echo's room and Lily stood by a couch under the window.

Echo strode over to her....and gasped out loud. Grant sat hunched and bleeding on the couch in front of Lily. Blood saturated his shirt that had been torn in several places. Gashes marked his face and crisscrossed his scalp.

He hugged one burly arm across his stomach and he kept wincing in pain. "My God!" Echo cried. "What happened?"

"Naught that need concern ye, lassie." He coughed and winced again. "It's naught but will heal in time. Not to worry."

"But...." She glanced toward the door. "You've only been down here.... maybe half an hour. How did this....?"

"The Laird did this," Lily interjected. "Grant's just trying to spare your feelings."

"My feelings! Why?"

"Because he......"

"Dinnae tell her ought, lass," Grant growled. "It's bad enough Elliot's gone again. Dinnae make it any worse."

"What the hell is going on? If this has something to do with me, you better tell me now." Echo rounded on Lily. "You have to tell me. Don't leave me in the dark."

Lily looked down at Grant, but he only looked away. "The Laird sentenced you to execution...."

Echo snorted. "Yeah. I know. I've been waiting for the big day."

"You don't understand," Lily murmured. "He sentenced you to execution as soon as we came down from the turret. You weren't even going to be taken back to your room first. He ordered the guards to take you straight to the gallows."

Echo's jaw dropped. "He.... what?"

"Grant stepped in...."

"I did no such thing!" he interrupted. "It wasnae like that at all, lassie."

"He's trying to stop you from feeling guilty. He tried to get the Laird to reverse the order....and you can see how that turned out."

Echo gaped at him. He looked absolutely awful. "You.... got in a fight.... against the Laird?"

"Ye couldnae call it a proper fight.... It was more of a route if I'm honest."

"Jesus!" Echo gulped. Now she really did feel guilty. "You didn't have to do that."

"Och, dinnae give me any of that tripe, lassie," he spat. "Of course I had to do it. Did ye think I was going to let them hang ye for standing up for Elliot?" He looked away and humphed again. "If I'd have kenned it would go that way, I would have launched me own self, but the Laird stopped me."

"He.... stopped you.... from launching......? You mean during the battle?"

"Do ye think I stood on the parapet and let him destroy me own wee brother without trying to save him? The Laird anticipated me. He bewitched me so I couldnae fly."

"And now he can't shift at all," Lily finished. "The Laird put a spell on Grant so he can't shift. This is going to put a serious crimp in our plans."

Grant snorted again. "Plans! We've wasted too much time on plans that have come to naught. I'm done with plans."

"So what are you going to do?" Echo asked. "How do you know the Laird won't kill you, too?"

"Och, he winnae ever do that," Grant replied. "He needs an heir even if he considers that heir a traitor and a coward."

Echo compressed her lips. "You're anything but that."

"Ye dinnae ken ought about it, lassie. Ye dinnae ken how I've spent these months scurrying about in corners trying to find a way to stop him." He turned to Lily gritting his teeth in pain and fury. "I winnae do any more scurrying, lass. Ye mark my words. Today's the last day of that."

She rested her hand on his shoulder. "Okay. I hear you."

"If the Laird is onto you, maybe it's too dangerous for you to help the offensive," Echo suggested. "Maybe you two should just sit it out and...."

"Och, dinnae say such things, lassie!" Grant's voice started to rise and he had to double over and check himself when another stab of pain gripped him. "We winnae sit ought out. Not a bit of it. We're in this. We'll be in it to the end and no mistake."

"How? We have no idea if Elliot convinced the rebels to help out or if Reid and Betty made it back to Icemeet. The Buchanans could still be in the dark. You might be putting yourselves in danger for nothing."

"For a start," Lily began, "the very first thing we're going to do is get you out of Tyrekirk. It will be dangerous, but you can't stay here. The Laird would only use you to make us do his bidding and he might decide to kill you after all. You have to leave and you have to go find Elliot."

"How can I do that? Duncan could have taken him across the ocean. I don't even know where to begin looking." Her voice cracked with emotion and she looked down at her hands in despair. "Duncan might lose his mind again. Today could have been a fluke. He could have forgotten everything and dropped Elliot from the atmosphere. We have no way of knowing if Elliot is even still alive."

"He is." Grant's bloody hand closed around hers. He crushed her fingers in a death grip, but when she looked up into his eyes, she knew he was right. "He's alive out there. I'd lay any odds on that. He's tougher than ye think. Duncan took him away to save him. Now ye have to find them both and bring them back. Ye're the only one that can go do it, lassie. We're all depending on ye."

He didn't say that *he* was depending on her to bring Elliot back, but she knew that was what he meant. Elliot meant as much to Grant as he did to Echo, maybe even more.

She had to find Elliot, not just for herself, but for Grant. Elliot couldn't have reconciled with Grant only to disappear again.

Lily crossed to the bed and picked up her weapons. She started buckling on her saber and sticking her dirk into her belt.

"What are you doing?" Echo asked.

"I told you. We're taking you out of Tyrekirk."

Grant hauled himself to his feet. He looked like he had gotten run over by a truck, but he started limping toward the bed, too. "Once ye get out of Kald, ye get back to the rebel camp. It might be the only place safe enough to keep ye out of the Laird's reach. Besides, if Elliot is anywhere, he'll go back there, too."

Echo watched him pick up a saber. He sighted down the blade and then tossed it back on the bed. He didn't use his left arm at all. He kept it pinned to his stomach.

"*You* aren't coming," Echo told him. "You look like you're going to pass out."

He snorted instead of laughing and ended up wincing again. "Tristan is coming with us," Lily announced. "He'll deal with Grant as soon as we leave this room."

"Tristan.... the wizard?" Echo asked.

Lily nodded. "He can use his magic to heal Grant's injuries and Tristan can also mask our movements from the Laird."

"To a point," Grant corrected. "It's only a matter of time before the Laird realizes what we're about, so we must move quickly."

"Once you get out of the castle, you'll need to take off as fast as you can and get to the forest," Lily went on. "Don't look back and don't worry about us. If you lose us, just keep going. Don't slow down for anything."

Echo stared back and forth between them with huge eyes. "Are you guys sure you want to risk this? I don't want anything to happen to you...." She glanced at Grant again. "I mean anything that hasn't already happened."

"Forget all that, lass," Grant told her. "Ye find Elliot. That's the best thing ye can do for us now."

She looked straight back into his eyes and understood exactly what he didn't say. He wanted her to find Elliot for him. She was doing this for him. He must have suffered the tortures of the damned after Elliot left. Grant couldn't go through that again.

She nodded and threw back her head. "I understand. I'm ready."

He hobbled toward her and squeezed her shoulder. "Thank ye, lass. Thank ye for me brother.... from the bottom of me heart."

Before she could answer, the door eased open and Tristan glanced in. "Ready?"

"Aye." Grant took a few painful steps toward him. "Do it now."

Tristan crossed the room, laid both hands on Grant's shoulders, and Tristan shut his eyes. He bowed his head for a second and, miraculously, all of Grant's wounds closed up. He straightened up and his arms relaxed at his sides. Blood still caked his clothes and hair, but he was perfectly whole and well again.

He spun around, grabbed his saber, and headed for the door. "Let's go."

The four of them slipped out of the room and a gleaming bubble of iridescent magical light surrounded all four of them. It floated along with them as they hurried away toward the stairs.

Grant led the way down into the deepest caverns that Echo and Elliot used to sneak into Tyrekirk. No one spoke above a whisper.

"We need to take you as far as possible from the castle," Lily murmured in Echo's ear. "You'll come out on the city streets, but you still won't be safe. As soon as you show your face outside, the Laird's magic will detect you. He'll send soldiers and probably wizards to either kill or capture you."

"Uh.... okay," Echo panted. "I understand."

"We'll slow them down as much as we can. Just keep running....and you'll probably have to fight your way out of town." The two women shared a knowing glance and Lily's eyes shone with compassion and longing. "I'm sorry we can't do more."

"You're doing enough. I'm really grateful."

Lily burst into a smile and squeezed Echo's arm. "You sound like them now."

Echo's heart flipped. She didn't have to ask who Lily meant by "them". She meant these Highlanders—Reid, Elliot, Grant, Alastair—all of them.

What would it be like to be one of them? Echo didn't have to wonder. She already was one. She was so far up to her eyebrows in this war that she didn't even think about going back to the present day.

Would she go back even if she had the chance? Would she leave Elliot....and all the rest? Her closest friends were here. Only Zero was missing, and if Liam was right, Zero would come through the portal soon, too, if she wasn't here already.

Grant reached the bottom of the stairs, entered the labyrinthian tunnels, and took off at a fast run. Lily, Tristan, and Echo ran with him and the bubble wobbled to and fro to encompass them all.

The party turned at an intersection and all four ran through the bubble's walls when they rounded the corner. The bubble took a split second too long to correct to their direction change.

"The spell's weakening!" Tristan warned. "The Laird's magic is overcoming mine. We dinnae have much time left!"

"Just a little longer, lad!" Grant called back. He picked up speed, but the bubble only lagged farther behind.

All four of them broke the field more than once. This couldn't last, and the next time they turned a corner, the bubble shattered completely.

"Run!" Grant ordered. "As fast as ye can!"

He charged forward racing like the wind. Lily and Echo stayed with him all the way, but Tristan hung back. He slowed on purpose to cover their retreat and he kept casting backward glances up the tunnel.

Echo had to run her fastest to keep up with Grant, and at the next corner, he ran full speed into a squad of soldiers. She saw at first glance that this passage had no side tunnels feeding into it. The soldiers could only have gotten here by magic.

Grant saw them a fraction of a second too late. He only had time to raise his saber before he charged right into their midst and started hacking in all directions.

Echo put on speed. She and Lily caught up with him and joined the fight, but in the heat of the battle, a starburst of blue light flared in the tunnel beyond. Another twenty soldiers stepped out of it and Echo's heart sank. The Laird would just keep sending more and more soldiers until he captured her and her friends. The fugitives couldn't win.

Chapter 28

Explosions went off behind Echo. Tristan blocked the tunnel battling ten wizards who bombarded him with spells.

"Get out, lassie!" Grant yelled over the noise. "Get through and go!"

"I can't leave you here!"

"Go!" he roared. "This is too important." He checked Lily's position and stepped away from her.

The soldiers separated into two flanks. One attacked Lily and backed her against the wall. The other cornered Grant and surrounded him in a semi-circle. His saber flashed everywhere, but he couldn't hold them at bay much longer.

The two flanks left a gap straight up the middle of the passage. It was now or never.

Echo raised her weapons to strike down anyone who stood in her way. She charged for the opening and some of the soldiers saw her making a break for freedom.

They turned around to stop her and Grant struck with stunning ferocity. He stabbed out and skewered one of the soldiers. The others had to turn back to defend themselves against his attack and she dashed between them.

Lily's words rang in Echo's ears. *Just keep running*. Echo had her orders. She just had to carry them out.

The hardest part was in front of her. *You'll probably have to fight your way out of town.* She tightened her grip on her weapons, but she didn't even know where she should go.

Yes, she did. She had to head west into the forest. She had to go back to Torran's camp and make sure the captains were organizing the rebels for the new moon assault. Nothing was more important than that.

If Elliot is anywhere, he'll go back there, too. Those words kept her going on and on down one dark tunnel after another.

She didn't have any wizard protecting her now. She had nothing but these two weapons. They would have to be enough to get her out of Kald.

She'd never faced danger alone—not ever. She'd always had her comrades in combat and she hadn't been alone since she came to this country.

Now everything depended on her, but that thought only made her more determined. She would do this. She would make it back to the fort and Torran better watch his step if he tried anything with her.

Elliot said he could take Torran by challenging Torran's leadership in a fight. Echo could do the same thing if it came to that. She would kill the bastard before she let Torran stand in the way of the assault.

Ye're the only one that can go do it, lassie. We're all depending on ye.

Yes. She would do it. She would become something more than she'd ever been. Elliot did it and now it was her turn. She would become something stronger than she ever thought she could be. She would destroy any obstacle to make sure she did the job that Grant gave her to do.

She had to do this to fulfill the vow she took on the turret. She had to bring down the Laird. That vow wiped out all the dusty old promises she ever made to the Last Division. This was her fight, her war.

Almost as soon as she thought that, her straining eyes spotted a gleam of light ahead. Was it another pack of soldiers coming after her?

She slowed and raised her weapons to defend herself, but she didn't stop. She advanced toward the light, but it wasn't more soldiers.

She came to the tunnel's end and looked out at the streets of Kald. They looked as squalid and destitute as she remembered. She paused on the threshold, but only for a second.

Once you get out of the castle, you'll need to take off as fast as you can and get to the forest. Don't look back and don't worry about us. If you lose us, just keep going. Don't slow down for anything.

Right. She took a deep breath and stepped out into the open. She didn't run. That would only attract attention.

She kept an eye out for soldiers. She saw plenty, but they were all busy harassing the townsfolk, beating up street children, and interfering with the few businesses that still had the nerve to operate in this wasteland.

She pushed farther west. How close was she to the city walls? How close did that tunnel get her to leaving Kald? She still had to get past the sentries once she reached the wall.

She wound her way through countless streets that all started to look the same. She checked the sun's position to make sure she was still heading west. She adjusted her course in the direction she thought would be the right one.

She turned another corner and spotted another group of soldiers. They were in the act of breaking the front windows out of a local grocery store. Several townsfolk stood across the square watching.

The women huddled against the walls and tried to shield their young children from the sight. The local men glared openly at the soldiers. No one tried to disguise how they felt about this treatment.

Echo skirted the area to avoid the crowd. She was just about to duck into another street and leave the soldiers behind when a voice shouted across the square. "There she is! There's the rebel spy!"

She didn't have to turn around to know who they were talking about. She bolted into the warren of alleys, but not fast enough. A whistling projectile smashed into the brick wall next to her head.

Broken mortar and shards pelted her face and arms. She ducked and tried to keep running, but a long, thin snaking whip slashed around her ankles, yanked her off her feet, and brought her crashing down on her stomach.

She struggled to free herself, but her legs remained bound together at the ankles. She twisted over on her back swinging out her saber to kill someone.... but there was no one there.

A long snake of yellow sparks slithered across the cobblestones to a tall, dark-haired man across the square. He looked nothing like Tristan. This man definitely didn't work for Grant. The wizard was nowhere near her. She couldn't hit him or threaten him in any way.

She had to get out of here somehow. She couldn't go back to Tyrekirk, not after Grant, Lily, and Tristan sacrificed so much to help her get away.

She lurched into a sitting position and hacked her saber down at the magical rope wrapped around her ankles. To her surprise, she sliced right through it and the part holding her immobile vanished.

The other piece darted forward, wriggled on the cobblestones, and shot out to grab her again.

She scrambled backward to get away from it in time, but she wasn't quick enough. She brought her saber down again and again chopping at the thing.

Another punishing smash struck near her and shattered brick fired into her face. She took a split second to look around and spotted more wizards advancing from all sides.

She staggered to her feet and whirled away to run on. She veered from one intersection to the next. She didn't have time to check that she was running the right way.

She only slowed enough to look behind her to make sure the wizards weren't in sight. She had to think. She might blunder into more soldiers running around like this.

She couldn't run anymore anyway. Her chest hurt and her knees shook from her narrow escape. She needed to stop somewhere and catch her breath.

She darted into an alley that looked dark and deserted.... until she got into it. She glanced over her shoulder one more time to make sure no one followed her....and walked straight into a tall, grizzled man blocking the alley.

He wore a tattered tartan of plain green marked with black lines. A hideous scar cut across his face from one corner of his forehead, through one eye socket, and down his cheek. A black eye patch covered his ruined eye and his other eye glinted a dangerous icy blue.

A dozen townsfolk crowded the alley behind him and they were all armed for doomsday. Echo braced herself for another battle she couldn't win. None of these people looked at all pleased to see her.

The one-eyed man glared down at her and snarled through a mouthful of broken teeth. "Ye're the lassie running from the wizards."

"Yes!" she gasped. "Don't make me go back out there! Please! I barely got away."

He scowled even more menacingly. "Ye dinnae speak as we do. Who are ye?"

She opened her mouth and stopped herself. She couldn't tell them the truth and she didn't dare to tell these people that she was a friend of Lady Lily Armstrong. The people of Kald hated all Creightons.

Echo took a wild chance, lowered her voice to a whisper, and blurted out in a heated rush, "I'm carrying a message from the rebels in the forest. We're launching an attack on Tyrekirk at the new moon to unseat Laird Balfour. Can you help us? Can you organize your people to rise up and join our offensive? Please! We need everyone who wants to drive the Creightons off the Seat of Armstrong."

The old man bared his teeth and curled his lip at her. "Ye dinnae speak for the rebels. Ye cannae. I ken Torran and I havenae seen ye before."

"I just came from his fort in the woods. His captains are Athol, Forbes, Frasier, and Gowan. He has a...."

"That's enough!" a second man snapped. "The Laird may have spells to overhear ye."

"I can't stay here!" She stole a peek outside. "I have to keep going and get back to the fort. The Laird's forces will be coming back for me. Can you pass the word....to anyone who wants to help? We need as many people as you can muster."

A few of the old man's companions glanced at him and at each other. They didn't look so hateful now. She must have guessed right. Anyone who was against the Laird's stormtroopers would want to help the offensive.

The old man sniffed and his one eye shot to the street outside before he came back to glaring at Echo. Then he held out his hand. "I'm Clyde McKay. This neighborhood is me own territory." He nodded toward the west. "Ye wouldnae best to go that way. Ye'll run into Clan Brodie over there and ye wouldnae ever come out."

She followed the direction of his nod, but every part of the city looked the same to her. "Do different Clans control different parts of the city?"

"Some." He shook her hand. "Now what's this about an offensive on the new moon?"

"Just what I told you. The armies that want to unseat the Laird will converge on Kald and assault Tyrekirk to overthrow him."

"Which armies?" someone else asked.

"I can't explain the whole thing to you now. I have to go. Just pass the word, okay?"

She inched toward the mouth of the alley, but when she tried to leave, Clyde caught her arm and pointed in the opposite direction. "That way, lassie."

"Oh, right. Thanks."

She set off down the street, and when she looked back toward the alley, she didn't see anyone there. The locals had vanished into the surroundings.

She pressed on doing her best to avoid Clan Brodie's territory, but she didn't know exactly where it was and where it wasn't. How should she know if she was trespassing on their patch?

She thought the Clan's territory looked slightly better maintained than the surrounding slum, but she might have fooled herself about that. The differences were so minute that she might have imagined the whole thing.

She finally came to an area that she knew for certain did NOT belong to Clan Brodie. She halted at an intersection where intact buildings lined one side of the street.

Mountains of rubble stood in heaps on the opposite side. Every single building had been bombed to powder and she didn't see a single person over there.

Wary faces watched her pass Clan Brodie's territory. Men, women, and children kept her under constant surveillance so they must have families living over there.

The other neighborhood had been pounded to a moonscape with not one living thing moving among the wreckage. Not even any birds, insects, or mice disturbed the ghostly stillness. This must be the boundary that marked the end of Clan Brodie's territory.

She looked down the street and her heart flipped. The city wall crossed less than a block away. She just had to get past the sentries and she was home free.

She started forward searching everywhere for the soldiers and wizards who would come out to stop her. She couldn't get out of this city without another confrontation. That would be asking too much.

She approached the wall. The entrance was shut with no sentries on the inside. They stood guard outside. Should she blow through the door at a run and try to make it to the forest before anyone tried to stop her.... or should she try a more understated approach? Maybe she should try to flirt with the sentries.

She blushed in spite of herself. Snowflake would never approve of a stunt like that, but Snowflake wasn't here. No one was here. Echo would use whatever resources she could to get out of here before the Laird sprang his trap to stop her.

Her heart hammered as she got near the wall. She sheathed her saber to push the door open....and a spark of electricity shocked her fingers. She yanked her hand away....and stared at a shimmering wave of energy covering the door.

She backed away, but the field had already expanded to cover the whole wall. No, it was coming toward her. It wrapped around her to form a large ball.

She spun around fearing the worst, but she was too late. The wizards who attacked her earlier stood on all sides. They advanced from different streets and different directions.

The field enclosing her seemed to get thicker by the second. She put out her hands to touch it and it didn't shock her again. It felt rubbery and flexible under her touch, but it didn't go away.

She pushed harder, but it only undulated to match her effort. It pushed back against her touch. She whirled from right to left getting more frantic by the minute. She was trapped in here. She couldn't get away.

She spun the other way to confront the wizards. She held out her weapons, but she couldn't fight them from in here. She stabbed her dirk at the field, but she already knew it wouldn't do any good.

The blade point indented the surface but didn't penetrate it. The field bounced back to normal the moment she removed her dirk. She thrust out with her saber and the same thing happened. The field adjusted to everything she did. It never budged except to accommodate her pitiful efforts to escape.

She turned the other way. Her heart threatened to explode from pounding so fast and so hard. She couldn't let the wizards take her back to Tyrekirk or she would die there if they didn't kill her right here and now.

Almost as though her own thoughts made it happen, the field started to compress and shrink. It got smaller exactly the way the Laird's net closed in around Elliot. The ball pressed in on her and the space left for her to stand became too small.

She crouched lower, but the field no longer adjusted to her position. It kept collapsing and now it felt hard and glassy to the touch. It would crush her and that would be it.

She dropped her blades, planted both hands on the surface, and pushed. She pounded with her fists and yelled out for anyone to help her, but the field swallowed all sound. She couldn't even hear her own voice.

Help me! Anybody—help me!

Nothing. Her voice vanished into a chasm of silence. Even the wizards were too far away to hear or care.

She kicked and punched the field, but it didn't move. She was finished.

She froze in stark horror staring out at the wizards. The tall one that caught her earlier moved his fingers around in the air like he might be massaging the ball from a distance. Did Clyde and his people realize what was about to happen to Echo within sight of freedom?

She gulped down panic, but there was nothing left to do but stand here and wait for the end. The field bumped into her head and she fell down on her knees to buy her just a few more seconds.

She stared out at the wizards about to take her life. Why were they the last people she had to see in her life? Why couldn't she see Elliot or Betty or Lily? Even Grant and Reid would be better than these venomous enemies.

Without warning, a catastrophic avalanche of fire smashed into the street a few feet away. It exploded the pavement, billowed far and wide, and enveloped nearly five blocks of Kald.

Flame and torrential heat engulfed the ball in which Echo crouched. The shimmering field snapped and she cowered under her arms waiting for the fire to consume her.

She hit the pavement as the last lick of heat seared her cheeks. It vanished a second later and left the surroundings leveled even flatter than before.

The strike had collapsed the city wall, incinerated the door, and torched the sentries along with the wizards. Nothing remained.

Echo didn't get a chance to stand up and look around before a huge gold-black dragon dropped right on top of her. His massive wings blocked out all view of Kald, and the next second, his iron claw closed around her body.

He exploded off the ground, took wing, and shot away over the distant forest to the west.

Chapter 29

Elliot landed on one foot deep in the forest. He shot a flinty glare in all directions to make sure no one was moving around out here. Only then did he dare to lower his other foot to the ground.

He uncurled his talons very, very carefully and Echo rolled out of his grip onto the soft moss. He bent his long neck and sniffed her. She smelled all right except that she smelled like Tyrekirk.

She scrambled to her feet, spun around, and flung her arms around his scaly head. Her cheek fell against his scales and she shuddered all over. "Oh, my God! Thank you so much! I thought I was dead for sure that time. You don't know how happy I am to see you! Are you okay?"

He growled low in response. He could shift back and put his arms around her, but he loved her so much like this that he didn't do it right away.

He wanted to relish the feeling of her clinging to him. His heart overflowed with love that she accepted him. She didn't hesitate to touch him and press herself against him. She loved him as a dragon. He didn't want that to end too soon before he had a chance to really enjoy the moment.

He shut his eyes and leaned his giant head into her. She felt magically soft and feminine....and she was his. She loved him. She had been worried about him and now she was happy to see him. Nothing could replace that feeling in his heart.

She straightened up and her bright eyes found his. She stroked his scales taking in the sight of him. "Don't you want to shift? Do you want to stay like this?" A secret smile played on her lips. "Do you like this? I don't blame you. You look amazing."

He growled back at her. He wanted to talk to her and he couldn't do that the way he was. Oh, well. He could always shift later.

He would never stop cherishing those words in his heart. She wanted him like this. She liked it. She didn't care if he shifted or not. His dragon form had its own attraction and its own pleasures.

He shifted and she attacked him even more enthusiastically. She flung her arms around him and kissed him all over his face. "Oh, my God! Thank God you're all right! How much do you remember? You must have gotten hurt when you fell. Did Duncan heal you again? How did you get here? Where's Duncan? We have to find him right away. The situation in Kald...."

"Easy, lassie!" He fought himself out of her rapturous embrace. "Slow ye down a moment and let a man get a word in."

"This is an emergency! We have to find Duncan and bring him back to Kald. The whole rebellion is depending on him—on me! You don't know what's going on at Tyrekirk since you've been gone. Grant and Lily...."

He held up his hand. "Ye'll tell me all about what's going on at Tyrekirk as soon as ye slow down enough to let me answer yer questions."

She opened her mouth to argue and checked herself. "Where *is* Duncan?"

"I dinnae have the faintest idea."

"But you're the last person who's seen him. He took you from the battlefield."

He cocked his head to one side. "Did he?"

"Yes! Don't you remember?" She froze staring at him. "How much do you remember about the battle?"

He frowned and scratched his chin. "Well, as it happens, not very much. I remember Duncan showing up and throwing spells at the other dragons....and then I attacked the Creightons....and the Laird threw a spell over me."

"That's it? You lost your memory when he threw the spell over you?"

He nodded. "I remember feeling that I was shifting back and I was miles up in the air. I remember thinking it couldnae be good when I hit the ground....and that's all."

Echo started pacing back and forth. "He must have done it. He must have...."

"Must have done what, lass?"

"Healed you. You slammed down on the ground from way too high. I thought you were dead.... or that you might be. He picked you up...."

"Who did?"

"Duncan. He shifted into a dragon and he...."

Elliot's eyes popped. "Duncan...shifted into a dragon?"

"Yes! He's big and black like you—only maybe bigger and blacker. He looks exactly like you except without the gold."

Elliot burst into a huge grin. He hadn't heard better news in years. "Good lad!"

"He tried to fight the other dragons, but they outnumbered him. He picked you up and flew off with you." She halted in front of him and frowned at him again. "What do you remember after that?"

"Well, I woke up in the mountains to the west...."

"Which mountains?"

"Do ye remember when I flew ye over the ocean....and there was a mountain range between this country and the coast? Those mountains."

Her jaw dropped and she gawked at him. "That far? You woke up all the way out there?"

"Aye. Dinnae ask me how I got there."

"I don't have to ask because I already know. Duncan must have taken you there. He must have used his magic to heal your injuries and he left you there. Did you fly down here? Is that it?"

"Aye. I didnae have any notion how I got there nor what had happened, so I shifted and flew back toward Kald to see what was on with the battle....and then I saw those blighted wizards attacking ye."

She smirked at him. "Thank you for coming for me. You really are a sight for sore eyes."

He could let himself kiss her now—kiss her the way she deserved to be kissed. He wrapped her in his arms and swam in the delight of her mouth and her fingers tracing through his hair.

They separated at the same moment and she blushed smiling at him. "I missed you."

"I missed ye, too, lass. I had to come back and try to find ye."

She laced her fingers into his and nodded to the right. "The Serpent Cave isn't far away."

"I ken as well as ye, lass. Why do ye think I brought ye back here?"

She laughed and blushed again. "I should have known."

"Aye, ye should have done."

They started walking through the woods, but neither of them hurried. Elliot didn't want this moment to end. He was too happy.

Echo filled him in on everything that happened at Tyrekirk after Duncan took him away. He scowled when she came to the part about the Laird injuring Grant and leaving him unable to shift.

"I'll pay that bastard out for this," Elliot growled under his breath. "I will nae let this pass."

"That makes two of us, but we can't go back to Tyrekirk now. We have to go to the fort and get the rebels geared up for the new moon offensive."

"Aye. But we dinnae need to go back tonight."

He led her into the cave and they both got to work. He built a fire while she unpacked what was left of the food supplies. She smirked at him when he got out the matches. "Are you sure you want to do that the primitive way?"

"I winnae fit in this cave the other way—not without flattening ye, lass—and I still have some use for ye before I do away with ye."

She laughed again and sat down on the floor next to him to prepare the food. He kept casting glances at her as the firelight grew up around the kindling.

"What's on your mind?" she finally asked. "You're making me nervous."

"I was just thinking...." He sat down next to her and put his arm around her shoulders. "I was thinking I wouldnae mind staying like this forever. I would rather stay here than ever go back to that posh room at Tyrekirk."

"Me, too." She kissed him and smiled down at her work. She really looked deliriously happy. His heart ached, he loved her so much.

"Tell me we can fly away and never come back to this country, lassie," he urged. "Tell me we dinnae need to bother about this daft war."

She laughed again. She laughed it off so easily. "I really wish we could."

He sighed and gazed down into the flames. "I suppose we must stay for Duncan's sake if not for ought else."

"I really wish someone could have talked to him. I'm not blaming you. You were probably half dead when he took you, but it sure would be helpful to understand what's going through his mind."

"If ye're right, lassie, he must ken all about this war. Why else would he come out to fight the Creightons the way he did?"

"I've been thinking the same thing. I just wish we could talk to him. This isn't the way to plan an offensive—when one of our most powerful allies is totally incommunicado."

Now it was his turn to laugh. "Ye have a strange way of speaking, lassie, but ye're right."

"Good man. Keep saying that."

She kissed him again and then they both settled back to eat the food. He looked into the flames in between checking that she was still here with him.

She brought up many interesting points. The situation certainly had evolved since he passed out hundreds of feet above the Boundless.

He brushed the crumbs off his hands, leaned back against a nearby rock, and pulled her toward him. "I dinnae want to talk about Duncan anymore tonight, lassie. I feel as though I havenae seen ye for years."

"Me, too." She cuddled close to his side and put her arms around him.

Chapter 30

Elliot woke up and looked around. It took him a long time to remember where he was and everything that had happened—or rather everything Echo had told him had happened.

He still reclined against the same rock. Echo lay sound asleep on his chest. They both must have drifted off in this position.

He didn't mean for them to fall asleep sitting up and now his back and hips ached from leaning against the unforgiving surface. He didn't stir, though. Not even this discomfort could make him to disturb her.

He had been so looking forward to getting her all alone in the cave, miles away from everyone and everything. He had worked himself up with so many fantasies about what he would do to her and with her during their one night alone before they went back to the fort.

None of those fantasies measured up to this moment. The fact that they could both fall asleep like this meant so much more to him than all his torrid fantasies. It was so sweet and it so perfectly represented everything that he felt for her. He would gladly spend any night and every night with her exactly like this. He didn't need anything else.

He rested his head back against the rock and shut his eyes. He sent up a silent prayer of gratitude to Duncan for giving him this—one perfect night with Echo.

Elliot was just starting to drift off again when she stirred, rubbed her face against his tartan, and sat up. She ran her fingers through her hair and looked down at the pile of dead ash where the fire had been. "Well, I guess there's nothing left to do but to go back to the fort."

Elliot leaned in and kissed her. He didn't mind going back to the fort now. He could face the future and he no longer wanted to run away. He wanted to be in this war with Echo, with Grant and Lily, with Reid and Betty, with Duncan—with all the dozens of people working for the same goal.

Elliot had grown up depending on one person—his brother Grant. He had never let himself rely on anyone else or seen himself belonging to anything larger. He didn't need to. He had Grant. That was enough.

Now he *was* part of something larger—something much more important—more important even than Grant. Elliot had Duncan. He had Echo and he had the whole country. The whole country needed him and that feeling gave him as much strength as being a dragon. It would carry him anywhere he needed to go.

Echo put the rest of the food away and they walked out into the grey morning. They joined hands and headed for the fort. This feeling carried him on his way. It would carry him to the ends of the earth if necessary. Torran couldn't stop this. Nothing could.

He pulled Echo to a stop in their old spot and shared a deep kiss with her. He devoured her with his eyes and she gazed up at him smothering him with so much love that he couldn't speak. Neither of them had to say anything. They both already knew.

They set off again for the fort. Elliot had to command himself to take his eyes off her face to see where he was going....and tensed.

Armed men advanced out of the trees, but these weren't Creighton soldiers from Kald nor were they the Laird's wizards. These men wore shabby clothes in a jumble of tartans from several different Clans.

Half of them aimed drawn bows at Echo and Elliot and Elliot recognized several of them. Fraser waved his saber at the pair. "Close them off, lads! Dinnae let them get away."

Elliot glanced to his left. "What are ye doing here, Forbes? Did ye forget about the offensive?"

Forbes shook his head. "There'll be no offensive—Torran's orders."

"Ye think not?" Elliot turned to his left. "What happened to ye, Bac? I thought we understood each other."

Bac pinched his lips and tightened his grip on his bowstring. He stood well back from the others. He didn't have to explain. Bac was no captain.

Torran must have reversed all Elliot's gains while Elliot's back was turned. Torran had demoted Bac back to the rank of an errand boy. Torran had also turned the other captains against Elliot's plan.

Fraser barged up to Elliot. "Ye're under arrest, lad. Hold out yer hands."

"What the devil for? Ye dinnae mean to bind me like a common criminal." Elliot forced a laugh. "If ye mean to kill me as yer enemy, do it now."

Elliot scanned the group fixing each of his former friends with an unwavering stare. Only Fraser would hold Elliot's gaze. They didn't want to be here. Torran must have coerced them.

Fraser grabbed Elliot's arm and tried to yank his hand forward. Fraser pulled a leather thong from his belt, no doubt to tie Elliot's wrists together.

Elliot shifted so fast that he didn't have time to think about it. He reacted on pure instinct. The dragon in his soul was so sick and tired of these puny humans pushing him around.

Elliot's neck shot out to an impossible length. He snapped Fraser in half before the man even realized he was in danger. The top half of his body fell to the right still clasping the thong in one hand.

His legs folded on the spot and all the other rebels blinked at the dragon erupting out of nowhere in front of them.

Elliot swung around to kill and maim and destroy, but when he saw Forbes, Athol, and Bac staring at him in stupid shock, Elliot checked himself.

He stopped himself from reducing them to ash on the spot. Instead, he swiped his giant tail in the slightest sideways flick. He leveled the whole rebel group in one quick movement.

The archers toppled and dropped their bows. Some of the others kept hold of their weapons, but his attack came as such a surprise that they took longer than he expected to straighten out their jumbled limbs.

He crouched there growling at them. Smoke puffed from his nostrils, but he still held back his fire. He would need allies when he got back to the fort. He wouldn't be able to find anyone better placed to help him than these men.

He glared at them with his fierce narrowed eyes. They quailed before him and a few of the archers retreated before his fury.

Echo strolled over to his side, rested her hand on his shoulder, and surveyed the rebels as they finally dragged themselves to their feet. "Get up, all of you. Stand up like men. Do you see this?" She gave Elliot an affectionate pat. "Elliot is Laird Balfour Creighton's grandson. He's a Creighton of the Royal Line and he's Grant Ritchie Armstrong's brother. Do you all understand what that means? Stand up, I said."

Several looked down at Fraser's remains, blanched, and eventually summoned the courage to straighten up and face her. What cowards they turned out to be. He would really rather step on them and be done with it, but he had to consider the larger game.

She waited until they pulled them together and then patted Elliot again. "You can come back now."

He shifted and almost laughed in their faces at their expressions of shock and horror. They looked a thousand times more terrified of him in his human form than when he was as a dragon. What wet blankets they were! To think he respected some of these men.

"Now take us to the fort," Echo commanded. "You—Bac! You go ahead and tell Torran exactly what happened here. Tell him we're coming in and we want to speak to him as soon as we get there."

Bac took off at a run and vanished into the trees. The other men retrieved their bows, fumbled with their arrows, drew them, and held Echo and Elliot at arrow point all the way back to the fort, but that only made these men seem even more ridiculous to Elliot. What were they thinking threatening him like this—as if they could ever threaten him?

The fort came in sight. The gate was shut—of course.

Torran stood tall on the sentry posts. Nearly the whole guard force had assembled to watch the advanced posse bring in Echo and Elliot. Bac was up there whispering furiously in Torran's ear.

Torran pulled his usual scowl at the approaching couple. "How do ye dare to come back here, ye Creighton bastard! Ye fouled our fort with yer presence too long. I should kill ye where ye stand."

"Now's yer chance, Torran, ye coward!" Elliot yelled back. "I challenge ye for the leadership of the whole rebel legion in these woods—and ye must accept the challenge yerself. I winnae accept any second—only ye. Are ye such a coward that ye'd hide behind another man's kilt to defend yerself?"

A murmur of tension went through the assembled rebels. No one could back down on a challenge like this. Torran had gotten away with using seconds in smaller challenges, but no one had dared to challenge him out in the open for leadership of the entire rebel contingent.

Torran tried to look properly furious that anyone would dare to question his authority, but Elliot didn't care about that.

"Fight me, Torran, you coward! Prove to these men that ye're strong enough to lead or step aside for a man who is strong enough. None of us will believe ye've the authority to lead if ye dinnae prove it now."

The guards murmured to each other and Elliot heard people running and exclaiming behind the wall. Every passing second made it more essential for Torran to accept the challenge. He no longer had any choice but to accept it.

"I accept yer challenge," he finally growled, "on condition that ye dinnae shift into a dragon. Ye must fight me as a man."

Elliot split in a deadly grin. "I mean to. I dinnae want any man to question afterwards that I won fair and square."

Chapter 31

E cho hurried over to Elliot and murmured low. "Are you sure you want to do this?"

Elliot looked past her shoulder. Torran was over there surrounded by his sycophantic followers, but Elliot didn't see Bac, Athol, or Forbes over there. Elliot was right about them. They all knew Torran was an imposter posing as a leader.

People assembled from all over the fort. Women and children watched from their windows and doorways as the guards led Echo and Elliot inside the gate. The guards didn't lower their bows, not even once the gate closed to shut everyone inside.

"Ye dinnae need those any longer, lads," Elliot mused. "Do ye plan to shoot me once I win the challenge?"

Two of the guards jumped as though they'd been slapped. They spun around and stared at him trying to understand what he meant.

They had to think hard before they realized that, yes, if he won this challenge, he would be in charge of them. They wouldn't be able to shoot him. He would be their new leader and Torran would be dead.

"Let me take him," Echo breathed. "I can do this."

Elliot chuckled to himself. "I'll tell ye what, lassie. Ye can be me second. If Torran kills me—*only* if he kills me—then ye can fight him and kill him in me place. Is it a bargain?"

She frowned at him and then sighed. "I guess I should have expected that."

"Of course ye did. I have to fight him. I have to beat him so we can bring the offensive. This is the only way."

Torran barged into the yard between the gate and the nearby houses. "Is this what ye want?" he roared and waved his arms at Elliot. "Is *this* the leader ye want—another Creighton?"

Elliot stood where he was and waited for Torran to finish. A few people looked sideways at Elliot, but most just observed Torran strutting around like the stuffed peacock he was.

"Follow the Creighton scum back to Kald if that's what ye want!" Torran bellowed. "Crawl back under the Laird's kilt where ye belong, ye spineless worms! Ye deserve him if ye follow him."

Elliot turned to Echo, unbuckled his saber, and handed it to her. He kicked off his shoes and socks and then unbuckled the beautiful sporran he put on when he left Tyrekirk.

He pulled his tartan down to his waist, stuffed it into his belt, and yanked off his shirt. "What are you doing?" Echo whispered.

"God help me, I'm turning into a Buchanan! I should have worn Alastair's tartan for the occasion."

She laughed under her breath. "That would definitely make a statement."

He grinned at her and a flood of the same exhilarating happiness overpowered everything else. He would put Torran in his place and then Elliot could get to work on the offensive. "Dinnae worry yerself about me, lassie. We'll be dining in Torran's apartment tonight."

He turned away from her and strode out into the yard. Several of Torran's supporters gave rude whistles that Elliot was standing out here in his kilt and nothing else. Then a few people laughed.

Elliot stood before them perfectly calm. He turned in a full circle so everyone could see him. The laughter died.

"Ye've all been out here in this forest for a long time now," he began. "Many of ye have been here a sight longer than I have....and why? Why did ye leave Kald in the first place? Why did ye turn yer backs on the Laird's service....and yer families....and all ye'd ever kenned in Kald?"

Silence answered him and he built to his subject. He was in command here. He didn't have to defeat Torran because Elliot was already in charge. He held everyone present in the palm of his hand.

He raised his voice and called a lot louder than he needed to. "Ye left yer homes and families and positions in Kald to bring the Laird down. Ye left all ye kenned behind to give yer children and yer families a better life—a better country than the one yer fathers handed down to ye. Ye sacrificed all on the chance that ye might do something no one else had ever done before. Ye did all that to take the chance ye might free this land from the Laird's rule."

No one breathed. Tension hung thick in the air and Elliot felt himself feeding off of it. The longer he prolonged the fight, the more he threw it in his own favor.

He took a deep breath and shouted with all his strength. "Ye have that chance now! The time has come to take yer blades and shed Creighton blood—to shed the Laird's blood and put a new man on the throne—a man who doesnae favor Clan and position—a man who grew up rough and forgotten just like ye! Ye stand a chance now, in all these generations, to put one of yer own on the throne and *this* man—!" Elliot spun around and pointed across the yard at Torran.

Eyes popped at Elliot's audacity. The assembled rebels stared back and forth between Elliot and Torran.

"This man would call ye back!" Elliot roared. "This man would tell ye—he would order ye under penalty of his retribution—to sheath yer blades and go home. He'd order ye to forget all about the offensive assembling in Kald. He'd have ye let the rest of the staunch hearts in this land do the dirty work while ye dig worms in the forest mud. Is *this* the man ye'd follow?"

People started to scowl in Torran's direction and grumble.

"Three days ago," Elliot went on, "I met with Torran in his apartment and informed him and his captains of this offensive. I gave them notice to arm the guard and equip our men to take their place on the western flank. The whole offensive depends on us....and what did Torran do? He reversed all me plans the moment I left the fort. He removed one of the captains he kenned was loyal to me and he ordered the remaining captains to come after me, arrest me, and kill me. He did all that to stop ye from taking part in this offensive as would be yer right as the Laird's true enemies! I can call up the captains to prove me claim. Is this the man ye'd follow?"

The grumbling got louder and quite a few people turned to Forbes and Athol for confirmation. Elliot waited for one of them to step out of line and contradict him, but he already knew they wouldn't. They wanted this offensive as much as anybody.

Elliot strode to the other side of the yard, turned around, and faced Torran. Torran glared at him in unvarnished fury, but that only played into Elliot's hands, too. Torran didn't say a word in his own defense. He couldn't.

Elliot spread his arms by way of invitation and Torran stepped out. He was at least three inches taller than Elliot, but in that moment, Elliot knew he would win.

He could release the dragon to crush this coward underfoot. Elliot could unleash dragon fire on Torran, but in the silence when Torran approached to take his place, Elliot realized he didn't need to.

The dragon's power—this feeling of being royal born—this sense that he could do no wrong—this raw power coursing through his veins—it was always there. It pulsed in everything he did even when he was just a man. He didn't have to become a dragon to conquer.

Torran started to circle to the left and Elliot copied him. Elliot was probably the first man ever to face one of these challenges barefoot and bare-chested like the Buchanans, but that only made him feel stronger and more in command.

He considered it an honor to copy the Buchanans. He could only hope he would be a man as honorable and upright as they were. He might not carry Buchanan blood, but they were still his family. They were Duncan's family and Duncan was his younger brother.

He would do the Buchanans proud and they would fight together to make this country great. His dragon soul would stand no other outcome.

Torran flexed his powerful shoulders. His eyes glinted with equal parts menace and triumph. The bastard was way too confident. How long had it been since he fought anyone? Torran hadn't fought anyone since Elliot came to the fort to join the rebels. It might have been quite a bit longer than that.

The spectators started calling out and cheering their favorites. Elliot heard Athol's deep, booming voice coming from over by the roundhouse. "Take him, laddie! Ye can take him no bother! That's it. Stay light!"

More people encouraged Torran to put Elliot in the ground, but Elliot hardly heard them. Elliot had the only people who mattered on his side.

Echo called from Elliot's other side. "Come on, Elliot! You can do this! Keep your hands up!"

Elliot circled for a while and waited for Torran to make the first move. Elliot had no idea what Torran might do. Torran might turn out to be crazy and ferocious.... but Elliot doubted it.

Elliot's mind turned on how to make this as decisive a victory as possible. He needed to find a way to humiliate Torran. That would be the best way to show the rebels what a shoddy leader Torran was. That would convince them that they needed a strong man to take Torran's place.

Elliot's practiced eye traced every move Torran made....and then Elliot had it. Torran shuffled his feet in the dirt. He didn't spring lightly on the balls of his feet. He moved quickly, but he didn't jump from one position to the next.

Torran's eyes darted around following Elliot's movements. Elliot danced in and out to check Torran's reactions. They were all good, and when Elliot feinted a punch, Torran reacted with lightning speed. He really could fight. His feet were his only weakness.

Elliot tried a few more times just to make sure. The last time he feinted, Torran lashed out to defend himself and then immediately charged. He thrust out with a devastating punch. It would probably have leveled Elliot if Torran had landed it.

Elliot made his move just as fast, darted forward to Torran's side, and danced to the right. He caught his foot around Torran's ankle and Torran's own momentum sent him pitching forward onto his face.

Elliot attacked with mindless brutality, pounced on Torran from above, seized the man's head, and snapped his neck in a flash. Elliot sprang to his feet and leapt clear while Torran's body flopped flat on the ground at Elliot's feet.

Elliot skipped out of range and whirled around spreading his arms to the onlookers. "Do ye see? Do ye see how easily this fool lost his life to a man who's been in this fort for less than two months?"

All the cheering died. The onlookers stared at him as though seeing him for the first time.... because they were. None of them knew the first thing about him—until today.

Now they did. He knew and they knew. They were done hiding in the forest. They were going to war with him as their leader.

He made sure no one stepped out to challenge him, but he knew they wouldn't. Athol smiled at him and Forbes nodded from the other side of the yard. Bac looked like he might burst into tears of relief and happiness.

Elliot strode over to Echo and pulled on his shirt, but he couldn't look at her. His gaze kept measuring everyone in the yard. He'd spent two months getting to know these people, but that meant nothing. Knowing each one in all their unique idiosyncrasies would be even more important, now that he would be in command of them all.

He took his saber and dirk from Echo, cast one last look around at the people staring back at him, and turned away. "Come along, lassie."

She carried his socks and shoes and followed him over to the roundhouse. Everyone in the yard remained silent and watchful until Echo and Elliot stepped inside. He heard a few whispers, but no one spoke until he got well out of earshot.

He strolled down the corridor and stepped into Torran's office. It was Elliot's office now.

He looked around and recognized for the first time how disorganized Torran was as a leader. Piles of papers lay jumbled on the desk. Elliot couldn't see any order at all. A few dishes with crumbs still on them stuck out from beneath the scattered documents. What a toad Torran was.

Elliot crossed to another door in the back of the office, threw it open, and looked in on a large apartment in an equally disreputable state of filth. This would never do. He and Echo would have to clean this up and make it their own.

Elliot grimaced to himself when he remembered Grant bending over his desk. Every piece of paper had its place. Grant could probably put his hand on any paper in his whole collection at a moment's notice.

Elliot took his socks and shoes from Echo, went into the apartment, and finished getting dressed. He straightened his hair, tucked his shirt into his kilt, and rearranged his tartan on his shoulder where it belonged.

He returned to the office to find Echo standing in the same place. She cocked her head to study him.

He kissed her once, but a second later, he pulled away when he heard footsteps coming down the corridor. He knew it would happen like this. It couldn't be otherwise.

He stepped over to the door as Athol and Forbes arrived. Athol nodded to Elliot. "Well, laddie, that was a wee bit more than we expected."

"Thank ye for supporting me."

"Not a bit of it, lad." The big man stepped into the office and slapped his sides. "Well? Where would ye like to start?"

"I already told ye. Arm our men for the assault." Elliot looked around. "Where's Bac?"

"Are ye still meaning that Bac should take over as captain?" Forbes asked.

"Of course. He's staunch. He winnae let us down. Did ye think I wasnae serious? I wouldnae have said it if I wasnae."

Forbes shrugged. "I told him just now to stay behind in case ye had second thoughts."

"No second thoughts. Go fetch him....and Brodie. We'll need someone to take Fraser's place. Brodie will be perfect for that."

"Brodie!" Echo blurted out. "Are there Brodies here?"

"Och, aye!" Athol replied. "There's packs of them."

"Why, lass?" Elliot asked.

She looked away. "I'll tell you later."

Elliot walked around the desk, pushed a few things aside, and lifted a few piles out of the way. "Where's a map of this forest?"

The two captains gaped at him like he might be speaking another language. "Map?"

"Aye. A map of this forest and all the land around the fort—all the way to Kald. Torran must have had one."

Athol and Forbes looked at each other.

"Are ye telling me," Elliot exclaimed with deliberate slowness, "that Torran doesnae even have a map of this forest?"

"I dinnae think so, lad," Athol replied. "I've stood with him in this office for close to eight years and I havenae seen any map."

"Nor I," Forbes added.

Elliot sank into Torran's chair—Elliot's chair. He buried his face in his hands and groaned. "Heaven preserve us!"

"Do ye want us to make ye one up?" Forbes asked. "I can get the lads to...."

"No! There's no time before the new moon. Ye put all your effort into preparing our men to march on Kald. Dinnae do or even think of ought but that." Elliot stood up and waved toward the door. "On ye go....and tell Bac to take over Gowan's place and Brodie to take over for Fraser. Pass the message to them.... Och, and get someone to bury Torran somewhere so he isnae lying out in the yard."

"Aye." The two men let themselves out.

Elliot sauntered over toward Echo. He still surveyed the desk with a disgusted feeling in his stomach. He had one week to reverse all the damage Torran had caused. That wasn't nearly enough time.

"Do you still want to fly away?" she murmured under her breath.

"More than ever. Can ye believe that crabbit auld gowk has been running this whole muckle disaster without a map of the area? Christ Almighty!"

"You'll handle it." She moved in and kissed him. Then she turned a critical eye to the arrangements and, for the first time, she betrayed as much distaste as he felt. "So.... where are we supposed to sleep tonight?"

He waved toward the apartment. "We'll stay in there, but not before we give the place a complete and thorough scourge with a mop and bucket...."

She laughed. "I thought you were going to say something about exorcising it with witchcraft to drive out the evil spirits."

"That, too." He took her hand. "Never mind. We dinnae have time for that now, either. Come along. I have another place we can spend the night where no evil spirits will haunt us."

"Let me guess—the Serpent Cave?"

He didn't take the joke. "I wish we were, but I dinnae see us getting back there for a fair wee while, lassie. In a few days, we'll be on our way back to Kald regardless. Even after the war ends and we come back here, we winnae be able to move around as we once did. We'll have to stick close to the fort if I'm to keep control of these people."

She sighed and accompanied him out into the corridor. The fort and the roundhouse had returned to their usual noise and activity with people coming and going from the canteen, fetching their food, and taking it back to their rooms and cabins.

"Where are we going?" she asked at last.

He opened the door to his old bedroom and led her inside. He shut the door and shot the bolt. "No one will bother us here."

She went over to the bed. The bundle made out of Alastair's tartan still sat where she had left it. No one had moved it since she and Elliot went to Kald. Was it only a few days ago? He found it hard to keep track. So much had happened and his life had changed so much. *He* had changed so much.

She sat down on the bed and Elliot went over to her. He cupped her face in both hands and brought her lips up to his mouth. Everything had changed between them because Elliot had changed.

He had changed into the man she deserved. He had become the leader he was born to be. Now he could command this force to act according to his wishes. He could harness their strength and their resources to help the offensive, but even that didn't guarantee success.

This offensive was doomed to failure if the rebels were the only force that carried it out. He had no way of knowing if the Buchanans had received Reid's message or if Grant and Lily would be able to do anything from inside Kald.

To make matters worse, none of the others knew that Elliot was in charge of the rebels now. He had no way of communicating with them and no time to do it even if he found a way.

He was going into this deaf, dumb, and blind while the other two forces were doing exactly the same thing. It was the worst possible battle plan in the history of warfare, but they just had to try it and hope for the best.

Echo snapped him out of his thoughts. "What are you thinking about?"

He swam back to reality and her beauty engulfed him. He had no reason to get distracted by problems outside his control when he had this majestic angel in his room, in his hands.

Her face turned up to him, so open, so loving, so attentive. He blocked everything else out of his mind and kissed her with all his heart. "Ye, lassie." He toppled forward and pulled her down onto the bed. "Only ye."

<u>End of book 3.</u>

Keep Reading

H ighland Heroes Series: Book 4: Clan Hero

With war devastating the landscape and Clan Creighton and Clan Buchanan at each other's throats, Dead Betty and Reid Buchanan get caught in a deadly race to track down the one man who can stop the war. No one can even find Duncan Buchanan, much less bring him to the throne to overthrow the deadly wizard Laird Balfour Creighton.

Betty doesn't want to get stuck in this bizarre version of Scotland, especially not with a man as enticing and charismatic as Reid Buchanan, but the Fates conspire to throw a wrench in the words when Betty starts using magic she never knew she had.

When worlds collide, Betty will have no choice but to embrace every aspect of this new life, including her feelings for Reid that won't be denied. When the dust settles and the war finally ends, there may be nothing left, not even the man she loves.

You can find it at your favorite book retailer.

Sign Up Once--Get all Theo Mann's free books including brand new releases

S ign Up Once--Get all Theo Mann's free books including brand new releases

Ian Wallace is tall, muscular, magnetically handsome, heroic, and passionately in love with the lady of his dreams--Lady Ada Ross.

Too bad he's just a character in a romance novel......or is he?

When Dayna Roberts finds a mysterious letter tucked between the pages of her favorite book, she decides to write Ian back to warn him of his enemies sneaking up on him. Little did Dayna know that one act would sweep her into a world of the past--a world of danger, intrigue, and powerful forces she never imagined possible. Disaster strikes when Ian's archnemesis Gavin Macauley intercepts her letter and conquers Grimlock Castle with Dayna inside it--but how could he intercept the letter when she wrote it in the twenty-first century?

If Dayna refuses to marry Gavin in Ada's place, he'll take drastic measures that could leave this whole mysterious world in ruins. Forget about Dayna finding a way to get back to the modern world. She'll be lucky if she survives long enough to escape from the castle. Is there any way out--much less a way to get back to the family and the modern life she knows?

Sign up at www.theomann.com to read it for free

About Theo Mann

I write 70 books per year—and yes, before you ask, all these books are my original creative work. Nothing written under my name is AI-generated or ghostwritten because I write better than AI and any ghostwriter out there.

People don't read fiction for entertainment or to escape from reality. People read fiction to see their humanity reflected in another person's character and story.

This is my promise to you. When you read my books, you'll see your own humanity reflected in the characters and stories. I take this commitment to my readers very seriously. My books are an intimate form of communication between us. I would never disrespect my readers by turning that over to a machine or another writer. This is my bond between me and you as my reader.

I write 20,000 words per day as my daily work output. If anyone with a public platform would like to challenge me to prove this in a controlled environment, feel free to contact me on this website's contact page.

I worked as a professional ghostwriter for fifteen years. Now I'm on a mission to set a Guinness World Record by writing 700 books over the next ten years and 1400 books over the next twenty years, all originally written by me. See my website for the full book list.

I'm also the author of *Proof for the Existence of God* and the *Crimes Against Fiction* blog. You can find all my nonfiction work at www.crimes-against-fiction.com.

If you have a story idea, or if you would like me to explore a series in more depth, or if you'd like me to explore a character by writing a spinoff series about that character or world, leave me a message on my website's contact page. I answer all reader emails, so ask me anything, tell me what you liked and didn't like, and let me know where you'd like your favorite series to go. I would love to hear your ideas and find out what you'd like to read next.

Find out more at www.theomann.com.

Also by Theo Mann (so far)